I0637046

Mysteries, Mayhem, and Other Mishaps

A Tess McGee Adventure, Volume 1

Tara N. Hathcock

Published by Quiet+Kin Publishing, 2025.

MYSTERIES, MAYHEM, AND OTHER MISHAPS

First edition. September 30, 2025.

Copyright © 2025 Tara N. Hathcock.

ISBN: 978-1737457695

Written by Tara N. Hathcock.

This book is dedicated to JM, who gave me the gift card that forced me to visit the coffee shop where this book was written.

And hopefully, many more books after.

And to The Mudhouse employees who suffer me week after week.

"I sat with my anger long enough until she told me her real name was Grief."

C.S. Lewis

Chapter 1

I t was a dark and stormy night on the mean backstreets of Detroit. The rain had ended not long ago, leaving a thick, murky fog in its wake. A few sickly flashes of lightning teased the edge of the horizon, briefly illuminating the bleak, dirty landscape. The old gumshoe pressed his back more firmly against the dirty brick of the wall he was leaning against and, reaching up, settled his hat more firmly on his head, the collar of his trench coat tugging up around his neck to block what wind it could.

The alley was deserted, save a stray cat crouched low beneath a dumpster at the far end, watching the detective cautiously. It had been perched on top of the half-open dumpster when he'd first arrived, licking its paw furiously to get every last drop of whatever its stolen meal had been. If the smell coming from the door cracked open beside the dumpster was anything to go by, the cat had dined like a king tonight. Unlike the detective, who was cold and hungry, and beginning to curse the great depression that required he take any job he could.

A newspaper, caught by a sudden gust of wind, blew down the alley and snagged on the gumshoe's leg. He stepped on it casually to hold it in place, then reached inside his jacket for a cigar and a lighter. There was nothing to see tonight, so a little smoke and smoldering ash wasn't going to give him away. Mission accomplished, he reached down and shook out the damp paper. Dated five days ago, the headline read Wealthy Philanthropist and Activist Dead at 65. The date of the *headline was the same date the daughter had shown up at his doorstep, unable to believe her healthy, vigorous father could have leapt to his own death, though he wouldn't be the first powerful man to have done so. Not these days. Stranger things had happened, the detective thought and had said as much. And that's when the crying had started.*

He sighed. And that had been his downfall. She had been willing to pay anything, any amount, to find out the truth - that her father had been killed. And he had agreed to look into it. And now, three hours and a good soak in the rain had changed his mind.

He started to turn away but stopped short. There was a snap towards the opposite end of the alley, and years of instinct locked him in place against the wall. Someone was coming. He flattened himself against the crumbling brick and sank to his knees, using the shadow of the fire escape to hide himself even further. He could hear footsteps walking slowly towards his hiding place and he held his breath, making himself even more invisible.

BAM, BAM, BAM. The sound of a fist against wood and the detective peered slowly around the dumpster. A huddled, shrouded figure stood in front of a decrepit door just opposite the restaurant. A pause, while the figure looked quickly towards the front of the alley, checking to make sure he was alone, and then again - BAM, BAM, BAM.

The door cracked open and the detective squinted. He could almost see -

BAM. BAM. BAM.

• • • •

TESS MCGEE JERKED BACK from the page, torn brutally from the world she was creating.

"MOM!" Tess yelled. "I am in the *middle* of something!"

How was she supposed to compose her masterpiece, the bete noire of her soul, when her mother insisted on her attention at the most inopportune of times?

"Middle of something or not, when your mamma calls, you come running with a *Yes ma'am* and a smile on your face, Tessa Lynn McGee." Her mother was all business today, leaning around the door frame with hand on hip and glare in place.

Tess sighed a martyr's sigh, thoroughly persecuted, and turned in her chair to face the warden.

"Yes ma'am." Her mother couldn't help inconveniencing Tess. That was just what mothers did.

"Uh hum," her mother nodded, clearly not buying what Tess was selling. "That's what I thought. Now, you get your cute little backside out the door. I called you twice before marching myself up these stairs."

Tess opened her mouth to make a very valid counterargument but was cut off by her mamma's finger-wagging in her face.

"Oh no, little girl," she said before Tess could get a word out. "There'll be no opinions from you. You know I love your writing, and your daddy loved your writing, but you can't keep tuning out the whole world while you're at it."

Tess didn't think that was fair at all. What was so great about the whole world, anyway? Nothing, as far as she could tell. And if her books could take her out of it, such the better, as far as she was concerned.

"Get those shoes on, little one," her mother called, sashaying her way back to her own room, where she would pretend to get ready for work until Tess left for school. "If you're late again, you'll be in trouble like you've never known."

Please. As though trouble didn't already follow Tess around like a bad habit.

Tess McGee was what adults outside the family affectionately referred to as *feisty*. Her mother called it stubbornness, her voice a mixture of exasperation and grudging fondness. Red-headed child of Satan and demon spawn of the south had been tossed about on occasion as well, but Tess preferred her father's description best. Ian McGee liked to say Tess was filled with pizzazz.

Pizzazz.

Tess liked the way the word sounded. It was strong, intense, colorful. It called to mind vitality, spunk, and panache - all the things Tess wanted to be. All the things her dad saw in her. Now though, her pizzazz was gushing out like a fire hose on full blast as she ripped out the latest notebook page behind her mother's retreating back, crumpling it roughly into a ball and launching it over her shoulder to join the other rockets of discarded garbage attempting to masquerade as literary genius.

She knew she needed to go to school, she really did. But she couldn't get the characters to do what she wanted, and it frustrated her to no end. They were *her* characters. She had created them, which meant she should be in charge. Tess was certain Agatha Christie never had this problem, and Conan

Doyle *was* his character, so Holmes would certainly toe the line written.

Tess sighed and rubbed her thumb absently across the back of the picture frame lying face down on her desk. It made her feel better, closer to him somehow, to touch the picture. And Tess knew exactly what her dad would say right now.

Tessie, if you quit every time something gets hard, you'll never get anything done.

He was right, unfortunately. And in that moment, Tess didn't need pizzazz. No, she needed what her mother saw in her. She needed to be stubborn.

Or Satan's offspring. Whichever got the job done first.

Tess picked up her pen, ready to wrangle brilliance onto the page come hell or high water, when the door of her room slammed back with force, causing her to jump one way, the pen in her hand flying the other.

"Tessa Lynn McGee, if you aren't out of this house in under five minutes, I will plant you in the backyard with the peonies and all the other teenagers who were late to school. You hearing me, little one?"

"Mom!" Tess screeched, clutching at her heart, "I was just about to-"

"Excuse me?" Her mother's hand flew once more to her hip and her eyebrows were raised in an expression of disbelief. If Tess didn't know better, she'd think this was the same woman who'd made dinner and rolled her eyes in exasperation at Tess's antics for the last fourteen years.

But Tess did know better. The woman in front of her talked the same talk and walked the same walk, but the spark where her heart used to burn hot was barren and cold. Desolate. Hollow. Vacant. Much like the look on her mother's face the night that...

"Were you about to argue with me?" Only Tess would see the strain around her eyes and the effort it took her mother to pretend to still be whole.

Tess knew the look and the tone even if the look in her eyes didn't quite match and the argument was forced. So she sighed and adopted her most angelic expression. If her mom was going to play the part, so was Tess.

"No, ma'am," Tess responded meekly. "I was about to say, 'Mom! I love you so much for reminding me!'"

Kate McGee sniffed. "That's what I thought." She dropped a kiss onto Tess's forehead, brushing Tess's unruly red curls away from her eyes, and then held up her hands like she was confused.

"Then scoot, why don't you!"

"I'm a scootin', I'm a scootin'!"

Tess grabbed her backpack and hurried out her bedroom door and down the stairs, fully aware her mother wasn't going to follow. No, with Tess taken care of and on her way, her mother would likely drift around the house like a ghost before wrapping herself in a blanket and settling on the couch to stare silently at the wall for the next eight hours.

Kate McGee had always been a beautiful woman and Tess knew it only too well. With her willowy height, dark, magnificent curls, and smooth, chocolatey skin, her mother was still the bombshell her father had fallen in love with so many years ago. Even wrapped in her husband's academy sweatshirt without a smidgen of makeup. Even without the spark of fire in her eye that Tess's dad loved to fan into flame.

Tess stopped by the front door, as was her habit whenever she went out. Ian McGee grinned down from his place of honor, full dress uniform pressed and neat, arms wrapped around his wife on one side and his daughter on the other.

Tess reached up, gently touching the place where his hand squeezed his daughter's shoulder tightly. "Look after Mom today," she whispered. "This house only has room for one ghost."

Chapter 2

Today, Tess decided as she walked, she wouldn't be the weird girl whose dad had died. The antisocial pariah who roamed the streets, driving off friend and foe alike as though nothing could touch her. It had been a worry for her mother, she knew, Tess's disappearing social life. Sports she no longer played, friends she no longer had. Classes she struggled to attend. Tess didn't mind being the odd man out, per se, the one who lived in books and said the things you weren't supposed to say. She kind of liked that about herself and always had. So what if her witty commentary had become sharper in the last year, cutting with a knife instead of painting with a brush? If she'd stopped reading and taken to her writing with a furor that defied explanation, what of it? Who needed friends, anyway?

It was the thing about the dad that she minded. She had gone from the girl with the dad who solved crimes and saved lives, the girl whose dad was a hero, to the girl with the dead dad, and she found she didn't care much for it.

Tess poured extra vigor into her steps, hoping to outrun that thought. But in the back of her mind, she was forced to admit the nugget of hope tucked out of sight: maybe if Tess could get back to normal, so could her mom.

Tess wasn't supposed to know her mom wasn't working, at least not at first. Every day like clockwork, Kate would raise Tess from her bed, prepare a lunch the likes of which most kids could only dream, and usher them both out the door just as she had every day of Tess's life. Dressed in her perfectly-pressed slacks, a crisp, white shirt, not a single curl out of place - the complete antithesis to Tess's t-shirt and worn jeans, hair escaping every hint of containment as though it had never met a brush it couldn't defeat. Until one afternoon, when Tess had snuck out of school and gone back home. She hadn't been running away from rumors or snide remarks, nor giving up in the face of severe oppression. Of course not. But kids were mean, and she'd rather work on her book, anyway.

Tess had stopped at the sight of her mother's car in the drive. She'd crept quietly to the window and watched as her mother sat motionless on the couch, wrapped in her father's old academy sweatshirt and a blanket, and stared blankly at the wall. No tears, just an empty stare where that zesty spark of life used to be. Tess had spent the rest of the day wandering aimlessly around a sun-dappled neighborhood she'd been too distraught to see.

Tess wasn't sure how her mother had known about that day, but she had stopped the pretense ever since. She still followed the same routine - getting Tess off to school, making lasagna for dinner every Tuesday, but something was missing and she didn't try to hide it.

Maybe her mother had never known about that day. Maybe she had just become too hollowed out to pretend any longer. But if Tess could be better, her mom could be better, too. So she squared her shoulders and reset her backpack. She was going to kill it at school today, and her mother would find the strength to go back to work. For her mom, for her dad, Tess could pay attention in Algebra and not argue with her English teacher's completely absurd interpretation of literary themes. She really could. It would be fine. In her defense though, how could someone with an English degree think *Wuthering Heights* was a romance? That Emily Bronte was seriously messed up.

Actually, now that Tess thought about it, *Jane Eyre* wasn't exactly sunshine and rainbows. Maybe all the Bronte sisters were messed up.

Don't get your hopes up, Tessie.

Sometimes, she could hear her father's voice so clearly. Usually when things were about to hit the fan.

Hopes and dreams are good, but a girl's got to do what a girl's got to do.

As Tess passed the back of the school, thoughts of disturbed Victorian authors in her head, she noticed a gaggle of kids gathered around a tree, hidden from view of any adult supervisory figures who may be watching from the school. Tess knew instinctively the huddle spelled trouble. Any kid who'd ever attended a public school knew the signs. And she knew, that if she wanted to avoid trouble, if she wanted to be *normal*, she should keep walking.

Curiosity killed the cat, Tessie.

That wise voice again, telling her what she already knew.

Just make sure you land on your feet.

He sounded like he was trying not to laugh.

Curses. Even dead, her dad knew her too well. Tess sighed, allowing her feet to follow her heart.

Oh well. She could try to be normal again tomorrow.

Chapter 3

Tess approached quietly from behind, just like her dad taught her. She could have tapped one of the onlookers on the shoulder and asked what was happening, but she preferred to draw her own objective conclusions.

Besides, this one was fairly obvious. There was a new kid in school, Ben Something or Other. If she remembered correctly, he'd moved in from somewhere in South Carolina. Or maybe North Carolina. She hadn't been paying that much attention when their science teacher forced him to introduce himself in front of the class. She had, however, sympathized as he'd sank into the only open seat in the classroom - right smack dab in front of all those prying eyes. Tess hated being looked at, too.

Now Ben was backed against a tree, looking unusually calm for the circumstances, the resident bad boys of freshman year surrounding him. A gaggle of others ringed the four, watching as two of the bigger kids tossed something back and forth over the new guy's head while the third dangled something just out of his reach.

Tess sighed. If it had been anything other than bullies, she could have walked away. Probably. Maybe. But bullies would eventually become criminals if something didn't stop them.

Enter Tess.

All hopes for normality wafted away like smoke drifting on a breeze as Tess shouldered her way through the crowd. As the kids realized who was pushing and shoving her way past them, they started moving aside all on their own. *Don't touch the leper. Don't make eye contact with wild animals.* Luckily, the three geniuses leading the pack didn't notice her coming and as Derrick Merrigan tossed what looked like a high-end camera back to Gage Shaw, Tess snatched it casually out of the air and shoved it back into Ben Something's chest without missing a beat, Derrick and Gage spluttering behind her as she strolled her way over to Mark Dunham, the undisputed ringleader of the three.

Mark was big and burly, with a football player's build and the dusky skin and dark hair of a movie star. He thought he was something special, and most of the girls in school agreed. Tess thought he was entitled, arrogant, and cruel. Or he at least pretended to be those things. Unfortunately, one thing he was not was stupid. Which would have been helpful, because Tess now needed to bluff her way out of yet another situation she should have bypassed.

See? Trouble, trouble everywhere.

"What are you doing, McGee?" Mark asked, perching a stolen pair of glasses on the end of his nose. "There's no need for you to get involved in this."

"What are you doing, *LaMarcus?*" Tess retorted, stressing his full name. Tess and Mark had been in the same class since kindergarten, neighbors for even longer, so she knew things. Like how much he hated his full name. Mark knew that she knew it, and now she was hoping he thought she might know other stuff, too.

"Tess McGee," he grinned, and the condescension in his tone needled her the same way she was hoping to needle him, "this isn't your fight. Go crusade for the downtrodden elsewhere."

"Plenty of downtrodden right here," she quipped cheerfully. "Why, take yourself, LaMarcus Dunham."

Mark narrowed his eyes, on the hook, and Tess plunged on, exuding cheerful confidence. "Always some injury or another, you know. You were limping pretty badly last week. Something going on at home everyone should know about?"

It was a pure shot in the dark, but Tess could tell she'd hit her mark. Mark was the best athlete in the school, even as a freshman, just like his dad had been before him. Tess had seen them after games, and Mr. Dunham expected greatness of his son. Mark played hard, and he played a lot, which meant he was also hurt a lot. And yet, he somehow managed to keep right on playing. Tess was of the belief that doping the pain away wasn't good for anyone, but the school didn't test at their level of competition, so no one was the wiser. Except for Tess, apparently.

She met Mark stare for stare, hers fearless, his contemplative. For a second, Tess could have sworn she saw a flash of fear, but it was gone before she could think more about it.

Mark ran his tongue around his teeth, a habit he had when he was thinking, and Derrick the minion piped in from the background, "Pound her into the ground, Dunham!"

Unbeknownst to Derrick, brain trust that he was, Mark had never actually hurt anyone. Tess wasn't sure why no one else had figured it out, but Mark was all bluff. Tess tilted her chin up, completely confident in her safety, and he finally broke the stalemate with a grin.

"Can't do it, man. She's so tiny, nothing would be left." He took the glasses off and tossed them back to the new kid. He could have twisted the frames, smudged the lenses, something. But he didn't. He folded them neatly and returned them undamaged, just like she knew he would.

"You're a real buzzkill, Tess McGee." Tess was sure it was meant as an insult, but Mark said it in a way that made her seem more endearing and sweetly obnoxious than a thorn in his side. How offensive. "Got to get to class anyway. Can't be late, you know."

At his pronouncement, the gathered crowd turned away in disappointment. Not one had considered stepping in, and they disgusted Tess to no end.

"You see more than you should, McGee." The words were quiet, uttered low enough that only the two of them could hear. Mark's size and status should have made them menacing, but Tess knew better. What was that she could feel? Surely not despair. Tess shook her head, certain she'd misunderstood.

"Watch that Irish nose of yours. It's going to cause you nothing but trouble one day."

That was better, Tess thought. Ominous, with a subtle hint of threat. Like a thunderstorm that hadn't broken the horizon yet, but foreshadowing destruction in its wake.

"Please," she scoffed. "This Irish nose has been causing me trouble for years. And I like a challenge."

Mark shook his head, an amused grin on his face, and grabbed his backpack off the ground like the rock star he thought he was, leaving Tess to watch him walk away.

Chapter 4

"**T**hanks, I guess."

"What?" Tess was still caught up in the glory of her deductive skills and had forgotten she wasn't alone.

"I'm always the new kid, so I would have worked it out," the kid said, adjusting his glasses. "But no one has ever tried to do anything either, so thanks."

"Uh-huh." Maybe there was a whole high school doping scheme right under her nose. She could blow this case wide open.

"Okay, then," he said when Tess remained lost in her own thoughts, slipping his camera around his neck. "I guess we'd better get to class."

"What?" Tess said again, snapping out of her plans for world domination. "Oh, no. You're new and I have a dead dad. First period is more like a suggestion for us."

The kid, Ben, stared at her for a moment, then shrugged his shoulders, accepting her words but not taking the obvious bait she'd dangled in front of him. *Dead dad.*

Instead, he turned back to the tree and lifted the camera. Tess peered over his shoulder. "What are you doing?"

"Robin eggs," he said, like that explained everything. He lowered the camera enough to gesture in the general vicinity of the small nest. "I've been shooting them every day at the same times in the morning and evening to document their development. They should be almost ready to hatch."

"I didn't know eggs did much changing," Tess said dubiously, peering over his shoulder at the perfectly-normal nest.

"'Much' is a strong word." He shrugged his shoulders again, and Tess was starting to think that was just an indication of his personality. "Color patterns change, location of the eggs shift as the chicks inside grow. I'm documenting the cycle for our life science project."

"You have Nelson, right?" She knew he did, but Tess asked anyway as the bell for first period trilled behind her. Neither paid attention.

"Third period."

"Me too." Tess should probably get started on her own project soon. Maybe there was something under her bed growing mold. That could be considered life science, right?

"I'm Ben, by the way." He moved to the side for a different angle. "Ben Lewis."

"Tess McGee."

"Oh, I know."

Tess shot him a look and he shrugged. Again.

"People talk."

Wasn't that the truth? "I'm sure they do. But they haven't talked about you yet. What's your story, Ben Lewis?"

He didn't seem the least bit curious or repulsed by her, the predominate approaches people took with Tess these days, and she found that fascinating.

"Sure you wouldn't rather make something up so you can threaten me with it later?"

His voice was casual, but he finally lowered the camera and shot Tess a lopsided grin.

Well, well. New kid Ben was as smart as he looked. She liked that, so she grinned right back. "Busted. But it worked, didn't it?"

"What do you think he's hiding?" Ben asked thoughtfully, carefully packing his camera away.

"You think he's hiding something?" It was a test. Of course, Mark was hiding something. But she found it interesting that new kid Ben thought so too when no one else in school saw anything other than that megawatt smile and beautiful brown eyes. Instead of answering though, Ben just looked down as he started packing his camera away.

"Drugs," Tess said confidently. "As often as he's hurt, he shouldn't be able to keep playing sports like he does. Never misses a game. I think his dad is doping him."

"Huh." Ben frowned. "That's not the conclusion I would have drawn."

Tess perked up. "Really?" What had she missed? "I'm all ears."

But Ben just shook his head. "We need to go."

"We have passes, remember? And besides, you haven't told me your story yet."

"We don't have passes, and we're already going to be in trouble for being late." Ben tossed his backpack across his shoulders and pulled Tess to her feet like they'd been best friends all their lives. "I live one block down from you," he said mildly, towing Tess towards the school. "I'll tell you my story on the way home."

And just like that, Tess realized she'd done one normal thing today, after all. She'd made a friend. How about that?

"Ben," she said, flinging an arm around his shoulders as Ben hurried her towards the school, "I have the feeling this is the start of a beautiful friendship."

Ben shook his head. "God help me."

Chapter 5

Tess waited impatiently for the final bell to ring. It had been a long day of waiting, and she had considered dropping into Ben's table at lunch. He sat alone and she'd get to hear his story that much sooner. But somehow, despite all odds, she'd managed to hook a friend. She didn't want to scare him off by suffocating him with all her pizzazz so instead she waited until the last bell rang. Tess hit the front door of the school going ninety miles an hour and slammed right into him.

Ben had been standing off the sidewalk beside the flag pole, and Tess's exuberance had thrown her clear of the usual foot traffic. The look on Ben's face said he was definitely not expecting a full-body hello, but he rolled with it as easily as he rolled across the ground.

"Nice tackle, McGee," Mark said, strolling by like he owned the place, that stupid grin firmly in place.

"Shouldn't you be in a gym or a locker room somewhere," Tess shot back without any real vehemence, not even bothering to look over.

"Nice one," Ben said, dusting off his pants. He stood and adjusted his glasses, touching his cheekbone gingerly. "That's going to be a black eye. You ready?"

Tess adjusted her backpack and tried to play it cool, though she doubted she could recover after causing physical injury to her new friend. "You said you lived a street down from me?"

Ben nodded and set off, and Tess fell into step beside him. "You're on Bon Ami Drive, right? I'm just down on Cher."

"You just moved in?" Tess knew Ben was new to the school, but she wanted to give him somewhere to start.

"My parents were both active military until just a few months ago." A muscle car rolled by stuffed full of high school guys. Tess wasn't sure which was louder, the car or the boys, but Ben paused to give it time to drive on. "I stayed with my grandma when they were deployed. But after she died, they realized they couldn't both stay military and leave me a potential orphan."

Ben said it casually, as though being left an orphan was just an ordinary risk of life, but Tess could hear what he hadn't said.

"I'm sorry about your grandma." Tess was fully aware of the hole that kind of loss left in a person's soul.

Ben shrugged those narrow shoulders of his. "Thanks."

"So, who retired?" Tess asked. She hadn't noticed Ben outside of school, and she hadn't noticed any new adults in the neighborhood. They lived one block down from Tess, and she rarely had the opportunity to go that way. So it was possible, she had to admit, that she simply hadn't been paying attention.

"Both. Instead of trying to decide who should give up their career, they both retired and we moved here. A new life for us all."

Tess couldn't decide if Ben was in awe that his parents would make such a sacrifice for him or resentful at the new life he was being forced to live. His tone was too bland to give anything of his feelings away. She also couldn't imagine what would bring two military lifers to a sleepy town like Lafitte.

"My grandma was born in Shenandoah, and we visited her sisters sometimes when I was younger. So my mom knew the area and wanted to move back," Ben answered without Tess needing to ask.

That made sense, she supposed. Still, she couldn't help but argue. "But Lafitte? At least Shenandoah has some life! It's got more people, more things to do." Lafitte's tiny population barely scratched the surface of Shenandoah's. "Plus, you can drive into Baton Rouge for the zoo. Ooh, or the Capitol Park Museum!"

Tess and her parents had visited both several years ago, but it was tough making a day trip to Baton Rouge over four hours away. Shenandoah was only two.

"I prefer Bluebonnet Swamp," Ben said mildly, "but my parents seem happy enough."

"Just your parents?" Tess asked, never one to tiptoe around an awkward question. After all, she was the girl who said what shouldn't be said.

Ben shrugged, hands in pockets, eyes forward. "It's fine. My grandma's only been gone for a few months and I miss her of course. But my parents are both home for the first time I can remember, so that's something."

Tess decided to let it go for now. She knew a little something of how it felt to miss someone, and even she was sensitive enough to not constantly pick at an open wound.

"They bought me this camera," he said suddenly, patting the case slung around his neck. "That's something. I've always drawn, but I'd never thought about photography until now."

"And you like it?"

"I do."

No one could accuse Ben of being verbose, but that was okay. Tess was verbose enough for both of them.

"Can I keep walking with you?" she asked as Ben slowed near her driveway. The streets were dappled in the sunlight streaming between the leaves of the mature magnolias that marked her neighborhood, and Tess knew she still had a couple of hours of daylight left. She might as well keep walking.

Ben shrugged again. "Sure." He turned and headed towards Cher, one block away. Tess shivered as a shadow fell over them, and she pointed out the old house on the left. "That's the old Brooklyn house," she said. "The one on the left leaking southern Gothic vibes?"

Ben dug out his camera, and even Tess had to admit it was a striking view. The old house was three stories of plantation manor glory, long-faded. The shutters were cracked and weathered and the lawn unkempt. Tess wouldn't have been at all surprised to hear a crow caw forlornly in the distance or see fog roiling over the ragged grass. There was something in the way the shadows settled around the house and anything it touched. The abandoned house had always been mysterious but with time and dilapidation, it was developing an ominous heaviness that shadowed the street. Malevolent, one might say.

Oh, yes. Tess liked that word. The house felt malevolent. Who knew what was watching from-

"I saw a van here a few days ago," Ben said, adjusting the focus of his lens and snapping Tess back to the real world. "Seemed like someone was moving in."

"It's been empty for as long as I can remember." Tess gazed at the house and realized it wasn't just malevolent. It seemed...sad, somehow. Lonely. Like it had a secret but no one to tell. "Having someone living there has to make it better."

The house sat on a diagonal from Tess's own and when she looked out her bedroom window, it filled the majority of the view. She'd spent many a night trying to imagine it in the context of a Gothic novel. That old house was just begging to be the haunting focal point in a gritty mystery novel.

Ben tucked his camera back into the bag. "Come on," he said. "My dad should be home. I'll introduce you."

Tess followed but kept her eyes on the house. For some reason, she couldn't bring herself to turn her back on it, and she shivered again as the chill of the house grew.

Chapter 6

"**M**y mom won't be home for a few hours," Ben said, unlocking the front door and pushing inside. "They both have offices upstairs but her car is gone, which means she's probably out on a case." Ben hung his backpack on a tidy rack by the door, and Tess grimaced. She usually just slung hers across the room with impunity, but she followed his lead and hung hers neatly next to his.

"Well, a case or the restaurant a few blocks over," he amended. "It's her night to cook and she loves Chinese, so it could really be either."

"What do your parents do now that they're out of the service?" Tess made herself at home as Ben wandered into the kitchen. He lived in a two-story bungalow with painted shutters, reading nooks in every corner, and high, airy ceilings. The whole thing had a very open, beach-style vibe happening, and Tess dug it.

"Mom was naval intelligence." Ben handed Tess a bottle of soda that he'd grabbed from the stainless steel refrigerator. Sugar-free. The soda, not the fridge. "She got her PI license after she rotated out, and now she takes private clients when she can get them."

"In Lafitte?" Tess had doubts about the existence of a seedy underbelly in their little hamlet but if it existed, she'd like to know.

"She does skip tracing and bail jumpers in between the real clients."

Now that, Tess understood. Any town big enough for a jail was big enough for bail jumpers. Not to mention the larger towns ringing their smaller, suburban area.

"What about your dad?" Tess took the can of fake soda Ben offered and wandered around the cozy living room. There was a fireplace on one wall, which Tess had never really understood in the south, picture windows facing a picturesque street, and French doors that opened to a small patio in the back.

"He opened a private security firm and provides consultation for corporations. Mostly, he gets to work from home too. Now and again, his clients are in other states and he flies out for a week or two to get them set up."

A framed photo of Ben and his parents, both in full military dress, and another of Ben and an older woman sat side-by-side on the mantle. Tess's fingers lightly traced the family photo, but she didn't mention it. Instead, "Is this your grandma?"

The older woman looked enough like Ben's mom there was little doubt, and Ben nodded slowly. He came to stand beside Tess, and they both kept their eyes on the picture.

"She died three months ago."

"Sorry," Tess said quietly.

"Yeah."

What else was there to say, really? Tess understood better than anyone what it meant to lose someone you loved. So instead of talking, they stood silently, sipping their sugar-free soda. It felt like forever but was no time at all before Ben turned to her.

"Come on," he said. "I've got a monarch butterfly in the final stages of pupation. You can use it for your life science project."

Tess was offended. "Why do you assume I need your leftovers?" she bluffed. "The project's due in four weeks. I have it completely under control."

"The project is due in three weeks," Ben answered mildly, "and I'm not using it. Do you want it or not?"

It was infuriating how Ben didn't even have the decency to sound annoyed with her. No, he sounded as if he already knew the answer. In fact, he was already heading for the stairs, not even giving her the time to accept.

The nerve.

"You can use the pictures and notes I've already taken, but you'll have to do the rest."

It only took Tess a second to swallow her pride. She knew a good deal when she heard it. Still, it wasn't in her to be completely gracious. "I would hate to waste all that effort. I suppose I can finish the project for you. Since we're friends and all."

Ben arched an eyebrow and Tess grinned. "Oh, yeah." She planted her hands on his shoulders and started steering him up the stairs. "You are definitely going to regret inviting me in."

"I didn't invite you," Ben pointed out as Tess shoved him up the stairs. "You invited yourself."

"Same difference."

After an hour, Tess had to admit the butterfly was a decent project. She was kind of looking forward to seeing what she looked like when she popped out of her shell.

"Chrysalis," Ben corrected.

"Potato, photahto." A bag was a bag, no matter what you called it. "Why do you have a random butterfly *chrysalis*," she asked, "just hanging out in your room?"

A door opened downstairs, and a man's booming voice found them easily. "Benjamin Michael Lewis, get down here right now!"

Tess glanced at Ben because she assumed that was his dad who sounded like a biker dude ready to brawl. Maybe she wasn't supposed to be here. She hadn't meant to get him in trouble. He was right though, he hadn't invited her. She'd invited herself. She knew she wasn't easy to say 'no' to. Maybe she could explain -

"That's just how he talks," Ben said, interrupting her internal dialogue. "He's not mad. He's just loud." He headed towards the door. "Come on. I'll introduce you."

Tess wasn't used to feeling hesitant, but he really had sounded mad. Catching sight of the giant standing in the living room didn't help matters either.

"Dad," Ben said, stepping off the stairs, "maybe tone it down. I have a friend over."

If Tess could have disappeared in that moment, she would have. Ben's dad didn't just sound like an angry biker, he looked like one, too. He had to be seven feet tall, with hulking muscle and a scar that wrapped from his jaw around his neck and disappeared beneath the collar of his shirt. He focused laser-sharp eyes on her, as though sizing her up.

He reminded Tess of a dog that used to roam the neighborhood. It had been a big pit mix with an ugly snout and mean eyes. It was dirty and gnarled and growled at anyone who came close. She had been sure that dog would tear her to pieces, and she had the feeling Mr. Lewis could do the same. So when he grabbed her up off the stairs and swung her around the room, she closed her eyes and prepared for death. Until she realized Mr. Lewis was laughing.

"Any friend of Ben's is welcome here!" he said, that booming voice echoing off the high rafters. He dropped her to her feet, and Tess staggered and rolled. "Oops," he said, sounding contrite. "I didn't realize you were such a tiny thing."

"Dad!"

Ben sounded so aghast that Tess couldn't help it - she burst out laughing. "I haven't had a ride that good since my dad took me to the state fair two years ago," which started Mr. Lewis laughing again.

He had a nice laugh, and it didn't sound so angry once she stopped to listen. Come to think of it, that dog had turned out alright too. Mrs. Sandoval next door, a little old lady with a whole lot of gumption, had been the only one with the nerve to scoop him up, give him a bath and a home, and now they took walks together every morning and every evening. Gary, as he was now known, wore a little sweater over his massive bulk and attended all of the neighborhood community events as the unofficial mascot of the street.

Which was just a good reminder that things in life were rarely what they appeared to be.

Chapter 7

For once, crime was slow on the mean streets of Detroit. The city was safe, in no small part because of his own hard work. But when the streets were safe, there were no cases. And when there were no cases, the creditors came calling.

It was hard to make a living when being good at your job meant there was less to do, but such was the burden of a grizzled old gumshoe like himself. He could always go back to the force, but toeing the company line was no life. Not for him.

Not anymore.

His secretary had gone home hours ago with many an admonishment not to stay too long himself. She worried after him, but she didn't understand. This was his home. This second-story walk-up of crumbling brick and twisting metal was the home he'd chosen, and he wandered to the window overlooking what once had been bustling streets. As he lit his cigarette, he had to wonder if maybe life had passed him by after all...

The knock at the door was the first in weeks, and he inclined his head as the door slowly opened. If he were very, very lucky, the streets would prove to be meaner tonight than they had in weeks. He was almost out of cigarettes, after all.

She was just a little thing, timid in her approach, but she was dressed to the nines in clothing that didn't come from the kind of stores he could afford. That was a good sign. The rich tended to overpay.

"Pardon me," she said, clearing her throat with a dainty cough, "but are you the detective who solved the Berrisford kidnapping and the Donaldson diamond thefts?"

Those cases had brought him notoriety and drinks on the house at the local watering hole, for a while anyway, and he gave a curt, silent nod. That was him.

"They say you can solve what no one else can solve. Cases that can't be answered. Cases that don't have an answer. Is that true?"

There was just a hint of steel in her voice, eyes that finally met his with determination, and even his winter-cold heart was intrigued.

"It's true that they say it." He nodded to the rickety chair across from his desk and, after a moment of hesitation, the young woman sank into it.

"It's my father, you see," she said. From her pocketbook, she produced a single sheet of newsprint, the kind he might get from one of the young news hawkers on the street. Or from the coroner's office.

"He, well, he died, not so very long ago and they say it was by his own hand." She held out the sheet to him, but he ignored it.

"I take it you don't agree?"

At this, the young lady straightened her spine. "I do not," she said with fire. "My father was a philanthropist. He dedicated his life to making the world a better place. And he loved me," she said with a sniff. "He would never have chosen to leave me."

The old detective recognized her now. The death of a wealthy businessman by suicide was big news in these parts, especially when his fingerprints were on the entire city.

He leaned back in his chair and steepled his fingers. "So, Miss McGuire, what is it you want from me?"

If she were surprised to be recognized, she didn't show it. Someone of her class, coming to this neighborhood alone at this time of night, seeking the help of someone outside the law? People like her didn't do things like that. Not unless they were desperate.

"I want you," she said vehemently, "to find the man who killed him."

• • • •

TESS HAD GOOD INTENTIONS of meeting Ben outside her house and walking to school with him the next day. She really did. But she'd had a particularly difficult chapter she'd been fighting with until the wee hours of the morning, and so sleep had become the priority.

But here she was now, leaving for school on time without her mother chasing her out of the house. So, goals. But Tess stopped short as she stepped onto the sidewalk, the sight of a moving van in front of the Brooklyn house making her pause.

Ben had mentioned someone moving in, but the Brooklyn house had been vacant since before Tess was born. Oh, there had been renters off and on, but only short-term. Tess watched as two men jumped from the back of the truck, one carrying two oversized duffle bags and the other with a large covered crate in his arms. Tess hoped they were only the movers because the two men looked like Disney villains. Both were dark-haired with pale, ashy complexions, one long and lanky, the other short and squat.

Something soft slipped from the crate and flopped against the ground as the man hurried on without noticing, and Tess realized it was a child's toy. A gray stuffed animal, with big feet and floppy ears. A bunny.

Movement caught Tess's eye, and she looked up to see a girl standing just inside the open cargo bay of the truck looking out. The girl was small, at least a foot shorter than Tess herself, with soft brown hair and oversize eyes that stood out in her thin face. Six, maybe seven years old, Tess guessed. She was wearing a soft, pink dress dotted with small white hearts, tattered at the hem. Whether it was her hair, her pale complexion, or the color of her dress, Tess didn't know, but the girl had a faded, washed-out quality that struck Tess as odd.

She seemed ethereal. Otherworldly. Tess knew a little of how that felt, so she raised her hand and gave the girl a welcoming wave and friendly smile.

"Is that your bunny?" Tess called out, voice raised to carry across the street. "I think he hopped out of his crate." She pointed towards the ground, in case the girl hadn't seen the toy fall.

The girl blinked but didn't move, and Tess frowned. The watery, early-morning sunlight was playing tricks with the shadows across the road, making it hard for Tess to see. The bunny looked old and worn, clearly well-loved, and Tess didn't want her to get lost. Maybe the girl hadn't heard? As Tess was preparing to cross the street to say hello in person, the screen door behind her slammed against the brick front of her house. Brick that had long been damaged from such treatment and could only sigh wearily and hold fast against the storm that had once been Kate McGee.

"Tessa Lynn McGee, what are you still doing here, sugar?" Tess's mom asked, stepping to the sidewalk beside her. A delicate hand moved to Tess's shoulder, and Tess glanced up. "What are you looking at, baby?"

Tess looked back, but the little girl was gone. Had she ducked back inside the truck? Tess didn't think she would have had time to dart up the sidewalk to the house.

"New neighbors, huh?" her mom commented. "It's about time that house was occupied again."

"They have a little girl," Tess said, pointing to where the bunny lay abandoned behind the truck, ready to be squashed when the men backed out of the drive.

"That will be nice," her mom commented, and Tess could tell she was really trying. "Let's not bother them right now, though. Why don't you grab it to give back later?" She gestured towards the bunny. "You can introduce yourself then."

Tess looked back towards the truck, but the girl had well and truly vanished. The Disney villains had closed the front door behind them so Tess didn't see any other options. She gave her mom a quick hug goodbye and darted across the street, picking up the stuffed animal and dusting it off on her jeans. It was old and worn, one ear hanging by threads and track marks in the fur where little fingers had gripped it tightly. It was obviously important to someone, so Tess tucked it gingerly into her backpack. She'd clean it up and look for the girl later. Maybe she could even invite her over. The girl might be younger than Tess, but that didn't mean she couldn't use a friend.

Oh, yeah. Tess had this *normal* thing down pat.

Chapter 8

"**S**o, my dad was murdered."

Tess was looking down at her feet when she said it, but out of the corner of her eye, she saw Ben skip a step at her pronouncement. She couldn't blame him. Ben had tracked Tess down at lunch after she stood him up on the way to school and they'd eaten in companionable silence, Ben cleaning his camera and Tess trying to work out the troublesome passage that had kept her awake until all hours. Now walking home, Ben had asked how her last class had been, and she'd blurted the thing that was always on her mind but never spoken.

It felt good to finally say it out loud.

The need to say it had been bottled up inside her for so long and Ben had become the perfect outlet. She and her mom never talked about how he died. They rarely talked about him at all, but certainly only about better times. Happier times. Tess knew her mom was doing the best she could, but Tess wasn't built the same way. How could she, or her father for that matter, truly rest in peace while his murderer was roaming free?

Tess's mom didn't want to talk about it. Her dad's partner didn't want to talk about it. Mr. Michaels, her school counselor, didn't want to talk about it. Well, that was fine. Ben would talk about it with her. Or he'd at least listen.

"I know you've heard the talk."

Ben nodded, acknowledging what they both knew to be true. Ben had only moved in last month, so he hadn't been around when it had happened, but gossip was everywhere and kids talked.

"He was a detective with the Louisiana state police. He'd tackled some major cases before, but this one was different."

Ben didn't say he was sorry for her loss or any of the other things Tess had come to expect. Instead, he went a different route. "Did they catch his killer?"

Finally, someone who understood.

Tess didn't need his sympathy, she needed someone to bounce ideas back and forth with. For a new friend, he already understood her pretty well.

"That's the weird thing." Tess's hands fisted at her sides, and she wanted to stamp her foot in frustration. "They don't even seem to be looking!"

That was what confused her. "They don't seem to be doing anything. I don't even think they're investigating."

It was maddening. To think the police would let the murder of one of their own slide...how could that even be?

"If the police don't believe he was murdered, why do you?" Ben asked, in what Tess was coming to realize was his naturally calm, logical manner.

"He was working on something before...you know, it happened." Tess felt a familiar twinge in her chest which she ruthlessly shoved aside. Now was no time for weakness. "The last few months, he looked pale and tired, definitely more than normal. I could tell he wasn't eating or sleeping and he spent all his free time locked away in his study."

Their free time was usually spent together, hiking trails and riding bikes. But in the last few months of his life, her dad would already be behind closed doors when she made it home from school. It was such a departure from what she'd always known that it had worried her, even then.

"When I'd ask if he was okay, he would just smile like he always did and tell me I shouldn't worry about him. That he'd work it out, same as always." Tess shrugged. "Even Sully changed."

"Sully?" Ben scrunched his nose and looked sideways at her.

"Dad's partner." Tess smiled fondly. "They met in the academy and worked patrol together. They got married together, made sergeant together, even took their detective exams together." She shrugged. "Whatever was going on, they were in on it together. Sully and Miss Angel - that's Sully's wife," Tess said before Ben could ask, "still came over for weekly dinner, but Sully just went straight to the study and they would lock themselves in there for hours."

"That does sound strange," Ben said thoughtfully. "Like they were working on something together. Something they didn't want to share with anyone else. It doesn't sound like Sully is someone who would overlook the murder of his partner."

Ben was right about that, which was more baffling than anything. "I'm sure he's working on it. He must be. He just won't tell me anything."

And wasn't that more frustrating than anything? The last time she'd gone to the station to ask about the investigation, the desk sergeant had only looked at her with his sad, sad eyes and ratted her out to Sully, who had popped around the corner almost immediately to take her home.

"I could help, but he keeps telling me I shouldn't worry. That I should focus on school and finishing my book."

Your dad wouldn't want you to worry, Tessie. He'd want you to finish that book for both of you.

Well, maybe so. But he'd also want his murderer locked up instead of roaming free, mindlessly destroying lives like they didn't matter. When Tess had helpfully pointed that out, Sully had only looked sadder.

"It sounds like he's just trying to look out for you."

Oh, Tess was well aware. Sully and Miss Angel still came over for dinner twice a week. Sully played hoops with her in the driveway while Miss Angel and her mom spilled some tea, whatever that meant. She knew they were trying to do right by her and her mom, for their sake but also for her dad. But that didn't mean she liked it.

They walked in silence for a few minutes, until Tess pointed to something down the street, content to change the subject. Like a pressure valve had been released, saying the words had released the pent-up pressure boiling inside Tess, at least for now. "Did you notice the van this morning?"

"The van?" Ben pushed his glasses up his nose as he looked at her in question.

"It was outside the Brooklyn house when I left for school today." Tess glanced down the street to where she could see the start of her own driveway. "There were a couple of guys moving stuff in, and they had a little girl with them."

"They must have showed up after I left. Doesn't look like it's there now."

Ben was right. The lane in front of the house was empty, save for some recent tire tracks and a scattering of leaves from the maple starting to shed.

"Maybe they finished unpacking already. I tried to talk to the little girl, but she must be shy. I looked away for just a minute but when I looked back, she was gone."

"Shy, sure. Or maybe you overpowered her with the force of your personality," Ben remarked wryly.

Was that a joke? Was there a sense of humor in there, after all? Tess opened her mouth to snap back, but was rudely interrupted by one of the last people she cared to see.

"Tess McGee!"

Why was he always around when she least wanted to be bothered? "Was that your bellow, LaMarcus, or did an ape escape from the zoo again?" Tess asked sweetly, batting her eyes like the southern ladies of old.

Mark Dunham laughed like she'd made a joke instead of being dead serious as he strolled their way. As though he owned the whole street, and it was infuriating.

"I've got a bone to pick with you, McGee," he said casually. "You mind?"

Mark nodded at Ben, who took it as the dismissal it was intended to be, which rubbed Tess even more wrong, like petting a cat backward. It just shouldn't be done.

"He minds," Tess snapped before Ben could respond. "My *friend*, here, is always welcome. Which is more than I can say for the non-friend types in my life."

To Tess's annoyance, Ben merely rolled his eyes. "She's all yours, man." He nodded at Mark as he abandoned her to her fate.

Turncoat.

"Nice guy," Mark said.

"Nicer than some," Tess shot back and this time, Mark was the one to roll his eyes.

"Tess McGee, I wasn't hurting your new little friend there, and I wasn't going to. I'm not as bad a guy as you give me credit for being."

"Uh-huh. I'm sure you and your posse were just offering the warm hand of fellowship to the new guy."

"Just like Pastor John taught us," he quipped. When Tess merely raised an eyebrow, he sighed. "They weren't going to hurt him, either."

Mark's tone was still calm and even, which only served to annoy Tess further. And she was not someone who could be accused of being calm and placid, even on her best day.

"Oh, I'm sure," she retorted. "It looked like his camera and glasses were in great hands."

At that, Mark grinned. "These hands, you mean? These hands that can cradle a football and create a perfect spiral?" Mark pulled back into a quarterback pose. "Or these hands," he went on, reaching into his pocket and pulling out something small, "that can carve the most delicate, exquisite art out of bits of spare wood?"

Mark tossed the small piece of driftwood at her, and Tess caught it without looking. "The reason I wanted to talk to you was because you said something when you were rescuing your new puppy yesterday."

Tess tried to think back. She was pretty sure she threatened him with nothing more than a made-up bluff with just the barest hint of truth. "What about it?"

Mark looked at her square, his face unusually serious. "Did you mean it? When you said something was going on at home, and everyone should know about it?"

Interesting. "Why, LaMarcus. Is there something to know?" Tess batted her eyelashes again and adopted the most innocent look she could. After another beat of silence, Mark relaxed his stare.

"That's what I thought. You got nothing, kid." He reached out and ruffled her hair fondly, increasing her red-headed rage exponentially. By the time she'd ducked out from under his absurdly long wingspan, he'd already spun on his heel and was slouching back towards his house, one block away.

"See you tomorrow, Tess McGee."

It didn't sound as much like a threat as it did a promise. "Stop calling me 'Tess McGee'!" she yelled at his retreating back.

Mark put up a hand, giving her an imaginary hat tip. "Just as soon as you stop calling me *LaMarcus*."

Chapter 9

"**T**ess has made a new friend," Kate McGee announced proudly at dinner that night. The reactions were wildly varied.

"Oh, sweet baby," Miss Angel gushed, hands to chest as though she were thanking her good Lord and Savior. "I knew she still had it in her!"

Miss Angel's husband, Sully, merely shrugged his shoulders. "Like that's so hard?"

Miss Angel elbowed Sully from where he grinned behind his forkful of lasagna. "Now you know this girl's had her troubles. Delightful though you may be," she said to Tess apologetically. "If our baby's made a friend, we will celebrate."

Sully merely shrugged again, needling his wife's outrage. But he did shoot Tess a wink on the sly as Miss Angel turned back to Tess's mother. "Tell us all about this new friend."

Kate turned skeptical eyes on her daughter. "Unfortunately, I have yet to meet this young man." She turned to the adults in the room. "His family moved in down the street a few months ago."

"A young man?" Miss Angel was practically salivating. "How exciting!"

"The beach shack on Cher?" Sully asked at the same time, focusing instead on what mattered. The cop at the table would, of course, know every house with new residents in their neighborhood.

Miss Angel rolled her eyes. "It's not a beach shack," she argued, in what sounded like a road they'd been down before. "It's modern coastal." As Miss Angel was an interior decorator, Tess supposed she would know.

"The Lewis's," Sully said. "Parents are career military. Retired to raise Benjamin, I think it is?" Sully shot Tess a look for confirmation, but Tess just rolled her eyes. He knew he was just trying to pull her into the conversation.

"Anyway," Kate said, attempting to regain control of the conversation, "they've been walking to and from school together, and Ben is helping Tess with her science project."

Sully harrumphed under his breath. "Teenage boys," he fairly growled, "are not good friends."

"Teenage boys," Miss Angel pointed out, "are statistically less likely to be kidnapped walking home from school. This *boy* keeps our Tessie safe."

"From the many kidnappers roaming our streets in broad daylight, sure. But is she safe from him?"

All three adults turned to look at Tess, who sat in mortified silence as her skin slowly adopted the color of her hair. She could feel the heat burning through her cheeks, and she shifted attention in the only way she could think of at the moment.

"How did you see us walking home together?" Tess blurted at her mother. "You don't get home from work until after five."

As so often happened when she opened her mouth, Tess wished she could pull it back the moment it was out. It was something they didn't talk about, her mother not working. And like the aftermath of a bomb dropped in the middle of a war zone, utter silence reigned as the dust and debris settled around the survivors.

It had worked, Tess supposed. She certainly wasn't the one humiliated anymore. No, now she was uncomfortable in a whole new way. Kate slowly brought her napkin to her mouth, blotting delicately as her mamma taught her before laying it across her plate in a flawless caricature of a southern belle of old. "Would you excuse me for just one moment," she murmured to the room before rising elegantly and disappearing up the stairs.

How many times would Tess end up cursing her stupid, sharp tongue or the way she blurted out the first thing on her mind without thinking? Her mother may have given up the pretense of trying to hide it, but they never talked about the fact she'd stopped going to work. They never talked about anything important.

Tess knew why. She understood. But it didn't change anything.

After a moment, Miss Angel rose. "It's okay, baby," she said, laying her hand gently on Tess's shoulder as she walked by. "I'll just go make sure she's okay."

Miss Angel shot a glance at her husband as she went, but Sully paid no attention. Tess was never quite sure if he was ignoring her or if they were so in tune that they didn't even need to make eye contact.

"Well," he finally said, after they were alone, "you sure messed that up, kid."

Tess sighed, pushing her mostly full plate away. "I know, I know," she grumbled. "No need to rub it in."

"Seems like plenty of reason to rub it in," Sully replied mildly. He rose and started gathering plates. Their weekly dinners ended like this more often than Tess cared to admit, though thankfully she wasn't always the reason. But they had a routine after almost a year of these tense throwbacks to more joyful times, and it was easier to just follow along. So Tess grabbed the salad bowl and the drinks from the table and followed Sully into the kitchen. Miss Angel had already filled the sink with piping hot water, and Sully slid the plates in carefully so they could soak.

"You knew, right?" Tess broke the silence as she covered the leftover lasagna and put it in the refrigerator.

"That your mother's not working anymore?" Sully asked. "We know. Didn't know you did, though."

Tess shrugged a shoulder, dumping the used silverware into the hot water beside him. "For a while now."

"Hmm. Now I wonder how you could know, what with you being in school and all?"

Sully didn't look up from where his hands were buried in the scalding water, but Tess wasn't surprised. She couldn't have hidden it from her dad, and she couldn't hide it from his partner either.

"I don't do it all the time," she said defensively. "It's just, you know, once in a while I need a little space. For my book," she qualified. "When I get an idea, I have to get it out."

"Right," Sully agreed. "And you can't write it down at school. That would make no sense at all."

Tess sighed and when she moved over to start drying the dishes, Sully bumped her shoulder with his. "Kids can be mean."

She just shrugged again. If asked, Tess would have testified under oath that her eyes were blurry because the dishes were so hot from the water. But Sully wasn't wrong. The Tess McGee she showed the world didn't care what the other kids said. She didn't care that her friends had stopped coming around or about the whispers that followed her through the hallways. She had a tough shell and a sharp defense. The whispers were uttered at their own risk. And yet, sometimes a girl just had to get away. It was exhausting with defenses set to stun for so long.

It wasn't something she wanted to talk about right now, though. Of anyone, Sully would be the person she would trust the most. He was the next best thing to her dad. But Tess lived with it all the time and frankly, she was sick of it. Instead, she wanted to talk about something else. As a cop, Sully knew everything about the newcomers in their neighborhood. That had been her dad's job and now, as his best friend, Sully had taken up the charge.

"What do you know about the people moving into the Brooklyn house?" she asked. Sully glanced at her but let it go as she'd known he would. Sully was quieter than her dad, less of a jokester. And he knew when to pull back.

"The Brooklyn house, huh?" He almost seemed surprised. "I didn't realize it was rented." That surprised Tess as much as it surprised Sully. He always knew.

"I saw them moving in a few days ago," Tess said, trying to remember exactly what day that was. "A couple of guys and a little girl. The truck has been back and forth a few times, but I've only seen them that once."

"It'll be good to have the house occupied," he said, and Tess understood. Her father had never liked that house. Unoccupied houses tended to attract squatters, and the Brooklyn house was a big place to squat. They'd never had trouble, but her father had kept an eye on it. It made sense Sully would feel the same.

"You said they have a little girl?" Sully asked, and Tess nodded. "That's good."

Tess understood that too. Families made for more stable neighbors, and children were a good excuse to get involved in the community. "The little girl was maybe five or six," Tess guessed. "Looked like a quiet little thing." Tess thought for a moment. "The men look like Disney villains. I'm calling them Horace and Jasper."

Sully laughed outright at that. "Well, you just stay clear of them for now, little Tessie," he said. "Let them get settled before forcing your rather...unique...brand of hospitality on them."

Waiting until Sully did a little background work was unspoken, but she heard it nonetheless.

Tess affected an indignant expression. "Forcing hospitality? Me? I would never."

But Sully just shook his head, and Tess could swear his eyes were a little more sad than before. "I swear, that attitude." He smiled, but it was bittersweet.

"Just like your father."

Chapter 10

B etsy McGuire, daughter of disgraced banking mogul Henry McGuire, sat across his ancient desk, spine straight, proudly daring him to disagree with her.

Anyone who could meet him stare-for-stare was worth a second look, so he silently slid the coroner's report across the wood, noting the signature with some measure of assurance. Dr. Holland was a seasoned professional who knew his business and never turned down the offer of a free drink, even from someone outside the force. He'd be able to buy the doctor's true observations, those not listed in the report.

"Dr. Holland is a seasoned professional who knows his business," he remarked dryly, for the sake of propriety.

"Indeed he is," Miss McGuire responded. "But rumor has it he doesn't turn down a drink, even from someone outside the force. I assume you'll have no problem buying the true story."

So, the girl had done her research. It meant she was smart, and she hadn't come to him on a whim.

"What do you know?"

She gestured to the newsprint. "I know that isn't true, despite Dr. Holland's reputation. And I know my father."

She was so assured in her beliefs that he almost smiled. Almost. One thing he'd learned in this business? You never knew what you thought you knew.

"Henry McGuire, sixty-two, founder of the largest banking conglomerate in the state. Calculating businessman who didn't trust his secrets to any man, leaving competing businesses bankrupt and broken in his wake. Found in an alley at the *bottom of Cadillac Hotel, the victim of a thirty-three-story jump."*

He'd said it straight but if he'd thought to induce tears, he was mistaken. Instead, Miss McGuire placidly responded. "Henry McGuire, sixty-two, founder of the Maryann Goff Home for Mothers and Children, the Charitable Institute for the Poor and Grieving, and the Public Youth Center of Detroit. A loving father who trusted exactly one person and included her in all his business dealings, dedicated to leaving the world a better place than when he'd entered it. Found in an alley at the bottom of Cadillac Hotel, the victim of an assault and a thirty-three story fall."

He had to give the girl her due, she had spirit. While most women would have succumbed to tears, Miss McGuire's resolve had only firmed. Interesting.

"He was working on something big," she went on. "A non-profit that would have shaken the foundations of the power-hungry world of medical and insurance profiteering. It would have changed the rules that give so much power and prestige to the rich, sharing it instead with the middle and working classes who need a hand up."

And now, finally, the tears threatened to appear. "He was committed to doing good," *Miss McGuire insisted. "He considered this the proudest achievement of his life. It would have been his legacy." She swiped angrily at her eyes. "Someone found out and killed him for it."*

The battered old detective closed his eyes and filled his lungs. If what she said was true, this idea was worth millions. Henry McGuire was known for making anything happen, and men had killed for much less.

"Do you know what the project was?" he finally asked, not sure if he wanted to know. The coroner's report was solid work. If Dr. Holland believed Henry McGuire had thrown himself off that building, it was likely true. And yet...

...her story was plausible. If McGuire was piloting a project that would cost the corporate world millions, there would be a line of suspects just waiting to end the threat to the lifestyles to which they'd become accustomed. He would be stepping into a lion's den of vicious, cutthroat men used to getting what they wanted.

Not that he minded. It was always a toss-up as to what would kill him first, his cigarettes or his job. And he had to admit, he was curious. And the payday, well - that certainly wouldn't hurt.

Unfortunately, Miss McGuire sighed. "He was keeping it a secret, even from me. He didn't want to involve me until he was certain about it. He only told me it would change the world. It was the legacy he wanted to leave behind."

That was unfortunate, but not necessarily a deal-breaker. He still had some avenues he could follow, and talking to Dr. Holland would be his first step.

If he decided to take the case.

"I want the killer caught," Miss McGuire said decisively. "But I want something else even more." She took a deep breath. "I want my father's name cleared. I want him remembered as the kind, decent man he was, and not a man who would take his own life."

He debated. If a case looked simple, it usually was. The business world was tough these days, and it wasn't uncommon to wake up to find another Wall Street man dead by his own hand. And yet...

...McGuire had seemed to be above it all. If his finances were clean, and if he was really on the verge of launching a foundation that would help the little guy recover from the worst economic depression the country had seen in its short life, it could be worth a look.

"I can't guarantee you'll like the results," he cautioned. "Or even that you'll agree with them."

"Your reputation precedes you," Miss McGuire replied. "You are honest, and you dig until you're satisfied you have the truth, no matter the cost. And for that, I will pay handsomely."

She withdrew an envelope from her pocketbook and held it out. After a moment of silent debate, he leaned forward and plucked it from her hand. Inside was a handwritten number with more zeros than he'd ever seen from a year's worth of jobs, let alone a single contract. Along with a thick stack of bills.

"I trust the total amount is acceptable," she said primly, "and the down payment suits your needs."

He raised an eyebrow as he mentally thumbed through the cold, hard cash in front of him. "I believe we have an agreement, Miss McGuire."

• • • •

THE VAN WAS BACK.

It was the first thing Tess noticed when she rolled out of bed the next day. It was sitting outside the Brooklyn house across from Tess's window, the back end slightly angled towards the house so she couldn't *quite* see in despite the back doors being open. As she watched, one of the men came from the house, head down, and made his way back to the van.

Tess wasn't sure why she was suddenly so interested in the house and the people renting it. Maybe it was the fact the information had caught Sully off-guard, which never happened. Maybe it was the fact the men looked like they should be shackled at the ankle, pounding rocks and singing a chain gang song.

Even now, the one she was calling Horace seemed furtive somehow, like a rat trying to slip beneath the watchful eye of the neighborhood cat as it snuck out of its hole for food. Like last week, they seemed to be unloading cardboard boxes more than anything, which made sense. If they had bigger cargo, like furniture and mattresses, they would have needed a moving truck.

Tess knew some cargo vans had a modified interior to make space for equipment, so they might have appliances and furniture in there. But so far, they seemed to be focused on smaller items.

The second man, shorter than the first, slunk out of the house and met his compatriot by the back of the van. A squat, barrel-chested little man, this one had a mean look about him that Tess instantly distrusted, and she snatched the binoculars she kept hanging beside her window to get a closer look. Tess watched as they debated something for a few minutes before the second man, Jasper, jerked several stacked boxes from the back of the truck and stomped back towards the house. Horace shook his head, either in frustration or exasperation.

It might have been Tess's imagination, but his shoulders seemed to slump as he picked up his flimsy pile of boxes. It didn't take long before Jasper was back, this time to slam the van doors closed and glance suspiciously around the neighborhood, as though he could feel her watching eyes. Tess decided she didn't care much for Jasper. He had a temper and a look about him that prickled the hairs on the back of her neck. Both times she'd seen him, he'd appeared agitated and jumpy, angry at his friend.

What were they hiding, Tess wondered. Because it suddenly seemed obvious to her that they were hiding something. The demeanor of the first man, jumpy and anxious, and the angry, hostile energy of the second man was enough to make her curious all by itself. But they only unloaded so much at one time and so far, she'd only seen them take boxes from the van in the early hours of the morning.

And where was the little girl she'd seen before? Was she already in the house? Was she still asleep? Tess only woke up this early on a school day to get some writing in. The little girl might have still been sleeping somewhere within the depths of the larger house.

Was she related to the men somehow? A daughter would be the most obvious answer. She didn't look much like either of them, though. A niece or a foster daughter perhaps? Neither man gave off the warm, fuzzy feelings Tess might expect from kind souls who would take in a young, orphaned ward of the state.

Tess dug around in her backpack until she felt the soft, worn fur of the little girl's bunny. Tess would like the chance to give it back to her, and that would be easier if the girl would make an appearance outside of the house. But maybe, well, it would be better to knock on the door and hand it over. Maybe the girl was shy or nervous? Maybe she wasn't a fan of the move and wasn't eager to explore her new surroundings.

Maybe she missed home and fought tears at night as she clutched at nothing more than a pillow, a poor substitute for her little stuffed friend.

Maybes and possibilities had never been Tess's favorite form of thought. What was in her wheelhouse, though? Taking charge. Taking action. She was certain her mother would not approve of Tess knocking on the door of an unknown neighbor's house, especially not a household that appeared to be two single, middle-aged men. Which was why Tess wasn't going to tell her.

Instead, Tess kissed her mother goodbye and headed out the door a little early. After Tess and Sully had cleaned up the kitchen last night, her mother and Miss Angel had emerged from their isolation and all appeared to be forgiven. Or at least ignored, like every other uncomfortable thing in their home these days.

Tess still felt queasy in the pit of her stomach when she thought of the look on her mother's face last night when Tess had called her out. So even though she was purposely doing something she knew her mother would not approve of, she still tried to make amends.

"I'm leaving a little early this morning," she told Kate, pecking her mother on the cheek. "I want to get to school in time to say hi to Maddie before classes start."

Her mom would like that. Maddie had been Tess's best friend since birth, right up until Maddie's life had taken a curve ball almost as bad as Tess's own would take six months later. Kate thought Tess had abandoned Maddie in her time of need, and Tess hadn't bothered to correct her. She would be happy that Tess was trying.

So Tess left the house whistling a jaunty tune for her mother's benefit, turning in the direction of the school and doubling back down the opposite street. She knew the men were home, and what better way to make new friends? Tess's logic wasn't exactly sound, but she used it when necessary. And this was necessary.

She thought of the little girl. She thought of the bunny, tucked inside her backpack. She would only hand it to the girl - about that, she felt very strongly. She wasn't sure why when she could just as easily give it back to Horace or Jasper. It might not be as pleasant, but it could be done.

Maybe she was just anxious to meet another girl on the street. As it was, she was stuck with a decidedly male population. Ben was proving to be someone she could grow on, but Mark lived just a block in the opposite direction and Tess felt like equal representation was important. Girls had to stick together.

Tess wasn't worried about her mother seeing her as she strolled up the cracked, pitted sidewalk to the front door. She had to climb a set of steep, crumbling concrete stairs to reach the door, tucked beneath a covered porch that wrapped around both sides of the house. It could be a very pretty porch with a little work. A coat of fresh, white paint, some leisurely lounge furniture, the requisite hanging ferns and such.

Tess could just see the southern veranda version of herself, sitting sedately on white wicker furniture, sipping sweet tea with her new little friend. For some reason, both wore the oversized, ridiculous hats favored by southern women at horse derbies. Like little girls playing dress up. Tess shook the vision out of her head. That was just silly. No hat, no matter its size, was going to be able to contain her hair. It would simply disappear inside the wild depths, never to be seen again...

Though it might be a useful scene in a book. A plot with a Southern Gothic flare, perhaps? She'd write it down, just in case.

The door in front of her swung open before she had a chance to knock, and Tess cursed her flights of fancy. Though frequent, they tended to come at the worst possible moments. She took a step back as Horace came through the door and almost ran into her. He looked surprised to see a girl on his front porch, and he said a word her mother often told her wasn't acceptable in polite company. Then he just stared. And stared some more.

Tess bounced from foot to foot, a little uncomfortable now that she was face-to-face with one of the men she'd been watching from across the street. From a distance, the man she'd come to think of as Horace was thin and lanky, with a slight stoop in his back that suggested poor health. Up close, that was still true. But now Tess could see he had a pale, somewhat greasy complexion that suggested he didn't get out in the sun much. His hair was slicked back, and he had a slight hook in his rather large nose, with a line of freckles running directly across the bridge. Tess would be willing to bet that nose had been broken more than once.

"Hi," Tess finally said, when it was clear he wasn't going to offer anything. He didn't look angry or upset, which was a relief. More confused, maybe a little wary though what he would have to be wary of, Tess couldn't say.

"I live across the street." She waved in a general direction behind her but made a point to leave off specifics. She was reckless, not insane. "I noticed you moving in last week and just wanted to welcome you to our street." She gave him a winning smile. Not one of her overly large, predatory smiles that she liked to use on her enemies. No, this smile was supposed to be charming. Comforting.

And yet, he did not seem comforted. And he still didn't say anything. Tess cleared her throat. How to proceed? Should she just ask to see his daughter? *Can the little girl I saw lurking in the van come out to play?* As she debated and Horace stared, Jasper yanked the door from Horace's hand, fully exposing Tess to the entryway of the house.

"What's taking so long?" he demanded, and Tess couldn't help but peer into the emptiness beyond. It was darker than she'd expected, and it looked like they'd hung some sort of makeshift barrier a few steps into the entryway, blocking the rest of the house from a view of the street.

Why would anyone do that?

"What's this then?" While Horace may have looked wary, Jasper was most definitely unhappy. "Unless you're here to install internet service, scram, kid."

He was completely dismissive, as though he'd already forgotten she was there when he turned back to the house. But in his haste to be rid of her, he slammed his hand against the door frame as he moved. The hand that was holding his wallet, presumably to pay for the internet service repair they were expecting. But when he hit his hand, the wallet went flying.

It was funny, Tess thought to herself, how certain moments can stand still in time or charge full speed ahead. In this case, time seemed to crawl as Tess noted the loose wallet, knocked from Jasper's hand, soaring through the air. The look on both men's faces as it flew free - Horace, slightly alarmed, Jasper, apoplectic. And then the wallet on the ground, laying face-up at Tess's feet, Jasper's unsmiling face peeking out from the fold. In the stillness of the moment, Tess felt herself shiver.

Easy now, Tessie.

Her father's voice cautioned her.

Be very careful now.

Both men froze, watching Tess watch the wallet. The pause felt unnatural, dangerous somehow. Maybe this was what people meant when they said a pause was *pregnant*. Regardless, the need to break the dangerous current in the air was palpable, and she heeded her father's voice.

She bent down and scooped the wallet up, allowing it to close in her hand as she held it out. "I'm clumsy, too," she said, as though she hadn't noticed the sudden tension. "I have school, so I have to go. Welcome to the neighborhood." Tess infused her smile with as much youthful charm and vigor as she could squeeze out of her suddenly narrow lungs, backing down the drive to create some distance. "I'm sure we'll see each other again soon!"

Once she was out of arms' reach of either man, she turned and darted to the street. Her breath was coming fast, and she forced herself to walk normally once she hit the sidewalk. She turned her feet in the direction of the school and counted each footstep methodically until she was certain she wasn't being followed. *One, two, three-*

What *was* that? She'd never experienced anything quite like it. Tess had been raised by a Southern mother. She had gone over to introduce herself like any good neighbor should. Sure, she'd had ulterior motives, but that shouldn't have been obvious. Nor should a southern welcome have ruffled the feathers she'd seemed to ruffle.

A little girl was living with two men, missing a beloved stuffed animal. Tess hadn't even gotten a chance to ask to meet their daughter, or whoever she was. She hadn't even remembered.

...eighty-nine, ninety, ninety-one...

And now she had an even bigger problem. Because this feeling in her stomach wasn't going away, school was fast approaching, she had a new friend, and she wanted to be normal.

But the feeling still wasn't going away. And on its heels was an unpleasant thought: what kind of people had something to hide from the kid across the street? They weren't just annoyed at her bad timing, they were cagey. They wanted her gone, immediately. And they definitely hadn't wanted her to see that wallet.

Or rather, what was in the wallet. The driver's license with Jasper's picture on the front. The one that proudly announced he was Thomas Jeffries from Savannah, Georgia. The one she'd pretended not to see.

The driver's license was a complete and obvious fake.

Chapter 11

Tess's father had taught her to identify fake IDs at an early age. It had started as a game.

Okay, Tess, which one is real?

A younger Tess took in two cards that looked identical and finally pointed to the one on the left.

Why?

Ian McGee held up the card Tess had selected to her eye level. *The surface of a real license should be smooth and clear. See the little bumps on the surface of this one?*

Tess had peered at the flat surface of the card, finally seeing the small imperfections bubbling up under the lamination when her father turned it just right.

And there will always be mistakes in the printing. A blurry photo, a misspelled state, a missing watermark. That's how you spot a fake.

Tess had only seen the license briefly from her bird's eye view four feet above. And yet, she'd noticed something.

It had been the photo. It was Jasper. A slightly younger and less greasy version, maybe, but still him. What caught her eye though was the slightly distorted image. Had she been anyone else, she wouldn't have even noticed. After all, it could have been a trick of the light, something in her eye, or just a flaw in the printing process.

Only, she knew better. She'd been drilled on ID printing since she'd been old enough to know what a driver's license was. If she had touched it, she knew she would have felt the tiny air bubbles littering the surface. But a printing mistake like that? It was lazy. A rushed job, which meant the lamination would have been rushed, too. Maybe even slight curling at the ends.

Did it matter? So the new neighbor had a false ID. Lots of people did. Her father and Sully both had several. Teenagers paid good money for bad fakes. Horace and Jasper weren't underage, and they sure weren't cops. Which left one very obvious subset of people who would be interested in having alternate identities on hand.

Criminals.

The way they'd reacted to Tess's mere presence, the way they'd frozen when she'd seen the wallet. The warning deep in her gut, her dad's voice in her head, telling her to get out. These were bad guys, and now she had a problem - did she let it go or did she not?

To be fair, the real question was *could* she let it go? At the front of the room, her art teacher, Mrs. Morales, was finishing up a comparison of pastels and acrylics, and Tess had occupied her hands by attempting to sketch her little neighbor's face. If these men were criminals, was the girl in danger? Certainly, in some form or another. Even non-violent infractions like check washing and credit fraud had victims. Even if she was well-cared for, she risked being removed from the home when Social Services found out or when her caretakers were arrested.

Had the girl looked healthy? Tess tried to think back. She'd been pale, but some people just lacked color. Like Tess herself, for example. As much as she loved inheriting her father's red hair and freckles, she surely wouldn't mind having more of her mother's darker tones. Kate McGee liked to refer to herself as burnt chocolate, but Tess had always thought of her mother's skin as a creamy caramel. One that only deepened with her time gardening in the backyard, so unlike Tess's fiery response to sun exposure.

Distractions. Tess shook her head, refocusing on the issue at hand. The girl had been pale, with light brown hair. Or had it been more of a blonde? Had it been long or short? Tess frowned as she tried to remember. She was usually so good with details - she prided herself on remembering even the most minute details with only a quick look, and the girl had made an impression. She didn't know why she was having so much trouble remembering specifics now.

She hadn't looked unhealthy, Tess decided. A little wan. A little thin, maybe. But not unhealthy or neglected. She was still living with criminals though, and that could get complicated.

What would happen to her if Tess exposed the men? She knew her dad had always hated that part of the job.

"There are no victimless crimes, Tessie. No man is an island," he used to say after a bad day. Every action has a reaction, and every reaction touches someone else.

Could Tess let it go? Of course not. But maybe she didn't need to decide right away what she should do, a thought that immediately eased her anxiety. The first step is always to gather more information, and so that's what she would do. Between Google and social media, the world was a very small place. If the ID was fake the way she thought it was, those might not yield many results. But Tess also had a sympathetic ear or two at the local Sheriff's Department who might run prints if she needed to pull any. Sure, they would think it was weird. They would be concerned, they would tell Sully. But they would do it.

Dead dad pass and all.

But one thing at a time. For now, she had a plan. A place to start. And that soothed her more than anything.

Mrs. Morales cleared her throat, and Tess snapped back to the real world. Where she was in art class. And her teacher had wandered over and was looking over Tess's shoulder having just asked her a question. And the rest of the class had noticed. Which sounded about right for how Tess's life was going.

"Sorry, ma'am," Tess said sweetly. "I was so involved in my work that I didn't hear you."

"Um hum," Mrs. Morales hummed, clearly not in the mood to be sweet-talked. "You're always so very involved in *your work*, Senora McGee."

Tess loved Mrs. Morales's voice. The lilting hints of South America were rich and sweet, lulling her students into a dreamy, creative space. It was uncanny. And it worked too well because before Tess could stop her, Mrs. Morales had swept Tess's sketch of the little girl from her desk and was holding it up, examining it.

"Not exactly the bowl of fruit I asked for is it, Senora?" Mrs. Morales turned a skeptical eye on Tess before returning to the picture. "But also not half bad." Tess perked up a little at that. She thought it was horrid, but what did she know about art?

"Who is it?" Mrs. Morales asked as she traced the various details with a sharp eye.

"My cousin," Tess blurted on a whim. She'd rather not admit to the entire class she was drawing some little girl she'd seen once or twice from across the street. That sounded weird, even to her.

"I see."

Tess couldn't tell if Mrs. Morales believed her, or if she just didn't care. Either way, she tucked the sketch under her arm with a *tsk*. "Why don't you turn your artistic talents to the actual assignment, yes? I'll just hang onto this while you do."

Well, that was just fine. Tess could pretend to draw a bowl of fruit as well as the next person. She peeked to her right, just to confirm. Michael Adams was in the middle of adding leaves to a misshapen lump on the page that could be an apple, and Tess was mollified. Yes, she could certainly do as well as that.

And besides, in those few minutes she'd been talking to Mrs. Morales, the plan had coalesced in her mind. She would investigate the identity of one Thomas Jeffries, gathering data on who he was pretending to be. That would give her a feel for how to proceed. She could slowly infiltrate their defenses with her bright, childlike enthusiasm. Offer to befriend their young ward, making sure she was safe. And then she could decide what to do with the information she learned.

Yes, that was a safe and solid plan. No jumping to conclusions or rushing in without thinking. This time, she'd do things the right way.

Her dad would be so proud.

Chapter 12

M s. Murrow was on a roll today, and Tess was here for it.

Her favorite teacher, by far, was hitting the strengths and weaknesses of today's criminal justice system. Tess thought it was a bit of a deviation from their current class topic of restorative justice, but it was vastly more interesting.

"That's a great point, Michael," Ms. Murrow said. Personally, Tess thought she was throwing the kid a bone. He was a junior in a freshman-level class, which wasn't a good sign. "Rehabilitation is hard in the best of conditions. And I'm sure no one would consider prison to be the 'best condition.'"

Tess hadn't realized her hand was in the air until Ms. Murrow said, "Tess, what are your thoughts?"

Was it Tess's imagination, or did the class collectively sigh around her? "Is prison really about rehab, though?" Tess asked. She'd never been one to shy away from a fraught topic before, so why start now? "None of the politicians will say it, but prison only serves two purposes: deterrent or punishment."

"Interesting," Ms. Murrow encouraged. "Go on."

That was all Tess needed to hear. "Prison can either be used as a deterrent for people before they commit a crime or used to punish them after. Rehabilitation, by its very definition, doesn't fit either scenario. If it happens, it's a happy by-product of the punishment. It's not something prisoners have earned the right to."

"Says the cop's kid," she heard someone whisper behind her. It was said loud enough for her to hear but not Ms. Murrow.

"Not cool, man," someone else said, trying to hush their friend, but it was too late.

"No, he's right," Tess said, turning and making eye contact with Derrick Merrigan. Mark, beside him, just shook his head helplessly. "I am a cop's kid. I've heard his side of the story every day, every night, for my entire life. So yeah, I have certain opinions that come from someone with intimate knowledge of the topic. Where do you get yours, Derrick? Google?"

"You don't get them anymore though, do you?"

It was like being slapped. Tess's mouth dropped open, and Mark grabbed his buddy by the shirt to try to pull him as far from Tess as possible.

"What's happening back there?" Ms. Murrow called. "Tess, is everything okay?"

Tess could hear her teacher's footsteps approaching through the blood pounding in her ears and feel the stare of every student in the class as they waited for her to respond. No one was sighing now. No, the class had drawn one, collective breath, and they were holding it in anticipation. That wasn't a low blow. That was a kill shot. Derrick Merrigan had just declared himself ready for a higher form of war.

And Tess smiled.

That's all. She simply smiled. It felt brittle and sharp, and she wasn't sure how long she could hold it, so she turned back to face Ms. Murrow. She heard Mark groan and felt content that at least he had interpreted her smile correctly.

"Everything is fine, Ms. Murrow," Tess said sweetly. "It seems Derrick and I have a difference of political philosophy on the subject, and we were having a spirited discussion. That's all."

Tone, inflection, smile. Everything about her response was designed to be bland and reassuring to adults. Ms. Murrow did not look reassured. Mark hissed, "Dude, this one is all you," let Tess know she'd hit the mark.

"Please," Derrick scoffed. "She's a pipsqueak. What's Lollipop Guild going to do about it?"

"Derrick!" Ms. Murrow exclaimed. "We don't treat others with disrespect in this classroom. You will apologize to Tess right now."

Again though, Tess simply smiled. "It's okay, Ms. Murrow. Derrick is simply under-educated on the subject. But I'm going to help him with that."

Ms. Murrow closed her eyes as the other students snickered. And something that sounded like Mark Dunham slapping his hand over his eyes echoed right behind her.

"Just," Ms. Murrow finally said, and Tess was pretty sure her favorite teacher was quietly cheering her on, no matter how terrified she sounded, "don't cause any permanent damage. Please?"

After that, Ms. Murrow forced them back to the theory of restorative justice and held the class hostage with a lecture that invited no room for open discourse. Tess couldn't blame her. After all, she was sure no teacher intended to start a blood feud mid-lecture. But Tess knew plenty about justice already so instead of listening, she started taking notes of a different kind.

She would have her revenge on Derrick Merrigan. Oh yes, she would. And while she would prefer to seek her vengeance quickly, there was something to be said for the slow burn. The methodical planning of the destruction of enemies. The cold fear as the target waited with bated breath for the plan to reveal itself. Oh yes, that was much better than immediate satisfaction.

Which was just as well. Immediate satisfaction could not be had this day anyway. Tess's pen stilled for a moment as she thought. She and Ben had agreed to start studying together after school, and she could plot her vengeance on Derrick under the guise of dutiful homework. She could tell Ben she was working on history, which would make him happy whether he believed her or not.

Chapter 13

Tess dropped into the seat across the table as Ben was taking a bite of his pizza. "You said you can draw, right?"

Tess really couldn't believe her luck in finding Ben. As a friend, he left little to be desired. As a male, they weren't accidentally buying the same clothes and fighting about who got to wear them. He was calm and placid, like a sea of glass undisturbed by a coming storm. And he rarely questioned her madness.

He didn't even blink now at her abrupt appearance or question. "Yep," he said instead, not bothering to look up. He had a book propped up against the edge of his lunch tray and was flipping the pages in between bites.

"Good. Here." Tess shoved her terrible sketch of the girl across the table at him and started digging in her bag for the pencil she knew was rolling around in the bottom somewhere. "I need you to draw her."

"Draw who?" Ben flipped another page. It looked like some kind of memoir, something thick and boring. Probably reading up on President Harrison or William Wadsworth or someone else so very...Ben.

"The girl, of course." There. Tess held up the pencil proudly before slamming it down on the sketch pad that followed. "I need you to draw the girl from across the street."

"What girl from across the street?" He finally closed his book, albeit ruefully, accepting he wouldn't be getting any more reading done, and finally looked up at her, which Tess thought was a wise move for as little time as they'd known each other. "And why am I drawing her?"

"I met the new neighbors this morning, and I want you to draw the little girl that lives with them. Something's off about them, and I want to figure out what it is."

Tess hadn't seen any toys, clothes, or signs that a little girl lived in that house but then again, they'd had the entrance blocked so she hadn't been able to see much of anything. Except for the fake ID, that is. But the girl had caught Tess's attention from the first.

She'd looked so small, her body half-hidden against the metal of the van. She'd almost blended in with the dusky colors around her - all the beige and tan and grays swirling together. The poor child had no color, but Tess could swear there had been a spark in her eyes as she'd peered across the street. Right at Tess.

And if Tess couldn't see her in person, she would bring her to life on the page. Proof that she was real, that she existed. "I'll describe her to you, okay?" Tess nudged the paper in Ben's direction. "You can copy what I say, like a sketch artist."

"I'm not sure it's as easy as that." Ben still picked up the pencil and pushed his glasses up with his other hand. "But I guess we can try."

"She was very...wispy," Tess started. "Barely there, if that makes any sense."

"Um-hmm." Ben did not sound enthused. "Wispy. Got it. But maybe we could start with something more solid. Face shape or hair type, for example. Or the slant of her eyes?"

"Well, fine. If you want to be all practical about it." Tess said *practical* like it was a dirty word. A word reserved for those with no imagination or creative flair. A great insult in her eyes.

"Could you try to put the dramatic license aside, just for a minute, and describe her as a police detective would? That should be easy enough for you, right?"

Well, Tess couldn't argue with that, boring though it was. "Okay, okay. Let's see." Tess squeezed her eyes shut, trying to think. "Her hair was long. Not unusually long, but down past her shoulder blades, I think." Maddening that she couldn't remember exactly.

"Straight. She had it down around her face, one side tucked behind her ear like this." Tess swept her wild hair over her left eye and tried to tuck it behind her ear, though it fought her the entire time. "Okay, maybe not exactly like that." She gave up on her hair and switched tactics. "She had what I might call an oval face, maybe?" Tess rounded her chin with the backs of both hands. "It sloped further than mine, almost coming to a point."

Ben nodded along, sketching out the rough shape of a face. "What about her eyes?"

Everything else about the girl was slightly fuzzy, but her eyes...her eyes were vivid in Tess's mind. "Large," she said, picturing how they stood out starkly in her wan face. "Very large. They had a kind of otherworldly quality to them. Haunting."

Ben glanced up wryly. "By *otherworldly*, do you mean almond-shaped? Wide-set? Symmetrical?"

Tess rolled her own eyes. "You've no imagination. But yes, I suppose I would describe them as *almond-shaped*," Tess mocked. "I haven't been close enough to see the color but with her pale skin, I might guess green or gray."

Ben sketched in a couple of rough eyes. "Nose and mouth?"

Tess didn't want Ben to know, but she was getting frustrated with herself. There was just nothing memorable about any of the girl's other features. Which was strange, as Tess fancied herself a wordsmith with fanatical attention to detail. "Her nose was small, and her mouth was just, I don't know, a mouth. How do I describe that? Regular, I guess."

"Regular nose and mouth, got it," Ben said. But he said it studiously instead of mockingly, and Tess got the feeling he did get it. Despite his misgivings, Tess noticed he still sketched in approximate placements for both. "If you can give me hair and skin color, I'll work on it tonight and you can give me adjustments tomorrow."

Tess was nodding along, trying to decide how to describe hair without any actual color until she felt a body slam down on the bench beside her.

"Hey, McGee," Mark said, shrugging his shoulder against Tess's and almost knocking her off the slanted plastic bench. "Lewis."

Ben nodded in Mark's direction, flipping the sketch pad shut and beginning to pack his textbooks back into his backpack.

"What are you guys doing?" Mark asked, cracking open a soda and the giant snack cake he ate routinely for lunch.

"There is absolutely nothing of nutritional value in that," Tess couldn't help but point out, nodding at his lunch. "Aren't you supposed to be a finely-oiled, athletic machine? Is your body not a temple?"

"I guess to some people." He leered down, but Tess just rolled her eyes and Mark grinned, despite himself. No matter how hard he tried to be a lech, he just couldn't quite pull it off.

Maybe it was the dimple buried in the corner of his left cheek or the fact she'd known him her whole life. Either way, his innuendo and mock flirting never made it past first base with Tess. And despite her outward disdain, that snack cake did look good. She was getting ready to go into a lecture on psychology, which was not a recipe for good fortune. Maybe some sugar...

"Want a bite?"

Mark dangled the last bite of chocolate in front of her, and Tess snatched it out of his fingers before he had time to react. She popped it into her mouth and swallowed it whole. "Sure do."

Ben just shook his head as Mark locked from his empty hand to Tess and back again. "You didn't even miss a beat," he mused, sounding awestruck.

"Why do you have a black eye?"

If Mark thought she was going to ignore the obvious, he was mistaken. It looked like someone had grazed him across the cheekbone, splitting the skin and causing him to grimace each time he talked. It wasn't the worst injury she'd seen on him, but it was obvious someone had hit him.

"I play football," he said, draining his soda and crushing it in hand. "I always have black eyes."

"Isn't that what helmets are for? Ow!"

Beneath the table, Ben had stomped her foot while managing to appear completely innocent. Tess needed to study that look because hers never seemed to fool anyone. She lacked any ability to produce innocence on command.

"What was that?" she demanded, but Ben kept packing his bag like he didn't hear her.

"I came to ask you for grace. The football season is almost over and we need Derrick. His sudden demise would be inconvenient for me. But this seems like more fun. What are you guys doing?" Mark had slid the sketch pad across the table and was peering down at the rough outline of the little girl's face.

"Drawing the new neighbor," Ben said mildly, plucking the sketchpad back and sliding it into his bag. "Tess has taken an...interest...in her."

Mark's face hitched in concentration. "New neighbor? You mean the guys who moved into the Brooklyn house?"

"Yes!" So Mark had seen them too. "Have you talked to them? Have you seen the little girl who lives there with them? She's this tiny little thing, three feet maybe? Mousy hair, freckles. Never makes a sound?"

But Mark just shook his head. "Can't say that I have. They keep weird hours. I've seen them leaving when I come home late from a game." He shrugged. "They seem like bad news to me."

"Yeah, I think Tess picked up on that," Ben said wryly. "Hence her interest." The bell rang and they all stood, Tess sighing heavily as she did. Another day, another dull lecture. Mark seemed to find her gloom adorable, which irritated her further. Until he grabbed her elbow. Then that became her new irritation.

"Hey, seriously though. Maybe give Merrigan a pass on this one, okay."

Tess raised an eyebrow, and Mark seemed to know what she was thinking.

"I know it was out of line, and I know he deserves it. But maybe cut the guy some slack. He's a jerk for a reason. We all are."

He had the grace to look slightly ashamed, which Tess did appreciate. And there was some meaning there, behind his words. Something she would love to poke and prod until she came up with the truth. Unfortunately, time was of the essence as kids streamed en masse from the cafeteria towards the next period. And her vengeance would not be denied. Even for an antihero like Mark Dunham.

"Hey, Lewis." Mark was already turning towards his friends who were hassling the younger students as they tried to rush to class, the moment broken. "Off-season baseball conditioning starts next week after school. You should come."

Tess blinked. Was Mark inviting Ben to play baseball? Did Ben *play* baseball? But Ben just nodded his thanks and Mark was already slouching towards the group at the door, hands tucked into his pockets, head down, before she could ask.

"You coming or what?" Ben asked, walking away. He had math, so he was heading in the opposite direction, but he still turned to remind Tess, "You've already been late to third period once this week. You don't want to push your luck."

"Yeah, yeah. Dead dad pass. It's a thing."

"I'll see you in a few hours for Life Science," Ben reminded her. Chastened her, more like. Then he shook his head. "And it's not a thing."

Chapter 14

B ut in a surprising turn of events, Tess was granted a reprieve from the horrors of her afternoon psychology class. The moment Tess stepped in the door, already focused on trying to unravel the next section of the novel that was giving her fits, Mr. Bishop was calling her name and holding a slip of pink paper towards her.

Every kid who'd ever been labeled "troubled" knew what that pink piece of paper meant, and Tess took it with a strange mixture of dread and delight. She was being summoned to Mr. Abrams's office, and he was a definite bummer to talk to. All counselors were, she supposed. On the other hand, she didn't have to pretend to pay attention to Maslow's Hierarchy of Needs while trying to unravel the mystery of who killed the client's father with the majority of her brain.

She tried to look meek as she took the proffered slip and fairly skipped back out the door. The counselor was an okay guy, and he let her ramble on about her book and where it was heading. She suspected he thought her writing was a knife intended to peel back the layers of her own battered heart, and she was happy to let him keep thinking that. She wasn't even opposed to tossing in some tears when it benefited her. Whatever got her out of class and let her work on her book was okay by Tess.

She managed to maintain that cheerful outlook down the hall, across the quad, and into the administration building. She even grinned broadly at old Mrs. Hildie, the office warden. It wasn't until Mr. Abrams ushered her into his office that the smile slipped from her face.

"Hi, baby." Kate McGee was sitting on Mr. Abrams's old, ratty couch, sipping something that smelled like burnt coffee and looking as uncomfortable as Tess suddenly felt.

"Mom." Tess looked up at Mr. Abrams suspiciously, smelling a set-up, but he just smiled and waved her towards the spot on the couch beside her mother.

"Have a seat, Tess," he said, as though he hadn't lured her into a cleverly disguised trap. Tess shot him what she hoped was a look of deepest betrayal before sinking warily beside her mother.

"Your mother and I have been talking," Mr. Abrams said, pulling the chair out from behind his desk and moving it over so he could face the ladies directly. Tess knew this move. Removing barriers, putting yourself on the same footing as your victim. Oh, yes. Thanks to Mr. Bishop and his insipid psychology class, Tess understood. She was about to be given "the talk". The "we love you, but we're so very concerned about you" talk. The "you have us worried" talk. The "you're so messed up" talk.

Well, that was just fine. It wasn't anything Tess hadn't heard before. She'd sit here, act like a teenager for a few minutes, then shed a few tears and apologize. The grownups would feel like they'd done their jobs, and she could get back to her book no worse for wear.

"I thought what you and I talked about was privileged," Tess interrupted, standing valiantly to her feet, kicking things off by engaging teenager mode. "I know my rights. Sacrilege!"

Mr. Abrams sighed and her mother rolled her eyes at the display of excessive drama. "Tess McGee, sit yourself down right now."

Tess sank back, eyeing Kate warily, and Mr. Abrams cut in. "Tess, I'm not a clinical psychologist. You're also not an adult. I'm happy to keep our conversations private unless I believe your mother needs to know. And in any case, she came to me."

Tess squinted at her mom. "You did?"

It was hard to believe. Tess often gave her teachers cause to call home. She came in late, she could be argumentative, and she tended to cut class when the mood struck. But they never did.

Dead dad pass.

At home, she did her chores. She toed the line. She avoided confrontation as much as her Irish nature would allow, and they both pretended like everything was fine. It was an unofficial agreement between them, which her mother had now violated without cause.

"I surely did. The renters across the street came by to introduce themselves, and they mentioned you've already met."

"Oh." Tess suddenly saw her mother with new eyes. Or maybe the right term was old eyes. Because this very much looked and sounded like her mother of yesteryear, and Tess was equal parts terrified and delighted.

"That's right, *oh*." Kate McGee focused on Tess with laser eyes. "Don't think I don't know what you've been up to. Sneaking around with that curiosity of yours, poking your nose where it doesn't belong!"

With every word, Tess's heart lightened. There was her mother! There was the fight Tess had been missing. Tess leaned forward, urging her on, eager for more. But as though she'd run out of steam, Kate stopped and took a breath. She shook her head and just like that, the new, tired version of the mother Tess had been living with for the last year resurfaced.

"I told you not to go over there," she chastised faintly.

Tess hated the look on her mother's face. She hated it. In Tess's entire life, Kate McGee had never looked anything but confident, controlled, and elegant. But now, she just looked...sad. Lost.

No one should look like that, least of all Tess's strong, proud mother. The lump in Tess's stomach grew, but she pushed it sternly away. Annoying teenagers felt no pity for sad mothers.

"What did they say?" Tess knew instinctively that neither Horace nor Jasper would have mentioned the incident with the wallet, but she was curious how they'd broached the topic of her visit. This could be an opportunity in disguise. At the very least, it was an indication she had rattled them, which just proved her deepening suspicions. Maybe here, Tess could learn something about them.

But her mother and Mr. Abrams just looked startled. "What did they say?" Kate repeated, clearly confused.

"What did they say?" This was important. Tess couldn't do anything about the annoying and upsetting feeling in her gut when she looked at her sad, sad mother, but she could concentrate on the feeling right beside it. The one that was churning.

The men across the street had approached her mother on the same day she'd paid them a friendly welcome to the neighborhood. Why would they be so suspicious of a teenage girl?

"Tess," Mr. Abrams began gently, and Tess could barely restrain the eye roll at the tone of voice. As though she were a rabid dog he was trying to settle. "We're not here to talk about them. We're here because we are concerned about your behavior lately. Approaching the neighbors is just part of the issue. You've been cutting class and when you are here, you pick fights."

"First of all, I haven't cut class in over a week, so I don't think that's relevant."

"Tess!" Mr. Abrams already sounded exasperated and she'd barely gotten started. "A week isn't exactly attendance goals."

"And I do not pick fights!" That was utterly absurd. "I may participate in some lively debate, but that's the backbone of a healthy society. Ask anyone!"

"A debate does not involve cleverly disguised insults and vows of revenge."

"It worked though, didn't it?" Word had spread surprisingly fast if Mr. Abrams already knew, and Tess felt pretty smug about that. If Mark was worried enough to approach her, if Derrick had told an adult that Tess was threatening him, that meant he was scared. She could work with that.

"Tessa Lynn McGee!" Her mother was aghast. "Who did you threaten?"

"I did not *threaten* anyone. I simply offered to help provide education."

"Lord Jesus," her mother said under her breath, looking skyward, "give me grace."

"What?" Tess sat forward, indignant in truth now. "I was participating in class. I was talking to people. And he said-" But Tess stopped. What was she going to do? Tell on Derrick? Tattle? She was no rat. And besides, if Tess hated the look on her mother's face now, what would happen when she told her what the jerk had said? She couldn't do that.

"What did he say?" Mr. Abrams prodded. "It's okay, Tess. We want to understand."

But Tess just shook her head, dropping back against the couch and letting the fight drain out of her. "It doesn't matter." She forced her shoulders to relax and adopted a look of defeat. "I was never going to do anything to him."

Not today, anyway.

Neither adult looked assured. "This is just one example of behaviors that have us worried," Mr. Abrams said. "The...lively debates...both in and out of school. The missed classes. The social isolation. You don't talk to your friends anymore."

"Correction," Tess pointed out, "they no longer talk to me. It was a mutual parting of ways."

"You and Maddie have always been such good friends," Kate said. "Why would you part ways? You have more in common now than you ever have."

Kate was referring, of course, to their wildly different personalities and their missing fathers. Maddie was tall, blonde, and even-tempered while Tess was a short, redheaded Irish devil. Where Tess was curious, meddlesome, and driven to poke her nose into every sort of mystery, Maddie was in pep club and on the honors list. It never really made sense why they were friends but somehow, it just worked. From the first day of kindergarten, when some boy made fun of Tess's corkscrew curls and Maddie punched him in the nose, they had been inseparable.

Then one Tuesday morning, Maddie's dad kissed his family goodbye and, instead of driving to the office like he had every morning of Maddie's life, had instead gone to his new family in New York and never returned.

Despite what Tess tried, Maddie had stopped calling and coming to Tess's house after school. She'd started sitting by her popular friends in class. She'd joined the cheer squad. And when Tess's father had...left...Maddie hadn't come to the funeral. She hadn't called. She hadn't spoken to Tess in the hall. She hadn't cared at all.

Which meant this conversation was approaching dangerous territory. The unspoken thing between Tess and her mother was getting closer to the surface, and Tess did not want to talk about it.

"I'm not isolated," Tess told Mr. Abrams in an effort to shift the topic desperately away from Maddie and their lost friendship. "Ben Lewis and I are friends. He's new, and we have a lot in common, too."

"Well, yes," Mr. Abrams admitted, "but-"

"We walk to school together in the mornings, eat lunch together, and study at each others' houses at night. We are," Tess declared proudly, "the best of friends." She would need to tell Ben that they were now the best of friends, in case he didn't know. He might be called upon to corroborate her story.

She could tell she was teasing a smile out of Mr. Abrams, which he managed to smother by stroking his mouth with his hand as though he were thinking. "Yes, you and Mr. Lewis have been spending time together, which is a good thing. You've been at this school your entire life, and it was good of you to reach out to him."

"Benjamin does seem to be a good influence," her mother agreed, and Tess glanced up at her, affronted. What, exactly, did that mean?

"Maybe it's time we meet his family."

Other than Sully and Miss Angel, her mother talked to so few people. In the past, her mother would never have allowed Tess to go to anyone's house whose parents she hadn't met, but things were different now. If she were suddenly talking about meeting the Lewis', maybe they should be having an intervention for her instead.

Tess was considering the political advantage of making that point when her mother threw a curve ball. "Tessa, you know what your father would say about you walking up to a house of strange men and ringing the doorbell. He taught you better than that."

Tess froze at the words. They didn't talk about Dad. They hadn't talked about Dad in almost a year. Tess *knew* what her father would think. She didn't need-

"They were very polite when they introduced themselves," Kate went on, not seeing the turmoil in her daughter's heart. "But they were also very firm. It's just not proper for a young lady to approach strange men in their homes, and the fact they felt the need to make that point speaks very well of them."

Tess narrowed her eyes as her mother shifted slightly in her seat at those words. She might not say it, but she was uncomfortable with the men, too. Tess might have been a cop's daughter, but her mother was a cop's wife for far longer.

"It's dangerous in more ways than one, even though they know your father was an officer of the law," she went on. "You have to think before you act, Tessa."

That threw Tess for a moment. "What do you mean? What do they know?" She blinked. "Did they say something about Dad?"

"They were very kind when they expressed their condolences. They must have heard about his passing through the neighbors," Kate explained to Mr. Abrams. "They were worried we would feel unsafe with unknown men living next door. Very kind."

Tess's mom sounded just a little uncomfortable about the last part, though Tess felt nothing but ice. Men who were living with fake identities had approached her mother and expressed *condolences* about her police detective of a father. That was...not right at all.

"Well, they were right to be concerned, and it was kind of them to express their sympathies. But your mother is right, Tess." Mr. Abrams looked at her sternly, as only an adult paid to be concerned could. "You know better than to approach unknown men in their homes without an adult with you. That could have been dangerous, and it's part of a pattern of behavior we need to address."

"You're right," Tess said, on autopilot now. Her brain was too busy for this, and it was time to initiate her exit strategy. "It was reckless, and I'm sorry." Mr. Abrams looked pleased, though Tess could tell her mother was suspicious. "And I won't cut class anymore. I don't even know why I do it." She did it because she hated being around mean, ignorant children who whispered about her dead dad as though Tess couldn't hear.

"And I'll make an effort to talk more to my old friends." Tess forced a hopeful smile and purpose into her dead eyes. "I do miss having other girls around."

She missed having other girls around as much as she missed the flu shot, but it was her golden ticket because the relief on Mr. Abrams' face was palpable.

"Thank you, Tess," he sighed. "I'm so glad to hear that. And, uh," he nervously adjusted his tie, "I'm sure that means you've reconsidered any plans for vengeance on Derrick Merrigan, yes?"

"Oh, yes." Tess smiled her sweetest smile, and her mother just sighed, seeing right through it. "Derrick didn't mean anything by it. He was being a silly boy. It's not worth my time."

"Oh, good." She had Mr. Abrams hook, line, and sinker, and he was pleased with his own brilliance. "In that case, I don't see any reason why you can't go back to class. Unless your mother has further concerns?"

This was the tricky bit. Her mother knew Tess better than to believe anything she'd just said. And a flicker of the old Kate McGee still lingered in the hollow shell of the mother just trying to survive another day. Tess had seen it just a few minutes ago and it was smoldering now, dancing in the back of her mother's eyes. Tess caught her breath. Whether she was hoping for full flame or not, she didn't know. But her plans for world dominance danced on the razor wire of her mother's emotions at this moment.

And then the spark of ember disappeared, extinguished by grief and loss and exhaustion.

"No, no further concerns," Kate said distantly, and Tess deflated, just a bit.

It was fine. She was fine. She didn't want her mother to be concerned. It would just get in Tess's way. Because now she had a new purpose. Those men had threatened her mother, even if Kate McGee, cop's wife though she was, failed to acknowledge it. And they'd dared to mention her father.

They weren't being kind. They weren't expressing sympathies. They were mocking her. And they were mocking him. And that fact, combined with the knowledge they had of his death, had planted a seed in Tess's mind. One she needed to carefully consider. The only people who would dare mock the death of a detective to his widow's face were cowards. Criminals.

Murderers.

Chapter 15

"**D**on't forget your mid-term project is due in two weeks!" Mr. Wright yelled after them, though no one paid any attention. The dismissal bell had rung, and all bets were off as students shoved books into bags and hustled for the door as quickly as possible.

"Want to come over and finish our projects?" Ben asked as he watched Tess haphazardly sweep every loose object on her desk into her bag ad nauseam. He looked slightly nauseated himself, which Tess thought was a beautiful sort of poetry.

"I can't," she said, slinging the bag over her shoulder and listening to the jumbled contents slamming together haphazardly. "I have a different project I need to work on at home."

At home, where she had access to pseudo-social media accounts she used to occasionally do a little snooping on murderers and such. And to plot the next step of her blood feud with Derrick Merrigan.

Tess bit her lip, thinking. She had only been intending to look into the Thomas Jeffries alias, but why couldn't she do both at once? Two birds, one stone, so to speak.

And while her father's murder was important, so was personal justice on a smaller scale.

"And I'm supposed to visit with Mrs. Sandoval after school," Tess blurted before the cogs she could see turning suspiciously in Ben's head had time to fully connect the dots between the homework he knew she had and the lie he knew she was telling.

Mrs. Sandoval had lived next door since before Tess was born. Her mother called Mrs. Sandoval a sweet soul. Tess liked the word *spicy*. She was supposed to do light housework for Mrs. Sandoval once a week but more often, they worked together for a little while before either retiring to the botanical gardens in the attached greenhouse or walking through the park-like backyard.

Tess loved her day with Mrs. Sandoval, and she could never decide which adventure she preferred. Mrs. Sandoval referred to her glassed-in sunroom as the "botanical gardens" laughingly, but it more than earned the name in Tess's opinion. It was as big as the lower level of the house itself, which was a massive throwback to the plantation era. Because of the glass, it acted as a natural greenhouse and was always warm and cozy. With the massive amount of greenery hanging from every available surface, it was like walking through a forest.

Mrs. Sandoval had over 300 species of plants from around the world, and she knew each of them by name. There was an ancient, stately olive tree in the center of the room, clearly beloved, almost eight feet tall with the most beautiful green and silver leaves spreading to the sky.

Mrs. Sandoval claimed the tree had survived the long boat ride on her grandmother's immigration from Spain, and who was Tess to argue? The tree had a gnarled, mature feel to it, as though it had seen many moons and remembered them all. Mrs. Sandoval called the tree *Anciana*, which meant *old woman* in Spanish, and when the olives were ripe, Tess would pick while Mrs. Sandoval sat on a bench nearby, regaling her with stories from her youth.

Tess loved garden days, but there was something magical about the backyard. It was a park, with a winding trail made of seasoned planks that wandered in and out of the trees, giving Mrs. Sandoval a smooth path to tread on her morning walks with Gary, former neighborhood torment and current mascot.

Though she would often say she wasn't getting any younger, Tess had to wonder. Whether it was the Spanish olives or just her natural spice, Mrs. Sandoval seemed as spry as Tess herself. The woman stood less than five feet tall, but she had a presence. And though she had professionals looking after her beloved landscaping now, Tess knew the woman and her departed husband had lovingly planted each tree and flowering bush themselves.

Tess wanted to be just like her when she grew up.

"My mom's bringing home Chinese tonight," Ben tempted. "Come over after you're finished and have dinner. Then you won't have an excuse for not finishing your project."

Something slammed into Ben's back, and he stumbled into Tess, catching himself on the desk in front of him.

"Oh, I'm sorry!" a voice said, sounding alarmed. A familiar voice, and Tess tensed. "Are you okay?"

Despite herself, Tess looked up as Ben righted himself and met Maddie's eyes. Cheerleader. Model student. Former best friend. Tended to avoid Tess like the plague.

"Oh. Hi, Tess." Maddie looked away, fidgeting with the strap of her backpack, but it was more than she had said to Tess in over a year. So naturally, Tess was suspicious.

Maddie looked back at Ben as though Tess wasn't even there. "I'm sorry about that. I caught my foot on the chair leg and would have fallen. You kept me from going down."

Ben shrugged without looking up. "Sure. Fine. No problem." Another shrug. "It's fine."

Tess's nose wrinkled. That was a messy string of words, and had she ever seen Ben turn that shade of red before? Granted, she hadn't known him that long but still, he hadn't turned that color the first time Tess had talked to him.

Typical. A girl with frizzy hair and wild eyes, no problem. Give a guy a well-groomed blonde, and it's a whole different story.

Maddie stood there for a second, probably to see if Ben could string a rational sentence together, before moving on. "Well, sorry again. Ben, right?"

Ben nodded, busying himself with his worn backpack straps.

"See you around, I guess." Maddie moved on, making sure to take a wide swing around Tess. Not that Tess cared. Not that she needed Maddie to say anything else. Not that she should still be expecting anything.

"Hey," Tess finally said as Ben continued to fiddle with his backpack straps and the color stayed high on his face. Anything to break the awkwardness of the moment. "Why don't you come with me to visit with Mrs. Sandoval?" Ben hadn't met her yet. "She's great. We'll probably learn more about history from her than we ever will in school. And then

I'll come over to finish my project and, since you twisted my arm and all, I might as well have dinner while I'm there."

Tess supposed, for the sake of a friend and the ever-elusive concept of normalcy, she could wait to do to her snooping until later that night.

"What do you and Mrs. Sandoval do when you visit?" Ben wondered as they made their way out of the classroom door.

"I'm not *visiting*," Tess said imperiously. "I'm *working*. Come on. You'll see."

Some hours later, as they were leaving, Ben gave her a side eye and a look of disbelief. "Working, huh?" he muttered under his breath as they left Mrs. Sandoval's house.

"Goodbye, mis queridas!" Mrs. Sandoval waved them off from the doorway while Gary roamed the yard in front of them, making sure the way was clear for his new friend, Ben. "I expect you back next week, Benjamin. I will make my gazpacho, and you will tell me of your travels."

Mrs. Sandoval's voice wasn't as strong as it once was, but it still held the lilting notes of her native Spain. It wasn't the Irish brogue her dad had, but Tess still loved listening to it.

"I will." Ben waved back until Mrs. Sandoval went inside, Gary almost knocking them over in his haste to return when she called, "Mi amor, come!"

"Seriously, what work did you do again?"

Tess sighed forcefully. "I couldn't exactly work while we had company, could I?" She grinned. "Besides, you've met her. What can I do that Mrs. Sandoval can't do better?"

Ben smiled, too. "I'm glad I went. I need more friends, and it never hurts to have one who served in the Spanish Armada."

"Now I'm going to have to look up the *Lazaga*. Do you think she served on a destroyer in the Mediterranean Sea?"

But before Ben could answer, Tess stopped short and grabbed his arm. "Look."

"What?" Ben stumbled to a stop and Tess nodded ahead, toward the Brooklyn house.

"There. The new neighbors, remember? I told you I met them on my way to school this morning."

Tess hadn't said anything to Ben yet, and she certainly hadn't told him about the little, impromptu family counseling session after lunch. She was still suffering from the weird weight that had settled in her chest after seeing the fake ID and learning they'd approached her mother. Knew about her father.

"Something's not right with them."

"What do you mean?" Ben asked as he started walking again. Tess hurried to catch up.

"I wanted to give the kid her stuffed animal back, the girl you're drawing. So I rang the doorbell."

Ben rolled his eyes. "Of course you did."

"Yeah, well, it's neighborly, alright?" Tess shook her head. "Anyway, they were real cagey. The short one, there," she nodded again as they drew closer on the street, "Jasper. He was not happy about me showing up. He couldn't wait to get rid of me."

"His name is Jasper?"

"No! I just call him Jasper. Keep up! I don't know his actual name," Tess paused for dramatic license, "because he isn't using it."

Tess relished the weight of her pronouncement, imagining the dread and horror creeping in around the edges of the scene. If this were an old gumshoe movie, instrumentals would accompany the moment's silence, amping up the creep factor. Maybe a little fog for effect. Alas, this was no movie and the moment didn't feel quite as fraught as she could have hoped.

"Okay, you got me. What is that supposed to mean?" Ben was humoring her, which was the opposite of the atmosphere she was going for. So she smacked him.

"Ow!" He rubbed his arm in annoyance. "What was that for?"

"In the books, the sidekick just believes the hero."

"Why am I the sidekick?" he murmured, a little resentfully.

"Because the hero is the girl with the guts to knock on the bad guy's front door!"

"Fine, fine," Ben said in defeat. "Tell me how you know Jerry isn't using his real name."

"Jasper," Tess corrected. "But yes, back to the point. He dropped his wallet and I saw his driver's license. It was clearly a fake." Ben shot her a look, and Tess sniffed. "I've been looking at fake IDs with my dad since I was three. I know one when I see it."

Ben accepted it as fact and shrugged a shoulder. "Okay, so that means-"

"Shh." Tess elbowed Ben again and they both shut up. Jasper and Horace had stopped outside the van and were watching them approach. They were clearly on the way out, and it bothered Tess more than she would admit the way both men were staring at them.

Her. Staring at her.

"Well, well," Jasper called out as Tess and Ben came closer. "If it isn't the friendly neighborhood welcoming committee. Out for another visit?"

Tess forced a smile she wasn't feeling. She may be on to them, but she had to play it cool. They were already suspicious of her. "Just making my rounds," she announced grandly. "Bringing joy and community wherever I go."

"Make sure you keep it on your side of the street from now on, little one," Jasper leered. His brother, because Tess was certain now that's what they were, started to say something but Jasper cut him off. "Just making conversation," he said, doffing his cap mockingly. "We wouldn't want our little neighbor to find herself in an *uncomfortable* situation."

Beside her, Ben stiffened. He grabbed her arm and tried to steer Tess around them. "Come on," he said, louder than usual. "My parents are waiting and will wonder if we're late."

Jasper grinned as Tess stumbled a few steps after Ben, clearly relishing their discomfort. Tess hated that grin. That grin said he thought he'd scared her. He hadn't.

"Tell your daughter I'm sorry I missed her this morning." Tess waved towards the house, in case the child was watching. "I'll try to catch her on her way to school next week."

The change was instant as smiles dropped from both men's faces and an icy silence filled the air.

Don't move, Tessie.

Tess stilled as her dad's voice spoke and Ben pulled on her arm, jerking her behind him. Jasper took his foot down from where he'd started to step into the cab of the van.

"What did you say, little girl?" he asked, pushing away from the van and advancing rapidly on Tess's position.

It was an act of aggression and Ben reacted before Tess, phone at his ear as he grabbed her hand and yanked her further away. "Yeah, we're almost there. Tell Dad if he looks out the window, he'll be able to see us." Ben waved towards his house, selling the act. "We're talking to the new neighbors just up the street. Yeah, the ones renting the Brooklyn house."

Tess was absolutely certain Ben hadn't had time to dial, but both men took a step back.

"No kids here," Horace said quietly, speaking for the first time. "You didn't see what you thought you saw. Come on," he said, grabbing his brother by the shoulder and forcefully pulling. Jasper had a look on his face Tess had never seen before, and it made the hairs stand up on the back of her neck. Horace shoved him back another step when Jasper didn't respond, and they locked eyes.

"We have somewhere we have to be," Horace said slowly, and Jasper nodded slowly. Tess hadn't realized until the moment he finally turned that she hadn't taken a breath since she'd said the word *daughter*.

"Yeah. Nothing else to say." Jasper turned back towards the truck. Horace watched her for another moment before turning after his brother. "Watch yourself, kid," he murmured. "The streets aren't always as safe as they seem."

Chapter 16

Tess was distracted and trying very hard not to be. Ben's parents had carried the majority of the conversation over dinner, and Tess struggled to follow even the most banal of topics.

Ben nudged her under the table with his foot, and Tess looked up. Ben's dad was holding the container of fried noodles towards Tess, waiting for her to tip her plate up. Ben's mom was looking at her with concern, so Tess cleared her throat and pasted a smile on her face.

"Thanks!" she said, holding up her plate and letting Mr. Lewis dump a spoonful of noodles over the fried vegetables already there. "And thanks for having me for dinner."

"You're mighty welcome, sugar," Ben's mom said, squeezing Mr. Lewis's hand as he sat back beside her. Ben's mom had been raised just a few hours away and her Southern accent was still strong. Despite being a hardened combat vet, she spoke softly and smiled often. Both Ben's parents smiled often, but his dad could never be accused of speaking softly.

"You look like you've seen a ghost, Miss McGee," he said gamely. "Tell me, where did you see it? Unless it was in our home. Then I'd appreciate you keeping that bit of information to yourself!"

Tess smiled for real this time, despite herself. "No ghost, Mr. Lewis. Just thinking about things."

Those *things* she was thinking about? Well, that was a bit confusing. She had considered the fact the new neighbors were criminals. They had false identification so of course they were criminals. She just wasn't used to being personally threatened. She hadn't misunderstood either man's meaning, though.

The streets weren't safe.

Horace was right about that. They weren't safe. Not anymore. Not since her dad had left. Having law enforcement in the neighborhood had been a natural deterrent in an area that saw little mischief anyway. Mature trees, cracked, well-traveled sidewalks, retirees mingling with young families. The most work her dad did from his own home was breaking up teenagers bashing the occasional mailbox or toilet papering the odd house around Halloween. It was an older neighborhood, but a safe one.

Until now.

These guys were new. They didn't know how the neighborhood watched out for each other. The threat had been oblique, but it was there. And what had Jasper meant by *no kids here*? Tess knew what she had seen. A waif of a girl, haunting the back of a moving truck, watching Tess from across the street. There was a stuffed bunny in Tess's bag to prove it. So why would the men lie?

Tess had to acknowledge that she could be a handful. And if the men were trying to hide illicit activity, they wouldn't want some spitfire from the neighborhood popping in and out, poking where she didn't belong. The poor girl had probably never had a friend over for dinner or to spend the night. And so far, Tess hadn't seen her walking to school. It could be the men drove her after Tess had already left, or they could be keeping her home. A lot of people home-schooled their kids. Tess supposed it was a viable option, though she couldn't picture Jasper being a model of scholarly rigor for his young ward.

"Tess, sugar. Are you sure you're okay?"

Ben's mom was looking at her again, so Tess took a big bite of her noodles. "Mm mm," she managed. "So good!"

She washed it all down with a big gulp of fake soda - no sugar, no calories, so where did the flavor come from? - then smiled and dabbed at her mouth with a napkin, a belated attempt at manners. "Yes, ma'am," she said. "I'm sorry about that. I was just thinking about..."

Usually, Tess was good at coming up with nonsense on the fly. She was definitely off her game. "I was thinking about how I need, to, uh -"

"How she needs to finish her science project. Tonight. Seriously." Ben stared her down, and Tess couldn't decide if he was helping her slide off the hook or if he meant it. Knowing Ben, he probably meant it. But it also did let her off the hook, so she took it.

"I know." Tess dropped her napkin back onto her lap and propped her chin up on her fist. "How much time do you think we have before the butterflies hatch? Another day or two?"

"*We*," Ben stressed, "don't have any time. *We* are not in this together. *My* science project was finished last week. *You* have until the end of the week at most. So *we*," this time Tess knew he wasn't just talking about school, "need to focus and get started on our homework now."

Ben pushed back from the table and collected his plate and Tess's. "May we be excused, please?" He waited politely until his mother nodded.

"Of course, baby. Just drop those in the sink and I'll get to them later. Oh, and Tess?"

Tess had already turned to follow Ben into the kitchen but turned back when Mrs. Lewis called her. "Ma'am?"

"I wrote that recipe out for your mama. It's lying on the counter beside the back door. Would you mind taking it to her when you go home?"

Tess cocked her head. "A recipe?" Had her mother acted so quickly on her threat to meet Ben's parents?

"She called a few hours ago, wanting to meet the people her daughter has been spending her evenings with." Mrs. Lewis arched an eyebrow, and Tess pulled the most contrite expression she had.

"Yes, ma'am," she said apologetically. "I meant to have her call you sooner, but it slipped my mind." It hadn't slipped her mind. She just hadn't been sure she wanted her mother to meet Mrs. Lewis.

Mrs. Lewis, who was so put together. Who ran her home like the ship she'd once been stationed on. Whose husband came home every night and gave her a big hug and a kiss, even when Ben was in the room. She hadn't been sure how her mother would react.

"I hope, well, did she sound okay?" Tess fiddled with an errant curl, not quite sure how to ask what she wanted to ask. Had her mother sounded awake? Had she sounded present? Did she seem to care? They had talked enough that Mrs. Lewis was sending her a recipe, so it had to have gone okay, right?

Mrs. Lewis smiled and reached for Tess's hand. "She'll be just fine, little one." She pushed back from the table to collect the rest of the empty plates. "She may not be herself just yet, but she'll find her way back."

Mrs. Lewis gave Tess a wink as she walked into the kitchen. "And so will you, even if it doesn't feel that way right now."

"You ready?" Ben asked, stopping beside her. Tess just nodded, watching as Mrs. Lewis made her way into the kitchen. "Here." He slipped the recipe for chicken gumbo into Tess's hand, and they both turned to the stairs without saying another word.

It was a short-lived silence, as it turned out. "You have to stay away from them, Tess," Ben said furiously as soon as the door was shut. It took Tess by surprise. In the few short weeks she'd known Ben, he'd been nothing but mild-mannered and calm. Like a tiny, nerdier version of Clark Kent, without the superhero side to shore him up.

"I mean it. Those guys are dangerous." He had hidden his feelings so well Tess hadn't realized he was having them, but now he was shaking as he ran a hand through his hair and paced back and forth beside his bed. "I mean, did you hear what that one guy said?"

"Horace."

"What?" Ben stopped pacing long enough to gape at her.

"Horace. I've been calling the thin one Horace."

Ben worked his tongue around his teeth, eyes narrowing. "Okay," he managed. "Is there some *reason* you're making up names for the killers across the street?"

"Oh, come on," Tess prodded. "You know. No? They look just like...on the cartoon...never mind." She threw her hands up and sank into his desk chair. The one pulled right up to the cocoons she needed to take pictures of before she left.

"You think they're killers?" Tess was curious. The idea had been playing in the back of her head since the meeting with her mom and Mr. Abrams, the idea these men were killers. That they might have killed...well, that they might have killed. But after the encounter on the street, that thin wisp of suspicion was starting to take shape in her mind.

"They threatened you."

Ben was stark in his pronouncement, and Tess found she couldn't argue the point. "Well, yeah, they did a little," she said weakly, but Ben wasn't giving in. "I heard, okay. I get what they meant." She sighed. "It's just not something I had to think about...before."

Before her dad went away. Before her hero lost a fight and left the criminals of the world with one less obstacle to fear. Before everything changed.

"I'll stay away, okay?" She didn't want to keep thinking about those things. Those things led nowhere good. "I'll just keep the bunny and if I ever see the kid outside, I'll slip it to her then."

Ben started unpacking his backpack, pulling out the math book Tess had utterly disregarded in her locker before leaving for the day. He sat it slowly on his bedspread before saying, slowly, as though he regretted coming out with it, "They said there was no one else in the house."

Tess had heard. *No kids here*, Horace had said. She found him the least menacing of the two, overall. Still, it had given her chills though Tess knew what she'd seen.

"I suppose she could have been visiting," Tess admitted reluctantly. "Maybe she was with whoever was helping them move. She dropped the rabbit while she was outside, forgot to pick it up, and went home without it."

It was possible, but Tess didn't think so. She had a strange, queasy feeling, like there was more meaning behind the words than she could understand.

"Well, good then." Ben dropped to sit on the end of the bed, facing Tess. "As long as you promise to stay away, and at least wait for me before leaving for school tomorrow. Let them cool off, forget they ever talked to you."

"What about you?" Tess demanded. She was a little insulted. She hadn't done anything wrong. She hadn't even gotten a chance to be precocious, let alone unleash her full uh on them. What made Ben think it was Tess alone that had deserved umbrage? "You were there, too. In fact," she proudly pointed out, "you were the one thwarting their threats with the fake phone call to your parents."

Ben just stared at her. "Come on, Tess," he said wryly. "We both know who was poking the bear. Those guys barely even knew I was there."

"And?" Tess prodded. She'd make him say it, despite the red that was slowly seeping up his face.

"And, what?" He picked up his book, flipping it open with a purpose no one studying math should display. "You should get those pictures taken. This could be your last chance before they open."

"And?"

Ben slapped the book shut with a pop. "Fine. Because you're a girl and I'm not. Which you know is true just as well as I do, it just sounds worse coming from me."

"Thank you." Tess let the smugness ooze, making sure Ben knew she'd made her point. It was true, though. Walking with Ben was safer than walking alone by the very nature of their genders. And it frustrated her to no end. But Tess had a feeling she was going to need Ben on her side. She wasn't quite ready to tell him what was bubbling up in her mind, but she would. Once she had a chance to flesh it out for herself.

She needed to do some research first and snoop around the databases she had access to. The idea taking shape in her mind wouldn't be denied for long, so for now she would let Ben believe he'd talked her down. But he was right about something else too.

"Alright, let's get this done." Sighing, Tess turned in her seat and pulled out her phone. She'd get a couple of shots of the cocoons, which looked the same as they had looked the last three times she'd taken pictures. Then she'd see what happened next.

As if that wasn't already the story of her life.

Chapter 17

D r. Holland was less helpful than he'd hoped.
"Of course I can't tell if he stepped off the roof on his
own or if he was given an old-fashioned heave-ho," the old
coroner said with disgust. "Of course he could have been
pushed! There's no way for minor bruising from a scuffle to be
distinguished from the pile of bones and skin on my table. And
who's to say there was a scuffle? He could have been bludgeoned
to death and dropped off the roof for all that's left of him. Come
on, man!"

Helpful *being a subjective term, of course.*

"Your report concluded suicide was the most likely cause,"
he pointed out while his companion ordered another Scotch.

"The most likely *cause, yes." Dr. Holland took another
drink. "The bodies of corporate financiers are piling up on the
streets around us. It's not a difficult leap to make."

*He could have pointed out the irony of that statement, but
Dr. Holland wouldn't have appreciated it.*

"There were no drugs in his system, not even alcohol, so
his faculties were fully intact. His wallet was found on the
body, along with a very expensive watch and diamond cuff
links, so he wasn't robbed. A bottle of expensive whiskey and
a half-smoked cigar were found on the roof overlooking the
body." The good doctor finished his drink and waved off the
barkeep. Two was his limit. "By all accounts, he took himself up
to the roof for a final drink and the finest of smokes, and then
removed himself from this world."

"But he didn't drink."

The old gumshoe drummed his fingers on the smooth, polished wood beneath them. The story did fit the details, but he had to wonder. The stock market crash had hit hard. If the man's finances were in shambles like most of the men in his position, the story worked.

Having lost multiple fortunes in the space of a week had been enough to end the lives of many an elite Wall Street man. Finances clearly weren't a problem for the daughter, based on the down payment he'd received. She would be the presumed heiress to her father's estate and if she had access to that kind of cash, likely the fortune was there to be had.

But he hadn't gained his reputation by assuming.

He clapped the old doctor on the back before tossing some bills on the bar and rising. "I may come to you again if I have a need."

"And I'll be happy to meet you here, over a fine Scotch."

The man might be old, but he certainly wasn't stupid.

• • • •

LATER THAT NIGHT, TESS lay sprawled on her bed, pictures of the butterfly cocoons in different stages spread around her like a rainbow on the verge of something great.

She hadn't noticed until she'd printed the pictures and placed them side-by-side, but they did look different. It was subtle, but each cocoon had minute changes in shape and coloring, enough that this project just might work.

Tess was currently labeling each picture with the date it was taken and laying them out in chronological order. According to the research she'd pulled up, the cocoons could break open at any time. She would need to drop by Ben's house every day to capture the butterflies in their earliest stage after emergence.

She supposed she could have brought the glass case home, but it was kind of nice having a purpose and a place to go after school each day. And she didn't think Ben minded her tagging along. He was still getting used to having his parents at home all the time, and she got the feeling he appreciated Tess's unique brand of extroversion to help dilute the tension of adjusting to a new life.

Ben had insisted on walking her home last night, but it hadn't been necessary. The van beside the Brooklyn house had been gone. It had yet to reappear, but Tess had marked the time of departure on the timeline she had created as soon as she'd shut herself in her room. She would watch for it to reappear for a while yet but if it came back after she was asleep, she would mark it as an overnight return.

Ian McGee had taught Tess that patterns were important, and she glanced now at the timeline she'd stuck to the wall beside her window. She would fill it in over the next few weeks, watching to establish the behavior of the men across the street. She would also watch for appearances of little Jane Doe, as Tess was now calling her. No matter what the men said, and no matter what Ben thought, Tess knew there was a girl there.

The bunny sat on the bed in front of Tess, legs crossed under her as she absently stroked its fur. It was soft and worn, as though a previous owner had done this same thing hundreds of times. Why would the men deny that there was a child with them in the house? Was it just to keep Tess from coming around?

Tess wasn't sure why men seemed to think girls attracted other girls, but that wasn't it at all. The girl had seemed...sad, somehow. Lonely, maybe. She had the look of a ragamuffin about her, as though a strong breeze could blow her away. Tess knew a little of what that kind of hollowness felt like. She just wanted the girl to know she wasn't alone.

There was a soft knock on her door, and Tess's mom stuck her head in. "Tessie, baby, you in here?"

"You can come in." Tess started sweeping the pictures of the cocoons into a pile as her mom came in and plucked one from the floor where the breeze from the door had caught it.

"What's this?"

"It's for class." Tess accepted the picture from her mother and tucked it into the pile. "Ben's helping me catalog the life cycle of a butterfly."

"Well, that's nice." Kate hesitated for just a moment, then did something she hadn't done in a long time. She swatted Tess's leg to scoot her over and climbed onto the bed beside her.

Tess made room and Kate leaned back against the headboard, shoulder pressed against Tess's. It was something her mom used to do most evenings, after Tess had finished her homework and before lights out. They would catch up on the day, Tess telling of her wild school-time adventures and Kate telling Tess silly stories of the things she'd seen at the law office. Then Tess's dad would stick his head in the door and demand his daughter return his wife at once, making both girls laugh.

Kate would kiss Tess's forehead and whisper, "Baby girl, find yourself a man like your daddy someday. He's a keeper."

Tess knew they were both thinking of those times now, and she glanced at the emptiness beyond the door, hating the stark silence that lay beyond.

There was that hollow feeling again.

"Baby," Kate finally said with a sigh, "can we talk about what happened at dinner the other night?"

It took Tess a minute to remember what her mom was talking about, but then it came. Sully and Miss Angel, and Tess making it clear she knew her mother wasn't going to work anymore.

"I'm sorry," Tess said, without looking at her mom. She kept her eyes on her ragged cuticles instead. "I shouldn't have said that."

"No," Kate let out a deep breath, "you should have. Or maybe I should have. I don't know. But listen," Kate turned and crossed her legs, looking at Tess head-on. "I thought I could protect you by keeping some things to myself. Or maybe I was trying to protect myself, I don't know."

From beneath Tess's wild fringe of hair, she could see the haunted look ghosting across her mother's face, there and gone in a blink. "But I forgot how much you see. How much your father taught you to see." Kate smiled at that. Not a big, happy smile, but wistful and fond. "That man was too much for all of our goods."

It was something her mother used to say all the time when Ian McGee did something wild and outrageous that made Tess laugh and her mother smile, even though as a grown-up she wasn't supposed to.

"The house is so quiet now." It came without Tess's permission and for a moment, she was afraid she'd broken the spell. She didn't necessarily want to talk about this, but she didn't want her mother to go away again, either. But Kate just gave her that same, wistful smile. "It really is, isn't it?"

They sat that way for a moment, knee-to-knee until Kate sighed. "I took a leave of absence from work about six months ago."

Tess nodded. "I skipped school about six months ago."

"I know," Kate said.

"Me, too."

Another minute of quiet. "Do you...think you'll go back?" Tess wasn't sure if she wanted to know the answer to that question. Her mother's return to work would be a return to normal, which would be good. Tess wanted her mother to be her mother again. But things would never be normal again, and she wasn't sure she wanted to pretend they were.

"I don't know, baby." Kate took one of Tess's hands in her own, examining her nails. "We'll work on these tomorrow," she said idly. "I don't know if I can go back to work there. I don't think I fit into my old life anymore."

"Me, neither," Tess said, and it was true. She was still the same, old Tess. Biting sense of humor, hair that wouldn't quit, and a voracious sense of right and wrong. But the bite in her humor had become cutting and her desire to right wrongs now came from a sense of obsession and not truth. Vengeance had replaced justice and while it was a fine line, she did know the difference.

If she could see those changes in herself, what must her mother see?

"Is that why you and Maddie aren't friends anymore?"

Tess knew her mother would eventually ask after their little counseling session at the school, but the topic made her uncomfortable. She didn't know if she and Maddie would still be friends in the aftermath of Tess's father leaving, because they hadn't survived the loss of Maddie's dad first. So Tess just shook her head.

"It started with Maddie's dad, didn't it?" Kate asked, giving Tess's hand a gentle squeeze. "I'm sorry I wasn't paying more attention."

Tess knew her own father's behavior had started to change around the time Maddie's father abandoned his family. He'd started spending more time in his study, and Sully had started coming over and spending evenings shut away with him. Tess knew her mom and Miss Angel had been worried, but she'd been so consumed with Maddie's troubles that she hadn't noticed the changes in her own house until later.

"People grow apart," Tess finally said. "It happens. Maddie has new friends and she's on the cheer squad, and I'm still breaking up fights and ruling the debate team."

"You're not still on the debate team," her mother chastened mildly, "but we don't have to talk about that now. You've been spending a lot of time with Ben lately."

It was a mild segue, which Tess appreciated. She toppled backward off the bed to grab her backpack as she remembered something. "Mrs. Lewis wanted me to give this to you," Tess said, climbing back onto the bed and extending the recipe towards her mother.

"Well, isn't this nice?" Kate took the card and glanced over it. "Chicken gumbo. I'll send her my lasagna recipe next week. Hey," she poked Tess's leg with her finger. "What if we had Ben and his parents over for dinner next week with Sully and Miss Angel? I haven't met them yet but if he's such a good friend to you, I would like to."

It was the kind of thing her mother would have done when her father was still at home, and Tess felt slightly encouraged. Maybe her mom wasn't ready to go back to work, but she wanted to meet Ben. And she'd gone to Tess's school because she'd been concerned about Tess's behavior. Those were all things her old mother would do. Her real mother.

Small steps are better than no steps, Tessie.

Tess smiled at the sound of her father's voice in her head. As an Irishman, he'd had no shortage of pithy sayings. Maybe she should write them down. She didn't want to forget.

Her mom leaned forward and pressed a kiss to Tess's forehead. "How about we hit the farmers market tomorrow morning, then the both of us get something done with these raggedy nails?" Kate wiggled her fingers in front of Tess's face and they both giggled.

"Okay, then." This time, Kate's smile was soft as she looked at her daughter. She climbed off the bed, hesitating by Tess's desk as she ran her fingers along the framed picture of Tess and Ian that lay upside down before she moved on. She stopped by the door to turn back to Tess one more time, and Tess could swear they both held their breath. And then, as though she'd never missed a beat, she said it.

"Baby girl, find yourself a man like your daddy one day. He's a keeper."

Chapter 18

A light breeze rippled across Tess's forehead as she browsed the racks of bracelets while her mother chatted with the lady at their favorite produce stand. They were debating the strengths of fall lettuce over spring lettuce and would be moving on to parsley next, which Tess interpreted to mean she had some time to kill.

There was a rumor that Fall in other parts of the country was full of crisp mornings and chilly bonfire nights but in Louisiana, heat and humidity were the names of the game, and Tess knew her hair was far bigger than it had been only an hour earlier.

The bracelets were made of some kind of reclaimed, carved wood, smooth and polished to the touch, and Tess liked how they sounded like wind chimes when the charms bumped together. This was their last stop on their usual rounds, buying the fruits, vegetables, and meat they would need for the week. Both her parents supported local businesses and bought only what they needed, ensuring income for their neighbors week after week. It was part of being a community, her dad said. You have to know and be known so you can know what others need. Once you know what others need, you can chip right in.

Tess fished some cash out of her pocket as she held up a bracelet with small chips of emerald glass interspersed between smooth circles of willow bark. If the sign was to be believed, the willow was harvested from a local bayou during clean-up from one of last year's hurricanes.

"That will look good with your hair."

The voice came from beside Tess, and she stiffened. She hadn't bothered to look at the other patrons milling about, and Maddie had somehow managed to slide in beside her without a sound.

And was speaking. To Tess. For the first time in a year.

Tess was proud of her restraint as she dropped the bracelet back onto the rack. "It's okay," she replied, not bothering to look over before fingering the row of necklaces above, moving on like she wasn't interested. She wasn't sure why Maddie would decide to speak to her now, and she wasn't sure if she cared.

Okay, fine. She cared a little. Tess glanced up from beneath the Chia Pet growing ever larger on her head to see if Maddie was following.

She was. Interesting.

"Sorry about bumping into your friend last week after class," Maddie said, trailing along behind Tess like it was last year and she'd never disappeared. "He's new, right?"

Of course Ben was new. Their school was small enough that you tended to notice when someone new showed up in class. Maddie knew that Tess knew that. So why was she asking?

"He seems nice," she went on, eyeing a rack of finely-knit scarves. They were delicate, with gold and silver filigree woven throughout. Tess eyed them herself, resisting the impulse to reach out and touch what Maddie was so clearly interested in. But come on, nothing could be that soft. They looked too fine and delicate to be real. What were they spun from, unicorn hair?

"Are you guys dating?"

The question came out of nowhere, jarring Tess from her dreams of wrapping that scarf around her hair to tame the frizz and strolling around with an emerald bracelet catching the sun on her wrist. "What? Who? Me and Ben?"

It was an insane idea, though Tess wasn't quite sure why. Ben was a guy. She was a girl. They'd been spending a lot of time together. But the idea hadn't even occurred to Tess and the mere suggestion of it now was enough to curl her nose. Dating was not in the cards for their particular brand of friendship.

But instead of answering, Tess eyed Maddie suspiciously. It was the first time she'd looked at Maddie since she'd made herself known, and Tess wasn't sure she liked what she saw.

Tall and willowy to Tess's short and scruffy, blonde hair pristine and neat, pulled into a high, casual ponytail that Tess's wild curls would never be able to achieve. Blue-eyed, with a light spattering of freckles across the bridge of a button nose and translucent skin. Maddie was the definition of the girl next door, and Tess didn't like this sudden interest in her friend. Ben was nice. He was new and still getting his sea legs back after losing his grandmother. And he was Tess's friend, not Maddie's.

But Maddie just smiled. "He seems nice. I like nice boys."

Oh, Tess knew. Despite being pretty and popular, Maddie had always been a *good* girl. She didn't lie to her mother and go to parties when she was supposed to be doing homework at the library. She couldn't abide the thought or smell of alcohol, and she wasn't shy in telling someone else exactly what she thought of underage drinking. She was part of a mentorship program at school and went to church every single Sunday. How she managed to be so popular was a mystery to Tess, but one that was surely tied not just to the way she looked but to that intangible, sparkly quality that surrounded Maddie at all times.

Tess never had been able to define it, but Maddie was one of those people who just, well, glowed. And she was so *nice*. Tess had never met a nicer person, and it burned her to no end. No one could dislike Maddie. Not other girls and certainly not boys.

Ben would be no different.

This was not at all what Tess had anticipated. "He is nice," she finally said, though it galled her. "He lives on Bon Ami, just down the street."

Maddie didn't live in Tess's neighborhood, but she was only a mile south. They used to walk back and forth to each other's homes all the time, so she would know the streets.

"Do you think he would care if I sat with him at lunch one day?" Maddie asked, those clear, blue eyes looking at Tess so innocently, and Tess just snapped.

"Just to be clear," she said, rounding on Maddie in what must have looked to outsiders like a mountain and a molehill situation, Maddie gazing down calmly at the tiny mouse attacking her. "You're talking to me for the first time in over a year because you're interested in someone I know. Not because you care about me, or want to see how I've been doing since, you know, my dad left, but because you like a boy and you want me to put in a good word. That about cover what's happening here?"

"Tess McGee!" Maddie looked horrified as she glanced around to see if anyone was paying any attention to Tess's outburst, and Tess felt a rewarding sense of accomplishment that she'd managed to ruffle those perfect feathers. Until Maddie grabbed Tess by the arm and steered her off the sidewalk and behind one of the tents, that is. Even in her embarrassment, Maddie was careful not to make a scene and even her grip on Tess's arm felt polite as they huddled amongst farm-fresh eggs and the fluffy baby chicks who were now peeping up a storm at the girls disturbing their quiet.

"Well, I'm right, aren't I?" Tess asked, pulling her arm back and fighting the urge to shake it out. For a polite grip, it sure had been firm. Both girls stood in the shadow of the tent, hidden in the small alley formed between the rows of sellers, and watched each other, Tess with determination and Maddie hesitantly.

Finally, Maddie caved. As Tess knew she eventually would. "Yes, I'm interested in Ben. He's cute and smart and new, and I want to find out more about him. I want to know if he would even be interested in me." Tess made a scoffing sound that Maddie ignored despite the rudeness. "And you are the only person he talks to and, well," Maddie cleared her throat. "Well, I guess I miss you, Tess McGee. Hard as that is to believe."

Tess just stared at the girl in front of her. The girl who had been her best friend all her life. Until she wasn't. And now she wanted to be friends again? Not that she'd said that, but still. That *almost* sounded like an apology.

All Tess had wanted out of today was to buy a bracelet. Maybe get her nails done like a normal girl. Why was normal so hard for her? Why did drama follow her everywhere she roamed?

Tess opened her mouth, though she had no idea what was about to come out when something caught her eye. Movement at the end of the alley, and the whisper of voices she recognized.

So long, normal. Hello, drama, drama, drama.

Tess grabbed Maddie's arm and pulled her around the side of the tent as two men slipped silently from the back of a stall directly across from them. Maddie started to protest but Tess hushed her, poking her head around the corner so she could see.

It was Horace and Jasper, and they were heading their way. Tess shoved Maddie back and they slipped around the corner as the men stopped even with their hiding place.

"Well?" Jasper demanded, and Horace shrugged his shoulders. "We wait and see," he said softly. "But he'll come through."

Jasper didn't seem happy with the answer, but Horace was unperturbed. "This was a stupid move," Jasper said. "It's too public, and we shouldn't risk it with that kid poking around."

Tess stiffened. Were they talking about her? Was she *that kid*?

"She didn't mean anything by it," Horace said calmly. "She was just curious about the new neighbors."

They *were* talking about her, and Tess did not like that one bit.

"Kids are nosy, but they have short attention spans. She'll move on."

Maddie tugged on Tess's shirt, but Tess waved her off.

"I don't like it," Jasper insisted. "She's that cop's kid. You know the one," he said meaningfully, and Horace gave a short nod. "And she was yammering about seeing a girl."

"We both know that's not possible," Horace placated. "She's just an overeager kid snooping around. And the cop's not going to be a problem anymore. You know that."

"We can't have it," Jasper snarled. "If she keeps it up, we'll have to take care of it."

Maddie's tugging had become insistent. "Tess!" The whisper was as frantic as any barely-there voice could be. "We have to get out of here!"

Maddie was right, and Tess knew it. The sense of danger was palpable - these men were dangerous, and Tess was in their cross-hairs. But that thing they said about her dad gave her pause. Like they knew him. Like they knew why he wasn't going to be a problem anymore...

"She's not keeping anything up," Horace said, talking his partner down. "We talked to her mom, and she's going to take care of it."

"She'd better." Jasper shoved Horace in the shoulder and he stumbled a step closer to Tess and Maddie, on the verge of discovering the frozen girls.

Horace seemed to think nothing of the shove and after a moment, he straightened up without reacting. "We need to go. He said there's a shipment coming in today, and we need to clear some inventory."

Jasper didn't respond, simply turning his back and stomping away. Horace seemed to accept this as an answer and ambled after his brother, and Tess breathed for the first time since she'd seen them. She allowed Maddie to tug her back into the main part of the Farmers' Market, into the crowds of people bartering and selling, families out sampling the goods, and catching up with neighbors. Where the sun shone brightly and danger felt all but impossible.

Tess's mother had moved on to the Amish bakery table, where three little girls in their handmade caps and aprons were playing jacks on the dusty ground. The retired couple three streets over from Tess's house were grabbing coffee from a parked truck while the single girl two houses down chatted with them, sipping her smoothie and laughing at some joke the old man told.

Gary was barking, and Tess could hear Mrs. Sandoval scolding him in her native language. A nice, normal day, but Tess could feel and hear everything, her senses on high alert. She craned her neck, trying to catch sight of where the men had gone. The wind lifted her sweaty curls from the back of her neck, and she shivered instinctively. A robin was chirping in the tree above her and his partner answered back. And somehow, Tess just *knew*.

"...stumbled into, Tess McGee?"

Maddie's claw grip of a hand shook her again, and Tess pulled back in. "What?"

"What are you mixed up in now, Tess?" Maddie demanded, and Tess was a little stunned to see tears in Maddie's eyes.

"What do you mean?" she asked, and Maddie sniffed. "Those men were talking about *you*, right? You're the girl poking her nose into their business that they're going to do something about."

"It's not so bad as all that," Tess soothed, snapping out of her shock and trying to calm Maddie. "I only tried to welcome them to the neighborhood, and they didn't like it."

"What were they saying about a little girl?"

Tess furrowed her brows. That was so weird. "They said they didn't have a little girl living with them, but I know they do. I've seen her! I mean, why would they-"

"No, Tess!" Maddie shook Tess's arm one more time before shoving her back. "No. It doesn't matter. You stay away from them, do you hear me? They are dangerous."

Tess thought back over what she'd just heard, and she knew Maddie was right. Ben was right. Her mother and Mr. Abrams were right.

Tess knew it too, but she couldn't let it go. And Maddie didn't need to know that.

"Trust me," she assured Maddie, "I don't intend to go anywhere near them."

It was the right words, and she wasn't even lying. She didn't have to get close to watch them. But Tess had forgotten something about Maddie. Tess may have been Maddie's best friend for years, but Maddie had also been Tess's. And some things just couldn't be erased with distance.

"So help me, Tess McGee," Maddie said, swiping beneath her eyes and somehow still looking flawless, "I will go to your mother if you don't leave it alone."

"You're going to tattle on me?" Maddie asked skeptically. "Really?"

"Most definitely." Maddie narrowed her eyes. "Without hesitation. I will go to your mother, I'll go to Sully." She drew herself up to her full, towering height with menacing effect. "I'll even go to Miss Angel, and you know what that means."

Tess frowned. She did know what that meant. Tess's mother might still be too sad to do much, though last night and this morning did seem to be a turning point of sorts. Sully had a job to do and couldn't watch Tess all the time. But Miss Angel could stick to Tess like glue, and she'd do it as loudly as possible. Tess was sneaky, but Miss Angel was on a whole different level.

So Tess did what she did best. She heaved a massive sigh and gave a big eye roll for effect. "Fine," she huffed. "I'll leave them alone. But not because of you." She looked Maddie right in the eye, and she didn't even flinch as she laid down the hammer. "Because my dad would have wanted me to."

Tess watched Maddie carefully, and the mention of her dad was enough to seal the deal. Maddie sagged backward, suddenly exhausted, and bought the lie.

"Well, okay then."

The girls stood, looking at each other for several minutes, neither quite sure what to say next until Tess felt a hand on her shoulder.

She jumped, whirling under the pressure, but it wasn't Horace or Jasper, discovering her subterfuge and ready to make good on their threats. It was only her mother, smiling at Maddie.

"Maddie Sue, it's so good to see you!" she beamed, and Maddie smiled back. If it was a slightly shaky, watered-down version of Maddie's usual smile, Kate didn't seem to notice.

"Hi, Miss Kate," she forced out. "Tess and I were just talking about school." Maddie looked back at Tess. "Don't worry, Tess," she said. "We'll work on it together. I'll make sure you keep up your end of the assignment." It was said with purpose, and Tess had to wonder how much of the lie she'd bought.

As Maddie disappeared back through the scarves and bracelets, Kate hooked her arm through Tess's and started steering them towards the outskirts of the market. "I stopped in at the salon and the girls can get us in. Manicures and pedicures, how does that sound, Tessie? Just you and me?"

Tess smiled at her mother and nodded. "That sounds great."

She tried to inject as much enthusiasm as she could but the truth was, her mind was right back in that alley listening to Horace and Jasper talk. Not about her. That, she should probably be more concerned about than she was but no, she was instead hearing them say, once again, how that cop wasn't going to be a problem anymore. Like they had known him. Like they knew what happened to him.

Like they killed him.

Tess didn't care what she'd told Maddie, and she didn't care what she'd told Ben. These men had threatened her, they'd threatened her friend, and they'd threatened her mother, even if she didn't know it.

Tess could move on from all that. But there was exactly one thing Tess could never move on from. One thing she would never forgive, and one thing she would never back away from.

Horace and Jasper had killed her father, and she would make them pay.

Justice, Tessie, not vengeance. You know better than this.

Well, she'd just have to take both then, wouldn't she?

Chapter 19

"**H**ere's what we know so far." Tess had rolled out the big whiteboard her dad and Sully used when working a case, spotlight snapped on for effect.

The rest of the weekend had gone smoothly, despite the unsettled feeling in Tess's gut. They'd gone to church the next morning, where Tess had officially introduced her mother to the Lewis', who'd swiftly invited them to dinner next Saturday night. After lunch, Kate had tugged on her gardening gloves and attacked the weeds that had overgrown her roses with gusto for the first time since everything had changed while Tess sprawled nearby on a blanket with a book in hand.

Under the shade of the magnolia they had planted together the week they'd moved in, the air was cool and much lighter than it had been the day before. Everything felt as normal as it could, and they'd finished up the night watching an old black and white movie that her father had loved, *Dick Tracy*.

And through it all, Tess kept her plan in the back of her mind, rotating and growing.

And now that the school day had finally ended, Tess had Ben trapped in her house after catching him up on her discovery over the weekend. They were in her dad's study, the one he would use to work on cases from home and where he'd spent so much of his last year. Tess thought it was poetic that his murder would be solved in the same room.

"Targets one and two," here, Tess pointed to the pictures she'd managed to get of Horace and Jasper as they'd arrived back home late last night. The pictures weren't great, dark as it had been, but they were enough to tell which man was which, "have moved into the Brooklyn house. The first date they were seen was October 12. We'll eventually need better pictures, but your camera should be able to handle that."

"Should I be taking notes?" Ben wondered aloud, but Tess decided it was a rhetorical question and continued with her presentation.

"Point two. They have a little girl who lives with them, let's call her *Jane Doe*. Jane Doe has been spotted beside the moving truck and in one of the front windows, here and here."

Another grainy image, this time of the house, had been added to the board, along with a rough sketch of the street where the van parked. Tess was no artist, but it could have been worse.

"She has light, brownish hair and pale skin. No distinguishing features I could see. She's roughly forty-two inches tall, between four and six years of age."

The girl had been standing solemnly in the front window of the house, tucked behind a ragged, sheer curtain. Tess had waved from her window but even though the girl appeared to be looking at her, she didn't wave back. By the time Tess had grabbed her phone and focused on the house, the girl was gone.

"'Jane Doe' sounds so big for someone so small," Ben remarked. "Can we call her something else?"

Tess rolled her eyes. "Fine. *Janie*," Tess paused to get Ben's approving shrug, "is roughly four feet tall and five years old."

"She's only ever been seen by you," Ben helpfully pointed out, "and you have, shall we say, a *vivid* imagination."

"Are you implying I made her up?" Tess might be imaginative, but she certainly knew what she had seen. "Then what is this?" She triumphantly pulled the girl's bunny from where she'd stored it carefully in her backpack. "Exhibit A, dropped from one of the moving boxes by Target One the day they moved in."

"Which was when again?" Ben asked politely.

"Oh, good grief!" Tess spun from the board, hands on hips. "This isn't even the hard part. Pay attention!" Ben had seemed a bit shell-shocked on the walk home, and she knew he wasn't taking her as seriously as he should. Disappointing, yes. But Tess knew she would convince him with time.

"That should be your first job," she decided, and Ben looked back up from his math homework, which was just insulting.

"What's my first job? And when did I agree to do a job?"

"You are my partner. Of course, you have a job." Tess paused, allowing tension to build so she could reveal the crux of her plan - evidence. "You will stake out the house and get pictures of the targets and Janie." She considered. "Pictures that are in focus. That's step one, anyway."

"We've been friends for two weeks but sure, I'm your partner." Ben suddenly looked up. "I'll do what now?" His eyes were wide, and he was staring at her as though he were sure she had to be joking. Which seemed odd to Tess. A stakeout was the least baffling thing about this.

"Didn't we decide to keep our distance from these guys?"

"Well," Tess hedged, "technically we decided that I would stay away from them. And I am! But we never said anything about you. And besides, a stakeout, by its very nature, is distant. Come on," she wheedled, "you'll be perfect for it!"

"How do you figure?" Ben appeared unimpressed, but at least he'd forgotten his homework for the moment and was tapping his pencil eraser against the desk, a sign Tess took to mean he was thinking it through.

"Well, for one thing, your parents are both in the game," Tess reasoned. "It's in your blood, just like it's in mine. The hunt, the chase, digging for the truth...it'll be great!" Tess could picture them now, lying in wait, anticipating their opponent's next move, a real-life game of chess.

"Okay," Ben drew out the word like she was missing a very big plot point. "But what's the purpose of this stakeout?"

"Purpose?" Tess had to admit, this one got her. What was the purpose of any stakeout?

"To find answers?" That seemed obvious, but maybe he needed to hear it.

"We're just kids, Tess," Ben said in exasperation. "We have school and homework and very solid bedtimes. And even if we do find proof, who's going to believe us?"

"Sully will." Tess was sure about that. If they could present Sully with hard evidence, he would believe them. He would act. For her. For his partner. For justice. "Wait. You still have a bedtime?"

Ben rolled his eyes. "I was making a point."

"Come on." Tess wasn't above wheedling when she needed to. "You love using that camera, and your parents did give it to you for a reason. You'd hate to let them down or, even worse," she pinned Ben with her stare, shaming him with the weight of her gaze, "let yourself down."

She could see Ben weakening, and she wasn't sure if it was from the fact that she was right or that she was persistent but either way, she exploited his hesitation. "Come on. Just imagine - Ben Lewis, capturing the photographic evidence of conspiracy and murder right here in tiny, little Lafitte."

Tess held up her hands, framing an invisible byline, and Ben's defenses crumbled. "Fine," he agreed, if not a little grudgingly, "just as long as it doesn't get in the way of homework or school."

"Or bedtime," Tess added gamely.

"Do you want my help or not?"

"Sorry, sorry!"

Step one accomplished. Now, for step two.

"Okay, what else do we know?"

"Are they buyers or renters?" Ben asked, begrudgingly joining in, and Tess considered.

"Renting would be most likely, although we shouldn't assume." Tess jotted the question on the board and linked it to the house. "I'll go down to the courthouse and check with the Office of the Recorder on Friday. That should be publicly available information. If they are renting, I should be able to see who officially owns the house. I'll also look for a floor plan so we can map out ingress and egress routes. "

"Why," Ben asked, closing his eyes as though he were afraid of the answer, "why, oh, why would we need to know how to get in and out of a big, scary house full of murderers?"

"It never hurts to be prepared, right? I like to cover all bases, but I'm sure we won't need to approach." At least for now.

"Have you seen them move anything in except for boxes?"

"No." Tess considered. "I know the house is full of old furniture." She may have peeked through the window once or twice in her youth, imagining all the places a small girl could hide in that big, drafty house. "I would have thought new owners or renters would have provided their own or brought in something a little nicer, but maybe two men don't care much what they sleep on."

"Still, it's weird. They should at least care what Janie sleeps on." Ben considered for a moment, jotting down an equation while he thought. "I guess they could have moved in the heavy stuff when we were in school." How Ben was managing to add to this conversation and work on math at the same time was maddening.

"I'm sure some of the boxes had toys," Tess picked the bunny back up, giving it a gentle squeeze. "This tumbled out of one of the boxes they were carrying, and usually people pack like things together."

Tess stroked the rabbit's soft, well-worn head. Little Janie would be missing her toy, and Tess had a soft spot at the moment for anyone lonely and missing something, or someone, beloved.

"That's true," Ben mused. "How old did you say Janie looked?"

"She was really small." Tess bit her lip, thinking it over. "I would say five or six, but I could give a little either way."

"Did she have any defining features?" Ben asked. "Did she have freckles, scars? Did she resemble either of the men?" Ben pushed his math to the side, finally, and rummaged in his bag for his sketch pad. He flipped it open to the rough sketch he'd started of the girl and stared at it.

Tess closed her eyes and tried to bring the girl back up in her memory. "Nothing that I could see. But she didn't look like either of them. Her skin was pale, but it didn't have the ashy, greasy quality they do. More clear, almost translucent."

Everything about the girl had been bland. Tess hadn't even seen her that first day until she'd moved and the fluttering of her dress had caught Tess's eye. "She could still belong to one of them. She could be a niece or a distant relation. She could be adopted." Too many scenarios to consider. "But if you can get pictures of all three of them, we can hopefully identify who they are and how they're related."

"You're thinking their identities could lead to criminal activity?"

"Everyone is online these days," Tess said confidently. "We just need names to go with faces." Thomas Jeffries might have been a bust, but you couldn't rent without providing some form of documentation. The proof was out there. They just had to find the right thread to pull.

"Okay." Ben shoved his math book into his backpack. "What's our timeline? My parents like us to eat supper as a family every night at six, and I have baseball every Friday after school until five."

Boys and their sports. Tess was still a little surprised Ben had taken Mark up on his offer of off-season workouts.

"Priorities, man!" Tess exclaimed, to which Ben simply cocked an eyebrow, and Tess could see she'd have to take what she could get.

"Fine, fine. Put academics and sports above truth and justice. I suppose we'll make due." But she didn't have to do it gracefully.

She considered the timeline she'd drawn out across the middle of the board. "Let's work from here after school Monday through Thursday. We'll say we're studying or something." She thought for a second before crossing to her window and peering out. "It wouldn't hurt to get a different vantage point now and again, and you can see the house from your window too. Can I come to your house on Mondays and Wednesdays? We can say we're working on the science project."

"One of us actually will be," Ben muttered under his breath, which Tess ignored. "We'll be able to see the back of the house from your room and the front and side from mine."

That sounded like a solid plan. They would surveil on the weekends when they could, but a couple of hours, four days a week, would have to do for now. It wasn't perfect but if they didn't make any breakthroughs in two weeks, they could rethink their plan of attack.

"Since tomorrow is Friday and you have *other obligations*," disapproval dripping from her words, "I'll head to the courthouse after school to see what I can find. We can officially begin our investigation on Monday."

"Okay, then," Ben stood, slinging his backpack over his shoulder. "If I leave, are you going to keep obsessing or are you going to work on your homework for a change?"

"We have left-over lasagna," Tess said, as much to avoid the obvious as anything. "Want to stay for dinner?"

Ben was intrigued. Word of the McGee family lasagna had spread, and a growing boy wasn't likely to pass up free food.

"I do love lasagna." He nodded. "Let me call my parents. I'm sure they wouldn't mind if I missed our family dinner, as long as I'm eating with a family somewhere."

Ben wasn't exactly a big talker, but it had to beat another supper where Tess said something awkward and Sully looked at her with silent disappointment and Miss Angel slapped her on the back of the head as she rushed out to comfort Tess's mother. Things had been better since last week when she and her mom had talked and spent an entire weekend pretending things were normal again. But Kate had retreated into her silent shell yesterday for no apparent reason Tess could see, and it hurt to hear the empty echoes of the house.

It was a work in progress. She knew this because Mr. Abrams kept repeating it over and over. "Give it time, Tess. Everyone grieves differently. It's a work in progress."

But Tess still didn't want to have to live through it alone. Plus, it was nice having a friend again.

"And you're sure?" Ben asked, hand on the doorknob. "You're sure this is real and not something you're imagining? You're sure these guys killed your dad?"

Tess met Ben's eyes without flinching. She was sure. She could feel it, deep down in her gut. These guys were killers. And they had to be stopped.

"I'm sure."

Chapter 20

The McGuire fortune wasn't housed in one bank but in many.

"Mr. McGuire knew the business better than anyone," the manager of McGuire Building and Loan said, opening the corporate office as he talked. "He would never keep all of his assets in one place.

"But he kept some here, in his own bank?" There were two avenues of thought amongst the financial elite - keep your money close or keep it hidden. You couldn't do both.

McGuire had found a way, though.

"How did his shareholders feel, knowing he didn't trust them with his fortune?"

It was a valid question. If the manager, Mr. Ford, could be believed, McGuire kept only a small percentage of his very large fortune spread amongst the conglomerate of banks he owned. Could be he didn't trust his own backyard.

Could be, he was right.

Mr. Ford shrugged. He seemed uncomfortable with the line of questioning. Or perhaps it was the idea that his deceased employer might have enemies out there, just waiting for an opportunity to act.

"Shareholders are never happy," he finally said, once the thick oak door closed the rest of the bank out. McGuire's office was front and center in the bank, with a wide view of the comings and goings and daily business of the bank. Another thing he found unusual.

"But Mr. McGuire was very clear as to why he spread his assets around multiple holdings." The man gave a wry smile. "And I guess he was proven right."

According to the man, McGuire's holdings were very nearly stable, despite the turmoil in the finance world at the moment. Because his assets were spread through a variety of smaller companies and locally-owned businesses, the stock market crash had taken relatively little from his associated coffers.

He took the thick files Ford extended. "Miss McGuire asked me to deliver these to you personally," he explained. "A complete listing of all assets from the estate in the months leading up to Mr. McGuire's death and in the months since."

Before he could ask, the man shrugged. "I am Mr. McGuire's executor, and his wishes were very simple: provide for his daughter and provide for his city. When Miss McGuire expressed discomfort with the official cause of death, I put a hold on disbursal of the estate."

He flipped through the files casually while Ford talked, but he saw nothing obvious out of place. He would look through them in full later but if the first glance was to be believed, finances truly weren't a problem.

"And what do you think?" he asked, interrupting Ford's listing of the current charities scheduled for benefit from the estate.

"Pardon?" The man looked blankly at him, and he wondered when the last time someone asked him for an opinion was.

"What do you think?" he repeated slowly. "Like Miss McGuire, do you feel discomfort with the cause of death?"

That nervousness appeared again as Mr. Ford seemed to debate the words and choose his own very carefully.

"One never really knows what happens behind closed doors, yes?"

Interesting. He waited, but Mr. Ford didn't go on. So he waited longer.

"Well, that is to say, there was a phone call that caught my attention."

The man adjusted his tie before running his fingers over his mustache, anxiously tugging and straightening. "Before Mr. McGuire, well, passed," Mr. Ford adjusted his tie once more, "he asked me to put through a call as soon as it came in. He was waiting most urgently, and I thought he would be relieved upon receiving the call."

Ford glanced around as though to make sure no one else was in the room with them. "I didn't see him again for two days. He dismissed the staff and closed the doors to the bank. He'd never done that before." Mr. Ford wrung his hands. "It cost the bank almost," he cleared his throat and leaned in, "ten thousand dollars in lost revenue."

Even more interesting. "How long before his death was this?"

Mr. Ford thought back. "I would put it at a month before his passing."

"And how did the shareholders feel about that decision?"

"As one might expect, they were, well, less than thrilled." Those anxious eyes darted to the door again. "A special shareholders' meeting had been called to discuss penalizing Mr. McGuire. But that was canceled in light of the obvious."

He nodded his head, thinking. McGuire had taken a phone call and decided to close the bank for two days without the foresight of the shareholders. As banks across the country attempted to crawl out from under complete financial ruin, the loss of several thousand dollars would be a fine motivation to kill.

Men had killed for less.

So had women.

"Did Miss McGuire know about this phone call and the lost revenue?"

At this, Ford blinked. "Miss McGuire?" he asked, clearly confused. "Why, I can't say, sir. They were close, as one might expect of a widowed father and his only daughter. But I can't say if he shared the phone call with her, or what happened next."

He nodded. "I see. And who owns the company and banks, now that McGuire is dead?"

Ford flinched at the word, and he realized he could try harder to soften the blow for those not exposed to the harsh realities of life. But not right now. "I take it Miss McGuire stands to inherit everything."

"Indeed, sir," Ford confirmed. "The estate in total will belong to her once various trusts for the city of Detroit are in place."

So, it wasn't just the shareholders who had a motive. Miss McGuire stood to lose a great deal if her father's rash actions became a habit.

He held out his hand and Mr. Ford took it in relief, clearly glad to have the interview over.

There were three immediate questions he now needed to answer. One, what had been the subject of the mysterious phone

call? Two, did Miss McGuire know about it? And three, why
had the police declared the case open and shut with a potential
motive for murder hanging in the air?

• • • •

TESS SLEPT LIKE THE angel she was and woke refreshed.
She had a plan. She had a purpose. She had somewhere to
focus her need for justice, and the relief she felt in simple
direction offered up the blissful sleep of a much younger,
much more innocent Tess.

After school today, she intended to get the deed and
floor plans for the Brooklyn house, and she needed a solid
plan to follow. She somehow doubted a 14-year-old could
waltz in and request copies of estate documents without
arousing some sort of adult suspicion.

What she didn't need was a nosy clerk getting her name
and deciding to call Sully, like they had when she'd gone
to the station to request a status report on her dad's case.
She had a false ID, but even Tess had to admit that, flawless
printing or not, she didn't look a day over fourteen. So using
the identity wasn't a viable option.

"Are you really going?" Ben asked when he saw her at
the end of the day. They had agreed by mutual consensus
to gather after class every day at the place they first met,
the tree behind the school. Ben was just finishing up his
photographic evidence of the hatchlings, and Tess didn't
mind waiting. They were awfully cute, after all.

"Of course I'm going." Tess watched as Ben captured
another picture of the babies, mouths open, cheeping for
their mama. There were five of the little robins, and they

were still covered in more fluff than feathers. But she could already tell they'd grown significantly since they'd hatched a few days ago. "I need details that only county records can provide."

Ben tucked his camera back into its case around his neck. "Do you have a plan for actually obtaining said records?"

Tess scowled. "Not yet. I am, however, pretty good at making something up on the fly. I'm sure it will be fine." She tried her best to ooze confidence, and she was pretty sure it almost worked.

Ben just shook his head. "Text me after, okay? Just so I know you haven't been arrested or fined for loitering on city property."

That was sweet. Ben was worried about her. "Go on with you," she said, shooing him on his way back towards the school. "Go conquer the baseball world. Become the Mark Dunham of Lafitte High School's baseball team!"

"Mark is already the Mark Dunham of Lafitte High School's baseball team. And Mark's not going to be there," Ben said calmly. "It's Friday and football season. And I'm no Mark Dunham."

Tess rolled her eyes. "No one is Mark Dunham."

"I actually am Mark Dunham," Mark Dunham said from behind them, and Tess fairly growled in frustration. How did he always pop up at the most inopportune times?

"Don't you know better than to spy on a lady?" she snapped, but he just laughed.

"If you see any ladies around, you let me know now."

He nodded towards Ben. "What mischief is Lady McGee up to today?"

"You should probably go with her," Ben said, already on his way. "It would make me feel better to know she has a chaperone."

"Turncoat!" Tess yelled at Ben's back. Benedict Arnold. The most traitorous of traitors. Her only friend, leaving her with her greatest annoyance.

"I would love to accompany the lady on her quest." Mark bowed deeply at the waist, and Ben tossed a hand in the air in farewell as he left them behind.

"So, where are we going?" Mark asked, and Tess found herself with a decision to make. She was burning daylight and the courthouse was only open for another hour. If she didn't go now, she wouldn't be able to go at all.

She accepted the inevitable with as much grace as the good Lord gave her and turned her feet towards the county seat. She hadn't come up with any brilliant schemes, so she supposed she would just go in and ask for what she wanted. Maybe she had a class project that she needed the records for.

Adults loved to think they were helping innocent schoolchildren with homework. Besides, the worst they could do was say no, and she had experience talking herself out of almost anything. Maybe-

She had momentarily forgotten Mark was still there, casually strolling beside her. He was being perfectly silent, which was a red flag any day of the week.

"What are you doing?" she asked. "Aren't you late for some kind of sporting event?"

"Not yet," he said. Everyone in a small town knew there was nothing more important than the bright lights of a Friday night football field. "I have all the time in the world."

Mark, as a freshman, was the starting quarterback on a team that was only average now but was expected to be a contender for the state championship in two years.

"And so...you thought you'd spend it annoying me?" This was poor timing. It wasn't that she didn't expect Mark Dunham to be a thorn in her side, but she wasn't interested in banter right at this very moment.

"No," he drawled, hands stuck in his pockets, "I wanted to ask you a question."

When no question was forthcoming, Tess was forced to look at him. "Did you want to ask it now, by chance?" And then she had a thought. "If this is about Derrick again, don't bother. It's in God's hands now."

Mark just laughed. "No, Derrick dug his own grave on that one." He was quiet for a moment and when he spoke again, it was with hesitation, which Tess had rarely heard him use. "I don't know why I hang out with Derrick and Gage. They're both jerks."

Tess arched an eyebrow, and he held his hands up to ward her off. "Listen, I know I'm guilty by association, but I'm not trying to be a bad guy, okay? Okay?!"

Though he doth protest too much, she let it drop. "So why do you hang out with them then?"

Mark looked away, and Tess couldn't tell if he was trying to figure out what to say or if he just didn't know. Finally, he shrugged. "Because they've been in every class and on every team I've ever been on. It seems like we're supposed to be friends."

"It seems like you don't like them all that much though," Tess remarked, genuinely curious for the first time. Was Mark having some sort of crisis of conscience? Had Mrs. Bishop's lecture on Maslow been more powerful than Tess had realized? Maybe she should have paid closer attention.

Mark wasn't wrong - she'd never seen him openly mock or hurt anyone. Not yet, anyway. The closest he'd gotten was that day with Ben before school started, but things like that, attitudes like that, were a slippery slope. He wasn't a jerk or a bully now, but he let himself look like one. How much longer until he dirtied his own hands?

"The longer I hang out with them, the more I start to act like them. I don't know if that's such a good thing."

This was a contemplative side of Mark she wondered if anyone had seen. "So stop hanging out with them."

He shot her a sideways look, a crooked half-smile that toed the line between gentle mocking and genuine curiosity. "It's that easy, is it?" he asked. Tess could have sworn she heard a tinge of desperation in the question.

"It was for me," she said quietly. It was her turn to look away, remembering Maddie, remembering how close they'd been. Or how close Tess thought they'd been. Before Maddie's dad had left. And before Tess's dad had...also left.

They walked on in surprisingly companionable silence for a few more minutes after that. Minutes Tess was surprised to realize she wasn't hating. Until Mark ruined it by slinging an arm around her shoulders and tugging her close. "So tell me, McGee, what are we actually doing?"

"Well," Tess replied, doing her best to shrug out of his ape-like grip, "I am visiting the courthouse to legally obtain publicly available documents. I don't know what you're doing."

"It's interesting, your need to label this a *legal* enterprise, as though that were in question. But you always have the best adventures," Mark said, "so I'm tagging along."

"You don't even know what documents I want," Tess protested. "Why would you want-"

"What documents do you want?"

Tess gave a deeply exaggerated sigh of annoyance. He wasn't going anywhere, and an unoccupied athlete was a danger to her mission. "I'm requesting a deed of sale and floor plans for the Brooklyn house if you must know."

"The Brooklyn house? That old house across the road from you that's been empty for years but has new renters?" Tess nodded, and he looked perplexed. "Why do you care about that? Other than the fact they look like Disney villains?"

"I know, right?!" Finally, someone who got it.

Mark looked stunned by the punch to the shoulder but also bemused to have elicited such a reaction. "I take it I'm not the only one who thinks so?"

"The new neighbors are definitely up to no good."

"Ah." That seemed to be enough of an explanation for Mark, though Tess was pretty sure more should have been required. "Well, whatever. I'm just tagging along for the show."

"You know," Tess said, inspiration striking. She came to a stop and turned, giving him a once-over. "You might be helpful."

"You're looking at me like you're about to murder me and hide my body," Mark said nervously. "That shouldn't be my fate, that should be Merrigan's. Derrick Merrigan. Remember Derrick and your quest for revenge?"

"Vengeance shall be had," Tess agreed, "so stop changing the subject. You're my age, right? Fourteen, fifteen?"

"Fifteen a few weeks ago," Mark confirmed warily.

"But you look older. At least sixteen, maybe even seventeen. Which is the age of legal adulthood in Louisiana."

"Okay," he said gingerly. "I know you're not asking me to buy beer. But you are about to ask me to do something so, so strange..."

"Nothing hard," Tess said, as innocently as she could. "Just something that would be easier for someone a little older." She emphasized the word *older*. Even if everyone in the town knew Mark as a crack athlete and Lafitte's best hopes for sporting glory, she doubted they knew his exact age. In fact, Tess was banking on it. "I just need you to ask the clerk at the courthouse for the records." Tess patted her bag. "I have the cash to pay for them."

"Oh." Mark squinted at her. "I thought maybe you wanted something hard." He chewed on it for a second, before shrugging. "This isn't a sting, right? I'm not going to ask and get busted for some sort of weird 'Tess' thing, while you watch from the corner laughing maniacally, right?"

Tess bit her lip. She hadn't considered that option, but it didn't necessarily sound bad-

"I'll do it," he said. "Before you change your mind." He looped his arm around her again. "No, we're in this together now, Tess McGee. So tell me, what crimes have your neighbors committed to pique your curiosity?"

Tess looked straight ahead. She'd only told Ben. She hadn't even said it out loud to herself. It had felt good at the time, like letting steam out of a pressure cooker. It might not hurt to let a little more steam out. Heavens knew, she tended to let it build. But Tess was aware enough to understand she was scared.

Ben was her friend, even though she'd only known him for a couple of weeks. He understood her. She'd known Mark all her life, but did he understand her enough to take her seriously? Would he mock her, tell everyone what she suspected? She was afraid she would be laughed at, and she didn't know if she could handle that. Not about this. She knew how it sounded. She knew there was no investigation. But she also knew she was right. She could feel it deep inside her chest.

Tess thought it would explode out of her like fire with the smallest of kindling. The only other time she'd said it aloud, she'd been bold and certain. And Ben hadn't laughed. But for some reason now, the words were a bare whisper.

"I think they killed my dad."

Mark didn't laugh. Instead, he stopped walking and, by means of their entangled arms, so did Tess. Mark stood dead still, right there on the sidewalk, staring straight ahead. It felt like hours, though Tess knew it was probably less than a minute.

"You think they killed your dad," he finally repeated, still not looking down at her. Instead, he stared straight ahead and Tess got the feeling he was debating something. His next move, alerting her mother to the fact she was crazy, heading straight to the locker room to spread the word about crazy Tess McGee and her dead dad, something. But she didn't get the feeling he was about to laugh.

"Yes." Another whisper and Tess hated herself a little for it. She sounded small. She sounded like a child about to cry when she wanted to sound like the Tess McGee of before. The stubborn Tess McGee, full of pizzazz. Why had she told Mark Dunham, of all people? Why would she trust her heart to someone like him?

Why indeed, Tessie girl? Why, indeed.

She shook off the voice and prepared to do what was necessary to reclaim her previously unquestioned status of daring and fierce but before she could speak again, Mark blew out a breath she didn't know he was holding and tugged her back into motion.

"Okay, then. Let's go get your records."

Chapter 21

Tess didn't know why she was even here.

So what if Mark had been helpful today? So what if he'd smiled confidently at the clerk and walked away with all of the documentation on the Brooklyn house she could have asked for?

So what if he'd gotten it for free?

Why should that have obligated her to waste her Friday evening on such a sentimental, meaningless pursuit as high school football?

Friday night lights, indeed. Tess squinted under the stunningly bright lights flooding the field and tried to watch the action below her. If the good ol' boys on the PA system could be believed, this was supposed to be quite a game.

Both teams were undefeated so far, which meant someone was going home sad. Both fan bases had turned out in force, which meant Tess was trapped, squeezed into one of the few seats left, squashed between Super Fan One on her left and someone's helicopter mom on her right. The goal had been to stay as far from anyone sporting a pompom as possible, and she'd thought she'd achieved her mission.

And then Maddie showed up.

Tess couldn't tell if Maddie had noticed her or not as Miss Popularity climbed the bleacher steps to Tess's right and slipped into a seat a few rows down, sandwiched in a gaggle of pretty, plastic girls.

Rumor had it that Maddie had left the squad. Tess hadn't thought much about it since she never went to games herself, but she did know that no self-respecting cheerleader would make her way to the stands to watch the biggest game of the year quietly, wearing jeans and a school sweatshirt no less. But her popularity hadn't seemed to dim at all.

Surrounded by other popular kids from school, all in their blue and gold, letter jackets proudly displayed, Maddie looked right at home. Her long, blonde hair was combed neatly, and somehow, she made a school sweatshirt look good. Tess watched as one of the girls near Maddie rose. She was making a concession run and wanted to get Maddie's order, only too happy to elevate her status with the top dog.

Tess watched for a minute in amusement as the other kids seemed to fall over themselves to be part of the larger group. Just a moment of attention, a minute of spotlight, a brush with glory - absolute certainty in the true meaning of life, as though high school would be the crowning achievement of their time on this Earth.

Tess supposed for some, it would. But what a sad statement about life. How could high school be all there was? Surely there was something more, something better, after? Tess herself used to have dreams of college. Emory and Clemson both had excellent writing programs and neither was so far away as to keep her from coming home when she wanted. Now though, she wasn't sure what she wanted or where she was going. She didn't even know if she'd have grades good enough to get into a prestigious university at the rate she was going.

You've still got four years to figure it out, Tessie.

She knew she had time but when she let herself think about it, time seemed to be both slipping away and dripping like molasses. She had become directionless, a ship without a rudder. Or a ship whose rudder had been wreaked beneath the surface of the waves. Floundering. Dead in the water.

Tess's fingers gripped her backpack, where she'd shoved the Brooklyn papers. She wouldn't be rudderless for long. Once she had closure, once she had justice, she would be able to refocus. Plus, what university wouldn't be impressed with a teenager dedicated enough to bring criminals to justice? Yes, what she really needed was to see her father's killers pay for what they'd taken. Life might not be normal after, but it would be better than it is now.

Mark took a hit on the field that sounded like a bag of bricks being dropped, which was enough to draw Tess's attention back to the field. It felt like the entire stadium held their breath as they waited in hushed, grotesque silence to see if he would get up. Even Tess felt a shiver of concern that she chalked up to mob mentality. No one wanted the star quarterback, the best athlete on the field, to suffer a season-ending injury. That would make him Clark Kent when what they truly wanted was a super man.

Slowly, as the seconds ticked away, he did what he always did. Limb by limb, he pushed himself slowly, painfully, to his feet. His teammates rallied around him, slapping him on the shoulders and other unsavory places as they headed back to the line. Unnecessary roughness had moved the ball up fifteen yards, and Tess judged that one more good play should see them in the end zone. But Tess wasn't watching the play. She was watching Mark's dad.

Mr. Dunham was sitting three rows down and to the right of Tess, and she'd spent most of the game watching him watch his son. When she'd first caught sight of him, she'd remembered Mark's reaction to Tess's insinuation that she knew what was happening in his home, and she'd been intrigued. Here was a man who would willingly provide drugs to his son in the name of sporting glory. What kind of father did that?

Now, his arms were crossed and his lips were drawn in a grim line. Anyone else might see it as a sign of concern, but Tess saw something different. Mark shook off hits like no one she'd ever seen, and he was only a freshman. He was a big freshman, sure. But in general, freshmen didn't make varsity quarterback very often.

Mark had always been good at everything he did. He was a natural athlete, sure, but he also excelled in any activity the teachers put in front of him. Tess knew his dad had been a big-deal college player, and she knew he and Mark spent a lot of time together doing sporty, male-bonding things. Practicing in the backyard, lifting weights, sprinting around the neighborhood.

It shouldn't seem that weird. Ian McGee had spent a lot of time with his daughter, too. Reading and writing, watching old black-and-white noir films, riding bikes, and playing board games mostly. Just because Mark and his dad did other kinds of things together shouldn't set off her alarms. But it did.

The clock mercifully sounded, signaling the end of the game, and Tess whispered a silent prayer of thanks. She had to admit, Mark had been helpful today. He hadn't asked any questions, and he hadn't laughed at her theory about the Brooklyn neighbors. She didn't know why she had even told him, other than he insisted on coming along and he might come in handy. She had a feeling he wasn't going to let it drop now that she had what she needed. *In for a penny, in for a pound was* something Mark Dunham seemed to live out loud.

Tess watched as the stadium around her began to empty. Parents, congregating near the locker room entrance, waiting for their little athletes to emerge. The pompom squad had already shoved their spirit into bags and were hustling off, no doubt to some after-party somewhere. Maddie had risen and was making her way down the bleacher stairs. She was bringing up the rear of her group and must have felt eyes on her because she turned and looked right at Tess, blonde hair swinging flawlessly behind her.

If Maddie was surprised to see Tess at a football game, she didn't show it. Instead, she raised a hand and offered a tentative smile before one of her new friends shouted for her attention. As Maddie hurried to catch up, one of her friends slung an arm around her shoulder and asked what she was looking at. Maddie just laughed. Nothing. She was looking at nothing.

It shouldn't hurt after all this time and yet, Tess was surprised to realize it still did. Casual rejection was a hard thing to bear from anyone, let alone someone who used to mean everything to you.

Tess was mostly alone in the bleachers now, and stadium workers were coming through to clean up the trash left after the crowds departed. Tess grabbed a couple of wrappers and half-full cups on her way down, dumping them into the garbage. It wasn't like it was hard. How grown adults could fail to do so was utterly amazing to her.

Tess's mom had insisted she call when the game was over. It was dark, after all, and her mom didn't want her to walk home alone, but Tess had no intention of calling her mother or anyone else. She was in a bit of a mood after seeing Maddie, and she wanted some quiet. Her mother would offer quiet too, but it was more of a depressing quiet than the contemplative solace Tess was looking for. That was her plan, anyway. Until she noticed Mark and his dad walking to their car ahead of her.

Tess wasn't close enough to hear what Mr. Dunham was saying, but he looked stern. Mark responded and his dad clamped a hard hand on the back of his neck, jerking him to a stop. Tess also stopped, ducking behind the entrance to the stadium so she could watch unnoticed.

Mr. Dunham held out his hand and Mark reluctantly offered up his right arm. His throwing arm. Mr. Dunham gripped his hand and flipped it over, poking at Mark's wrist and forearm until Mark flinched. He said something, shaking his head in apparent disappointment, and dropped Mark's arm. He strode off towards the parking lot, expecting Mark to follow. Which he did. Reluctantly.

Tess found it inherently disconcerting to see LaMarcus Dunham as anything other than exuberant. He was bigger than life, buoyant. Whatever his dad had said managed to take the wind out of his sails, and after a win, no less.

Tess knew she shouldn't intervene. She knew it deep in her bones. And yet, the memory of the day outside the school, where Tess had alluded to what was happening at home and convinced Mark to back off was playing in her head. She found it hard to believe parents would actually resort to doping their kids for something as trite as athletic glory, but she did know it happened. Which was why she found herself hurrying after the Dunham men in the parking lot.

"Mark. Hey, Mark!"

Mark's hand, his left hand, had just reached for the handle of his dad's fancy car when he looked over his shoulder. For reasons unknown, the urge to rub some dirt on the fender and give the tire a good kick hit Tess hard. Who drove a car that was impeccably clean in Louisiana? Was it surrounded by an invisible shield impervious to mud and dust? Or was Mr. Dunham's wrath enough to repel even the most determined of bird droppings?

Mark's expression was hard to decipher, and it looked like he was trying hard to adopt his usual, carefree attitude when he realized it was her.

"Tess McGee. Can't a man relish his victory for a few minutes before being brought down a peg?"

"You relish your victory, and I'll relish mine." Mr. Dunham had already slid into his chariot, so Tess plunged on. "However, this night I come for a favor."

"Is that right? Well, how might this brave knight serve the Lady Tess?" The words were right, but the delivery was off and he still seemed ill at ease. Like he was wearing a jacket that was supposed to fit, but it settled in all the wrong places. Tess didn't like it. She didn't like it at all.

The passenger window rolled down and Tess could see Mr. Dunham's impatient glance. "Mark, what's going on?"

"Hi, Mr. Dunham!" Tess chirped, as perky and cheerfully as possible. "My mom doesn't like me walking home after dark alone, but I hate to ask her to come get me this late. Would you mind taking me home?"

Tess had lived near the Dunhams for as long as she could remember. Mr. Dunham knew exactly where she lived. It was exactly one block out of his way, but she could tell he didn't like it. She also knew he wouldn't sacrifice his reputation by abandoning a girl in a parking lot after dark. So she smiled as brightly as she could and thanked him before he had a chance to think it through. Mark smirked, finally, as he held open the passenger door for her.

As she was crawling in, he said, low so his dad couldn't hear, "Really? That's the best you've got?"

"What?" Tess shrugged her shoulders as though she didn't know what he meant. "It's dark and cold, not safe at all. Smart girls would never walk home alone under these conditions."

"Oh, you've always been smart, McGee," Mark said. "I just never knew you cared about being safe."

Chapter 22

"How are you doing, kid? Really?"

Sully and Tess were sitting on the bench outside the lion habitat, as was their routine one Saturday morning a month, snacking on giant pretzels, and Tess had to swallow to answer.

How was she doing? Such a loaded question.

"Depends on who you ask." She paused to dunk her next bite in the cup of cheese they'd splurged on. "My counselor says I'm *healing*. My former friends say I'm a different person. My mom can't bring herself to go to work. Oh, and I'm going to fail if I don't scrape something together for my life science project this weekend."

"Well, they're not asking. I am." Sully took another giant bite himself. "How do *you* think you're doing?"

"Five by five." She punctuated this with her dad's famous, megawatt smile. She couldn't do that with her mom anymore, but Sully seemed to appreciate the reminders. "I at least know what my science project is about, I have a new nemesis at school who will allow me to bring my full wrath upon his head, and I have a new friend who seems utterly unconcerned by my desire for said wrath."

Tess's shoulders sagged ever so slightly, though. "I'm having trouble working out this one, specific chapter, but that happens. Writer's block, you know?"

Sully took another bite. "Who are we destroying this week?"

And that's why Tess loved Sully.

She smiled as she gulped her soda. Real soda that is full of sugar and artificial colors and everything bad for you. "Some guy at school said something untoward. I see it as an educational opportunity and if I don't instruct him, who will?"

"Who, indeed."

As much as Tess wanted to tell Sully what Derrick Merrigan had said about her dad, she knew she couldn't. That knowledge would have shattered her mother's heart, but Sully was a man of action. And men of action...take action. Tess didn't actually want Derrick to disappear, no matter how she'd felt at the time. This was something she could handle on her own.

They sat in silence for a few minutes, watching the lions roll around in the sun like giant house cats while they finished their pretzels.

"Tell me about this friend who is unconcerned with wrath, destruction, and chaos."

"Ben's new."

Sully raised an eyebrow. "Uh-huh. You covered that part."

Tess grinned. "We talked about him at dinner a few weeks ago. He moved in a block down on Cher. His parents are both retired military, and he was raised by his grandmother while they were deployed." Tess grimaced. "Mom invited them to lunch after church tomorrow."

"I know," Sully said. "Angie's at home right now, making roughly seven desserts for the occasion." Sully shook his head. "Tough being new."

"It's weird, though," Tess said, scratching at her chin in thought. "Mark Dunham and his merry band of idiots were picking on him the first day we met but the next thing I know, Mark is asking him to join the baseball team and Maddie wants to ask him out. So I'm not sure if he's a nerd or if he's cool. High school is confusing."

That got a laugh out of Sully. "You said it, kid."

One of the lions sat up and shook his shaggy head, letting out a chuff that made the hair on the back of Tess's neck stand up. She'd learned a long time ago that lions, unlike the typical house cat, don't purr. They chuff. And chuffing is loud.

He must be feeling pretty good, with his lady friend asleep at his side and the sun warm on his face. Unlike Tess, who had to hide every inch of her Irish-fair skin from the sun. She flicked the Saints baseball cap she was wearing in irritation.

"So. Maddie." Sully stretched his arms out wide and slouched down contentedly beside Tess, resting his arms across the back of the bench. "That's a name I haven't heard in a while."

Tess rolled her eyes. As though he could convince her it was just a casual question. "And you won't again. She's only sniffing around because she's interested in Ben and I'm her way in."

Tess hadn't meant to place extra emphasis on any particular word, but Sully wasn't a detective for nothing.

"And that bothers you?"

"No!"

Sully didn't say anything to that, but Tess could feel the weight of what he didn't say. "I don't care if Maddie likes Ben. I don't like him like *that*. It's just that, you know..." Tess trailed off. What was it, exactly, that bothered her about Maddie liking Ben?

She tried again. "It's just that she hasn't talked to me in almost two years. Not one word. Until a boy enters the picture and she thinks I can get her closer to her prize."

"Is that Maddie, though?"

It was a quiet question, simply stated and left to percolate. Sully knew Maddie, too. And as much as Tess didn't want to admit it, that wasn't Maddie's way.

"She does like Ben," Tess insisted, trying to hold on to her anger. "But, I don't know. Maybe she wanted something else too."

Sully nodded thoughtfully. "Something like talking to her best friend again, maybe?"

Tess just shrugged. She didn't want to talk or think about it right now. And Sully, being Sully, seemed to pick up on that. He stood, stretching out, and tossed their wrappers in a nearby trashcan. "So, ultimate destruction, huh? You started working out a plan yet?"

Tess smiled and stood. She hadn't told Sully the details, but he hadn't needed them. Sully was always on her side.

His phone went off and he glanced at the message. "Give me a second, kid. I need to relay a message to the station." As he stepped away, Tess considered.

Sully was adamant that she shouldn't be concerned with her dad's case. Sully was his partner and loved her dad like a brother. She was the niece he and Miss Angel didn't have.

She could take her theory about Horace and Jasper to him, and he would listen.

But without evidence, he wouldn't be able to do anything. Being unable to act hurts men of action. He shared that with Ian McGee. It was one of the things that made them so close. Sully would be on Tess's side, regardless. But his hands would be tied unless she brought him evidence. Actionable evidence he could do something with.

"Okay, kid. Where to next? The giraffes are to the left and the elephants are to the right. Which way are we going?"

Which way, indeed. But Tess nodded, mind made up. She'd keep quiet for now. She and Ben would embark upon surveillance beginning Monday. It was a good plan, and it gave her a place to start. Once she had the proof she needed, she would take it to Sully. He wouldn't brush her off or treat her like a silly little girl. He would listen. He would take her seriously. And together, they would bring justice to her father's memory. Her dad could finally rest in peace.

I'm already at peace, Tessie girl.

Are you though?

"Tess?"

She'd hesitated at the sound of Ian McGee in her head, and Sully had caught the shift in her eyes. So she shook it off. She'd heard it wrong anyway. Her father had been murdered. He couldn't be at peace. And neither was Tess. But once she felled the Goliaths across the street, they could both rest easy.

So she pasted on that sunny smile one more time. "Giraffes. Definitely the giraffes."

Chapter 23

To Tess's utter surprise, lunch with Ben and his parents was an absolute delight.

Mr. Lewis and Miss Angel hit it off, both loud and happy enough to carry the conversation to the most unlikely of places. During dinner, Mr. Lewis regaled them with his tales of derring-do in the most secret of places, somehow making black ops sound like a comedy special, and Miss Angel picked up any slack, turning the life of a culinary queen into a series of combat missions. Tess would have thought they'd practiced the routine if it wasn't the first time they were meeting.

While they relaxed around the table over Miss Angel's collection of desserts, Tess shot a glance at her mother. Mrs. Lewis had been drawing her into quiet conversation during breaks in the entertainment and now she sat contentedly, sipping sweet tea and listening to the conversations around her.

She looked peaceful, Tess decided. Content and comfortable. Her eyes were sharp, and she was paying attention to the conversation. Sully caught Tess's eye and gave a quick nod, and Tess understood. Sully thought her mom was going to be alright. Tess wanted to believe that, too.

Ever since that night in her bedroom, where they'd sat on Tess's bed together and giggled over their day as they had so many times before, Tess had wanted to hope. But hope was a fearsome thing, and Tess was afraid to touch it or look at it for too long. Hope wasn't certain. Hope was frail and easily shattered.

Tess's heart had already been shattered once, so she'd locked hope away. She'd patched herself back together with a combination of sarcasm and devil-may-care attitude, but a girl could only take so much. Only time would tell if her mother returned in full force. Tess would just have to wait it out.

Ben was sitting across from Tess, and he leaned towards her to be heard. "Still no movement on the butterflies," he said, and he looked disappointed. Which Tess thought was both sweet and a little weird.

"You should start checking them every day," he went on. "You'll want to document as soon as they emerge. They'll change fast, so it's best to get them early."

"Uh-huh." Tess herself wasn't overly concerned with it. Did a butterfly change that much once it was free? Tess had her doubts. "I'll do that. But you know, there's another project we should talk about today. We need to finalize our plans."

Tess said it knowingly, and a disturbed look crossed Ben's face so she knew he understood. It brightened Tess immensely.

"May we please be excused?" she asked her mother politely during a lull in the conversation. "Ben and I need to hash out the details of a project we're starting tomorrow."

If Tess didn't say exactly what that project was, and if Ben was turning a particular shade of green, no one seemed to notice. No one but Sully, that was. Sully, who had spent most of lunch listening quietly. Adding a word here and there only where necessary. Sully, who was always watching.

"Clear the table first please, baby," Kate said with a smile. "And then you and Ben can use your daddy's office if you want."

That pulled Tess up short, but Kate had already turned back to Mrs. Lewis and resumed a conversation about transplanting peonies from the McGee yard to the Lewis yard.

Kate never mentioned the office. She didn't say anything when Tess spent time inside, but she never opened it herself. Tess had noticed she rarely even walked down the hall if she could help it. So to openly refer to her father's office, during lunch, in mixed company...

...maybe hope wasn't quite as fragile as all that.

Tess stood and started collecting plates while Ben went after silverware, and all the while Sully watched with a knowing look. Tess just smiled back, knowing what he thought. He thought she was roping Ben into helping her plot revenge against Derrick Merrigan. Tess had her thoughts on that, and she was making initial inquiries. In the interim, she had taken to watching Derrick when she knew he was looking, simply smiling her sweetest smile until he looked away. It was creeping him out, and anticipation was building. He knew something was coming, and he was afraid.

Exactly as she had planned.

But right now, she and Ben were beginning surveillance of the Brooklyn house tomorrow and there were details to finalize.

Bringing about ultimate destruction to the men who had murdered her father, in the room where he'd spent his last days and weeks, was poetic justice.

Ooh, poetic justice. She could use that for chapter seven.

Don't count your chickens so soon, Tessie. They'll scatter before they've finished hatching.

Chapter 24

Were stakeouts always this...Tess didn't want to say *boring*, but nothing else seemed appropriate.

Were stakeouts always this boring? She'd been sitting, chin propped on fist, in her bedroom window staring across the street for what felt like hours but in reality, was approximately fifty-six minutes.

The cargo van had been missing since she'd gotten home from school. White paint, dark windows, nondescript in the most obvious of ways - the only legitimate reason to drive a van like that was if you were a painter or plumber. Tess could think of several illegitimate reasons to drive a van like that though, and all of them revolved around the crimes you could commit with it.

The van had been missing when Tess had gotten up this morning, but she'd heard it creep back into place while she was deciding if she should attempt to brush her hair or if it was already a lost cause. She'd dashed to the window, tangles swirling over her eyes, and watched as both men got out without saying a word.

Jasper eased the driver's door closed in a way that made Tess think he didn't want to attract attention while Horace tossed a jacket over the top of a packing box and carried it towards the house. It wasn't the first time Tess had seen a box like that. Janie's bunny had fallen out of one just like it the day they had moved in. What was in that box and why cover it with a jacket?

Tess made a note on the paper she'd taped to her wall beside the window. *Mystery box.* She was going to need to see what was in those boxes. Eventually. After they established the timeline.

Tess knew Ben would not be happy with that conclusion. But Ben wasn't here, and it annoyed Tess somewhat that he would miss their first stakeout. Were they in this together or not? He had looked apologetic yesterday when he'd told her about his dentist appointment after school, which was why Tess had started the stakeout at her house instead of his. But he had promised to come over if they got home before six.

Tess glanced at her watch, the one her dad had received for meritorious service on the job, and sighed. It was only just after four. Why had her dad never told her how slowly time slunk by on a stakeout?

It's not like Tess had expected to break the case in one afternoon, but she had expected *something*. Movement. Unsavory characters sneaking in and out of the back door. Shifty glances from behind dark curtains. Even a glimpse of Janie would have been nice. Tess hadn't seen her since she'd enlisted Ben's aid in sketching, and he wasn't going to get any further until Tess could renew her memory. She'd pay more attention to the details next time.

Janie must have been home while Horace and Jasper were out. She seemed a little young to stay home overnight without a babysitter, but Tess supposed one could be in the house, having arrived before Tess had started her vigil. If she would only come outside, to play in the yard or look around for her bunny, Tess would have an excuse to cross the street.

She could introduce herself and ask some non-intrusive yet probing questions that would make her dad proud. Make sure Janie was okay. But until she made an appearance, Tess would have to wait.

She knew better than to approach the men again.

She did.

She really did.

As boring as the stakeout had been so far, at least Tess had the documents provided by the courthouse to keep her company while she waited. It was easy to be annoyed by Mark Dunham, but she had to admit that he'd come through on this one. The girls in the County Clerk's office had practically swooned when the hero of Lafitte had waltzed in and graced them with a smile.

They had very few questions about why he wanted all paperwork filed on the Brooklyn house in the last six months, completely satisfied with the idea that he was doing a school project on historical Lafitte residences.

Tess had to admit, it was a pretty good cover. And the way he'd said it, full of confidence and utterly unconcerned that anyone might question his motives, had been impressive. Tess herself had no such poise, though she fancied herself a good liar.

There was just something about Mark that made people bend to his will. Probably why the minions he hung around with followed his lead as much as they did. Tess accused Mark of being a bully but the truth was, he limited the damage the rest of the goon squad did.

When he'd handed the documents over, he'd grinned like he knew she couldn't bring herself to thank him.

"My lady," he'd said, bowing over her hands as she snatched the file from his. Tess had stood there awkwardly, knowing she should be polite but being utterly unsure of how to do so. He'd headed back to the school after that, cocky grin still plastered to his face, leaving Tess to decide between going home or, Heaven forbid, repaying the favor by watching the game.

Now, Tess had the documents from the file spread out on the window in front of her to make it easier to flip through while keeping an eye on the house across the street. The Brooklyn house was formally owned by the Lockley Foundation, a trust created after the death of the original owner, Mrs. Alta Lockley. Old Lady Lockley had more money than she could burn, and her lawyers helped her tie it up in charitable causes.

The house was just one of many properties the foundation owned, but it seemed to be the one they cared about the least. Very little work had gone into fixing it up, and Tess wondered why the foundation kept it around. Selling it seemed like a better option than letting it sit idle.

There was no information on the current residents, but Tess hadn't expected to find anything. What she needed was information on the rental company managing the property. Then she would have an avenue to explore Horace and Jasper's real identities. Unfortunately, the documents didn't provide that information either. No matter. They did provide basic floor plans, which was like handing Tess the keys to the front door. Not that she would use the information to take a look around-

-would she?

No. Tess set her shoulders determinedly. She'd promised both her mother and Ben that she wouldn't purposely incite the men, and there was no reason to pour gasoline and light a match. She'd keep that idea on the back burner, just in case, but she could gather plenty of information just by watching an empty house.

She would establish patterns of comings and goings. Did they ever have visitors? How did Janie get to and from school, if she even went? There was a chance, though small, that the men home-schooled her. The elementary school started earlier than Tess's own school day, which meant it would get out earlier. There was every chance Tess's schedule ran opposite of Janie's. But she'd see if Janie ever had friends over. If she played any sports. Food delivery, band practice, something.

As Tess glued her eyes back to the house across the street, she found herself wishing Ben was there. He was someone to talk to. Or someone to listen to her talk, at least. She could picture him now, sprawled across her bed working on an art project. Or the ever-looming science project he'd finished before she'd even started. Unfortunately, he'd been right. She really could work on the project while keeping an eye out the window.

He'd given her two weeks' worth of pictures and, by all that was holy, Tess really could see differences in the shape and position of each chrysalis. Minute differences, for sure, but they were there.

Tess fished the pictures out of her backpack, taking a moment to smooth her hand over the soft fur of the rabbit stashed in the front pocket, before flipping through the images. The butterflies should be ready to hatch any day, which meant she needed to pay attention. She would need pictures as soon as she could get them after hatching to stick with the essence of the project. But she could do that.

Stakeout aside, homework after school with a friend was a perfectly normal thing to do. Ordinary. Tess's attempt to be normal, take two.

Right, like this attempt wouldn't be utterly thwarted, just like last time. The odds of a surprise hurricane cropping up and blowing this far inland with no warning or a 6.0 earthquake shattering the streets of Lafitte were unlikely, but add Tess to the equation and she suddenly wasn't so sure.

She caught movement in her peripherals and looked up. The front door opened and Horace wandered onto the front porch, taking a lazy look around before speaking to the air, and Jasper stepped out behind him. He locked the door and then...Tess snatched up her binoculars and watched as he snapped a large hunk of metal, dull but with enough heft to be a beast to cut through, to the outer hinge.

They padlocked their front door.

A chill ran down Tess's spine as Jasper looked right at her. After a moment, his gaze moved on and Tess took a breath. It was unlikely he had seen her, she knew. Between the distance and the glare of the late afternoon sun on the window, her luck would have to be extremely bad for him to catch her watching. But she still swallowed reflexively at the thought of those hard eyes aimed her way.

Who padlocked the outside of their house when leaving? Murderers, of course. Tess reminded herself she'd known they were killers. But seeing it reminded her that this wasn't a game. These were bad men who had killed her father. Very bad men who dared to set up shop right across the street from the family of the man they had killed. They thought they'd gotten away with it.

Tess set her jaw. They were wrong.

She turned to make a note on the timeline - almost 4:30. She would keep watch for another hour or two to see if they were just out picking up dinner. If they hadn't come back by then, she would check again before she went to bed. If they didn't come back until the next morning, she would have the beginnings of a pattern.

A flutter in the corner of her eye pulled her away from the timeline and back across the street. What had she seen?

Tess watched, straining her eyes until the curtains in the back corner of the house shifted again. It was such a small movement, she wasn't sure how she'd seen it. But she had, and now Tess watched as Janie stood highlighted in the window. She was just a waif of a thing. But Tess focused. She didn't know how long she had, and she needed more details.

But the longer Tess looked, the more trouble she had pinning the girl down. Her hair was fine and long, but Tess couldn't tell if it was brown or more of a dull blonde. It could even be gray for all that Tess could make out. Tess couldn't see enough to make out the shape of the girl's nose, but she had the impression of a heart-shaped, cherubic face. Skinny but with baby fat still rounding her cheeks.

Her dress was the same as her hair, watery and difficult to make out. Tess could see the hint of a collar, one of those lacy ones that southern mamas put their babies in for school pictures but no one wore in real life, but the color of the dress was washed out. Tess pulled back and rubbed her eyes. It must be a trick of the light, but it was very frustrating. She rarely had a sighting of the girl, and she needed more details for Ben.

When Tess looked back, the curtains were still and nothing moved in the window across from her. Tess couldn't help but grin, just a little. That sneaky little devil. She moved through the world as though she wasn't a part of it, and Tess could admit that she was a little jealous. Tess herself had many talents, but stealth wasn't one of them.

At least she had a few more details for Ben if he ever bothered to show up. Tess jotted the few details she had been able to make out on the timeline so she wouldn't forget and reluctantly pulled the pictures of the butterflies in their dormant state back over. The pictures were one thing, but she still needed to write a paper to go with them.

This was the part Tess dreaded, which seemed ironic to her. Tess took pride in calling herself a writer, but she would much rather write about murder and mayhem than science or school. And yet, Tess acknowledged, the time had come. It cheered her to think of the shock on Ben's face when she could honestly say she was finished, and it helped her set to work.

As Tess debated the merits of adding an overabundance of prose to what would otherwise be a rather dry paper, the strangest thought crossed her mind.

Even Mark Dunham would be better company than this.

Chapter 25

B en was waiting on the front step when Tess stepped out the door the next morning.

"Hey," he said, by way of greeting. "Sorry I never made it over. I-"

"I saw her again!" Tess had been trying her best to remember every detail of the little girl ever since she had seen her, and she whipped out the list she'd made. "Petite and bird-like. Delicate, heart-shaped face. Hair to here," she gestured towards her shoulders, "very straight and fine. She's just a little bit of a thing..." Tess trailed off. Was she getting enough to eat? Were Jasper and Horace taking care of her? They didn't strike her as the kind of men to invest in raising a child. They didn't even acknowledge she existed...

"Earth to Tess," Ben said, probably not for the first time, snapping his fingers in front of her face. "So, I guess the stakeout went well?"

"Very productive." Tess wrenched Ben's backpack from his shoulders. "Sit down. We need to sketch out the details while they're still fresh."

"Um, we're not exactly leaving for school with plenty of time to spare," Ben objected. "I know Mrs. Morales likes you, but there's only so many times you can be late without getting in trouble."

"You mean, there are only so many times *you* can be late without getting in trouble." Ah, there. Tess pulled the sketchpad from Ben's bag. Now, where was that pencil...

"I mean," Ben qualified, yanking the sketchpad and backpack out of Tess's hands, "that I care that we're both about to get in trouble. You made a list," he said, slinging his bag back across his shoulders. "It will hold until lunch."

"But-" Tess tried to protest. Who was this assertive Ben and where had he come from?

"But nothing. If you want the freedom to investigate after school, you have to toe the line. Getting grounded or stuck in detention will throw a wrench in your plans, don't you think?"

Curses. He had a point, but Tess didn't have to be graceful about it.

She sighed heavily as she followed Ben's determined steps towards the school. She couldn't help but glance across the street, even though Ben stayed as far on their side as he could. The van had returned at exactly 6:30 again that morning. Tess heard it pull up and watched as the men once again carried in a single, office-sized cardboard box. The lid was secure, but Tess could tell by the way Horace was holding it that it carried some weight.

What was in those boxes they came home with every morning? She needed to know.

"What?" Ben looked sideways at her. "What boxes?"

Tess grimaced. She tended to work through thoughts out loud, which had, on occasion, caused all sorts of troubles for her. But Ben was her partner, so she could tell him.

"The van was parked when I got home from school yesterday," she said. "Our villains left at 4:30, carrying an empty box. When they got back at 6:30 this morning, the box was full but I couldn't see what was in it."

"Paperwork?" Ben suggested. "Supplies for whatever job they're going to? If the timing becomes a pattern, we can infer that they work an overnight job."

"Let's remember that whatever they're doing isn't legal," Tess reminded Ben. "Whatever *job* they're doing is bad news."

"Let's also remember that we don't have actual proof of crimes just yet." Ben didn't even miss a beat. "Isn't evidence important, you know, in the grand scheme of things?"

"We'll get our evidence," Tess said confidently. "Once we do, we'll turn it over to Sully, and he'll make sure those guys don't hurt anyone else ever again."

Tess hadn't meant for that to come out as solemn as it had, but even she could hear the touch of grief in her voice. It was easy to distract herself from why they were watching Horace and Jasper, but it was always there in the background. Her dad was gone, and these guys would pay for it.

It was easier to focus on justice than on loss.

"Anyway," Ben cleared his throat. "I have some news, and I don't think you're going to like it."

Tess grew immediately suspicious. "What did you do?" Ben was shifting nervously from foot to foot, and Tess's suspicions grew sharply.

"Nothing!" Ben protested, a little too shrilly. "Listen, you've already let him help once so I didn't think you'd mind if-"

"You'd better not be talking about Mark Dunham," Tess threatened. "Because if you are, I'll-"

"You'll what, McGee?"

How Mark always managed to appear beside her at exactly the right moment was maddening, and Tess suspected collusion as Ben and Mark nodded at each other.

"I'll be very unhappy," she snapped. "And you know what happens when I am unhappy."

"Yeah, yeah. Hell hath no fury, vengeance, and other things of that nature." Mark was entirely too casual when his life was on the line. "I want in."

"You want in? On what?" Tess eyed Ben, who was studiously avoiding her.

"The stakeout, of course. You want these guys, and I want to help you get them."

"I never told you we were watching them." Ben. That little rat.

"Please," Mark scoffed. "I've known you since we were five. If you think these guys killed your dad, you're not going to leave them alone. You're memorizing floor plans of their house, for Mr. Abrams' sake! You need a voice of reason, and Ben isn't going to be enough to stop you on his own."

"Hey!" Tess protested. "I told you that in confidence. You're not supposed to be spouting it all over town!"

"'Mr. Abrams' sake?'" Of that entire exchange, that's what Ben picked up on?

Mark looked affronted. "I would never take the Lord's name in vain, Lewis. But Mr. Abrams? His name is fair game. And all over town, McGee? It's Lewis. You telling me you haven't told your new best friend?"

He had a point, but still.

"You can't just assume someone knows something. What if I hadn't told Ben? What if I didn't want him to know his new friend thinks killers are living on their street?"

"Then you wouldn't be the Tess McGee I've known and loved my whole life," he said confidently. Like he knew her or something.

"Why do you look like you got run over by a Mack truck?" She had decided not to say anything about the walking train wreck beside her, but he didn't deserve her circumspection. "Football getting you down?"

Mark winced, his hand moving towards the bruising on his face. Which only showcased the bruising on his hand and forearm. "Yeah, took a couple of hard hits in practice last night. It happens."

Now that she was looking, she could see the slight limp he was trying to hide. "It happens to you a lot, doesn't it?" she asked. "Maybe you need to have a word with your offensive line."

Ben cleared his throat nervously, but Mark let out a laugh tinged with relief. "You know what, McGee? Maybe you're right. Maybe my linemen are out to get me. We'll investigate them next, okay?"

Tess rolled her eyes, though she couldn't help the slight smile that curved her lips. She knew how it sounded, but Mark wasn't making fun of her. He was laughing with her, not at her. She could appreciate the difference.

"Fine." She didn't want to give in too graciously, though. "How do you propose you assist our investigation when you're playing football every night of the week?"

"Easy. I take weekends. Oh, and Tuesday nights after practice." He winked at her. "I've been hearing about the McGee family lasagna for ten years now. I want in on that action."

"It really is good," Ben chimed in from her other side, and Tess knew she'd been set up. Had Ben recruited Mark to the cause? Did she care enough to find out?

"The more eyes we have," Ben said logically, as though he knew the thoughts spinning inside her head, "the more quickly we'll find the evidence we need so Sully can take care of them. That's what you want, isn't it?"

She ignored the look Ben and Mark shared above her head. It didn't matter, because Ben was right.

Tess stared determinedly ahead, her mind made up. "Yes. That's what I want."

Chapter 26

"LaMarcus, sweetheart, can I get you another helping?" Tess's mother asked in amazement as Mark finished off his third serving of lasagna. Kate, Ben, and Tess had all watched, caught between shock and awe, as Mark had inhaled a truly impressive amount of food.

It was a good thing Tess's mother still made such a large pan, even though it was usually just Kate and Tess, otherwise they would have run out long ago.

"Yes, ma'am." He enthusiastically mopped up the last of the sauce with his fifth piece of garlic bread and held his plate out. "I'd never turn down that offer."

Did the boy never eat? Like a man starving who was getting the most out of his last meal, Mark acted as though he'd never eat again.

He'd come over after practice, freshly showered and looking much better than he had on the way to school. Odd how playing a sport where he was brutally tackled daily seemed to refresh the soul. Tess hadn't allowed herself to think about it at the time, but she hadn't liked the look in his eyes on the walk to school.

His usual smile had seemed forced and his eyes dull. He'd been more than tired physically. He'd been soul-weary, only playacting his usual, annoying self. Luckily, that frustrating, natural buoyancy of his had returned in full force with some unnecessary roughness and carbohydrates.

"Football must take a toll," Kate remarked, handing back the plate overflowing with a double portion of lasagna and bread. "The calories will do you good. Put some color back in those cheeks."

Sitting at the table, Tess was conscious of the fact that Mark looked more like Kate's child than Tess herself. They both had straight noses and the most beautiful, smooth skin. Mark's was a lighter brown than Kate's, but both had the airbrushed quality of fresh chocolate. Tess had her father's Irish coloring and freckles, and her eyes were green instead of the deep almond of her mother, but she did have Kate's hair.

Tess reached up and patted said hair, attempting to smooth it behind her ears while knowing it was a lost cause. Somehow, her mother's curls were always well-kept and under control while Tess's had a life of their own. Maddie used to get frustrated with Tess's complaints about her hair. She would roll her eyes, not understanding that pins and ball caps were only pipe dreams for hair like Tess's. Bandannas could momentarily contain the beast, but trying to wrangle her hair under control long enough to get the wrap in place was like trying to hog-tie cattle. No fun, and the patience required was not in her wheelhouse.

"Thank you, ma'am," Mark said, digging right in while Kate smiled indulgently before turning to the other male at the table.

"Benjamin, how are you and your mamma doing this week? I know your grandmother's birthday is tomorrow. Those kinds of milestones are hard."

Only someone who knew how hard those days were could ask something like that. But Ben only nodded. "We're going to drive up to the cemetery in Montgomery this weekend to drop off some flowers."

Kate reached over to squeeze his hand briefly. "She would have liked that."

Of all the things about her mother that Tess hadn't inherited, this was the one she most envied.

Comfort. Grace. The ability to say the right thing at the right time. Kate McGee was the personification of motherly charm, knowing what to say at any moment. Had Tess asked Ben the same thing, she would have struggled with her awkwardness, only succeeding in reminding him that his grandmother was gone. When Kate asked, it was like a warm southern breeze rifling the hair. It made you feel peaceful and content, the memories sweet instead of stinging.

Tess wasn't sure how Kate did it, but she admired it.

"Thank you for having me for dinner tonight, ma'am," Mark said, heaving to his feet painfully and gathering the empty dishes around him. "I'll take care of clean-up if you don't mind."

"Now, LaMarcus," Kate argued, "you're a guest. Guests don't do chores in this house."

Kate began to rise, but Mark cut in politely. "Pardon me for saying ma'am, but I just ate my weight in lasagna. And it was the best meal I've had in months. Cleaning up is the least I can do."

And then he smiled that stupid, charming, Mark Dunham smile and her mother folded like a wet paper towel.

"Well, if you insist, sweetheart." Kate smiled. "I'll make sure your mamma knows what a gentleman she raised."

"As long as you don't tell her how much I ate, I'll thank you kindly. I'm not sure she'd approve of my poor manners in someone else's home."

Mark winked at Tess as he scooped her plate out from under her nose. "I'll just take care of the kitchen real quick so we can get started on that homework."

Kate fairly beamed at the sight of her daughter surrounded by school friends, as though it were perfectly normal for Mark Dunham to drop by for dinner and homework after football practice.

Ben slid his chair back. "Thanks for dinner, Miss Kate," he said. "My dad is out of town this week, and I told my mom I'd be home before it got too dark."

"Oh, wait. I wrapped up some dessert for her." Kate disappeared briefly into the kitchen and popped back out with several pieces of cheesecake in a covered dish. "And tell her next time, work can wait. She doesn't need to stay home and eat alone."

Ben smiled. "Yes, ma'am." He looked over at Tess, and his grin dimmed. "See you tomorrow, Tess."

Tess smiled back and walked him to the door like her mother taught her. "You little weasel," she said politely, also like her mother taught her. "You are not sneaking out and leaving me with Mark Dunham."

"I'm not sneaking anywhere, and you'll be fine. He just wants to help."

"But *why* does he want to help?"

Ben paused and looked over Tess's shoulder, back towards the kitchen where they could hear Mark and Kate laughing together. "I think he's lonely," Ben said quietly.

"Lonely?" It seemed like the last word on earth to describe Mark Dunham. "He's surrounded by groupies day and night. Whether he's making game-winning plays or strolling the halls of academia, his little minions are there to do his bidding."

Ben pinned her with a look. "You're the one who asked him why he was friends with those guys. He's not like them, and you know it."

"Funny, considering how you met."

Ben hitched his backpack a little higher. "Yeah, well, I think we both know a thing or two about pretending so you don't have to deal with what's really going on in your life."

Tess felt like the air had been punched out of her lungs at that, which Ben must have seen because he relented. "Look, it's easy to assume things about a person because of how they look on the outside. That's all I'm saying."

Ben opened the front door and Tess followed him out, making sure to close the door softly behind her. "You know something's not right in his house," he murmured, as though saying it out loud somehow made it worse.

Tess's mind flashed to her throw-down with Mark the day she'd met Ben. Her threat implied she knew things he wouldn't want her to share. Her suspicions about his dad pumping him full of painkillers and performance enhancers. How bruises seemed to grow overnight.

"He helped you get information on the house, right? You're the brains, he can be the muscle, and we'll have all of our bases covered."

Tess had to admit, he wasn't wrong. But Tess couldn't help one parting shot as Ben strolled away.

"If I'm the brains and Mark is the muscle, then what are you?"

Tess could hear the grin in Ben's voice, though he didn't turn around. "I'm the grownup who knows better."

Chapter 27

"What are we working on tonight?" Mark had slung his backpack onto Tess's desk and was unpacking his books, as though homework was the reason they'd escaped to her room after dinner.

The corner of his bag caught the edge of the framed picture sitting on her desk and knocked it askew.

"Hey, did you know this was upside-down?" Mark picked up the picture and turned it over so he could see, but Tess snatched it out of his hands before he could make any other comments.

"I like it how I like it," Tess snapped, settling it back into position, frame-down but close enough to touch while hashing out a particularly difficult chapter. "And you're as bad as Ben, what with the homework and all. Aren't athletes supposed to be dumb jocks and such?"

Mark rolled his eyes as Tess brushed past. "Dumb jocks who don't do their homework are dumb jocks who don't play," he said practically. "It's all perspective."

Tess didn't reply as she killed the lights, tugging the curtains over her window to the side and settling in to watch.

"McGee, why are the lights out?" Mark sounded distinctly uncomfortable, which amused Tess. Big school hero, scared to be in a dark room with her. Not that she could blame him, but she didn't think it was for the reason she would prefer.

"Ben said you wanted to help, so you're helping." She waved him over. "You can't watch from the window at night with the lights on. You'll be seen."

"Oh, right," he said wryly. "That. I do have some homework that I need to-"

"You can do homework at your own house. If you want in, you're in. But right now, we watch."

In true Mark fashion, he rolled with the punches. "Copy that. So, fill me in." He dropped his books back to the desk and settled beside her to watch, not close enough to touch but close enough she could smell the soap from his after-practice shower. He smelled minty and fresh, giving Tess pause. She wasn't sure how she smelled, but it was too late to do anything about it now.

"I'm working on establishing a solid timeline of their daily activities," Tess explained. "Both men leave every night at 4:30. The tall one carries an empty box, and they get in the van, and drive east. They're back every morning at 6:30. The box is full, but I can't see what's in it. They arrive home from the west and park in the same spot."

"And...that's it?" Mark sounded a little disappointed. "That's all you've got?"

"What?" Tess protested. "I've only been watching for a week. Building a timeline takes patience!"

Mark snorted. "Well, patience *is* your middle name and all." He shrugged. "It's just, I don't know. Nothing exactly shouts *murderers* to me so far."

"When you were talking to your new best friend about joining the baseball team, didn't he tell you about our run-in with them on the street a few weeks ago?"

"Aw, McGee," Mark said fondly, reaching over and ruffling her hair. "You know you're my best friend." Tess slapped his hand away and Mark went on, both ignoring how oddly heartfelt he'd sounded. "He said they aren't guys you want to hang around with, and that you need to be careful."

Mark was suddenly serious, beside her in the dark. "He said they got aggressive, and that he's worried about you being on their radar."

Tess remembered Jasper's parting words, and she felt her skin crawl like it had in the moment as he'd warned her that the streets weren't always as safe as they seemed. "Well, yeah," Tess said, trying to shake it off. "They're bad guys. Murderers. They killed my dad, and I'm not going to let them get away with it."

Tess kept her eyes glued resolutely to the house across the street, but she could feel Mark beside her, taking in her words. She'd told him her suspicions when he'd helped her get the blueprints of the Brooklyn house, so she knew he wasn't surprised. No, she was the one surprised. At how he'd helped her. At how seriously he was taking her claims.

Not once had Mark Dunham made her feel stupid for her theories or too small to handle them. Instead, he'd jumped right onboard her crazy train.

Maybe Ben was right. Maybe Mark was a better guy than he pretended to be.

"Tell me about him." Mark's quiet words reached her in the dark and again, there was no hint of mockery or laughter in his voice.

"About who?" She didn't have many other details about Horace or Jasper, though she could tell him about the fake identity. How Thomas Jeffries wasn't listed in any-

"Tell me about your dad."

Oh. *Him*, him.

"You knew him," Tess argued, defensive and not sure why. Everyone had known her dad, and Mark's quiet, solemn request made her feel...Tess didn't know. Weak. Soft. Vulnerable. All things she didn't want to be.

"I knew who he was. I knew him as Mr. McGee, the cop down the street who liked to laugh and was always spending time with his kid. But I didn't *know* him, know him. Not like you did. What was he like as a dad?"

There was a hint of wistfulness in Mark's voice at that, and Tess didn't know how to take it. But it was hard not to respond to the longing she could feel in that simple question and if she were being honest, she missed talking about her dad.

"He was my best friend." She said it honestly, not worried that Mark would mock her for it, though she supposed she should. What teenage girl thought of her dad as her best friend? But it was true, and she wasn't ashamed of it. "I could talk to him about anything."

And wasn't that one of her problems? She'd talked to her dad about everything and now that he was gone, who was she supposed to talk to? Tess wanted to talk to her mom. She wanted to be able to say, "Hey, remember that time when dad did something crazy but it worked out anyway?"

She wanted to smile across the table as they both remembered whatever crazy thing he had done, then talk about how that story reminded them of another story. But her mom wasn't ready for that yet, and Tess wasn't sure if she ever would be. She could talk to Sully, and she did. But she hadn't realized until this very moment that she wanted a friend of her very own to talk to. And Mark had known her dad.

"I hear how the kids at school talk." Tess kept her eyes locked on the house across the street, afraid the magic would break if she looked at Mark beside her in the dark. "I know what happened with Maddie's dad. I know not every dad is like mine." Ian McGee had spent time with Tess, not because he had to or because that was his job, but because he wanted to. She'd never wondered if he liked spending time with her or if he loved her. He had, and she'd known it.

He'd taught her how to shoot baskets and look for patterns in behavior. He'd taught her to love noir in all its forms and to spot fake identities. They'd adopted zoo animals and identified robin eggs in the backyard.

He stimulated her curiosity and encouraged her passion for writing. Ian McGee was a man who would thrive on his child's athletic prowess, but he was every bit as excited by Tess's next chapter as he was at the thought of her joining a team.

Whatever Tess did and wherever she went, her father's exuberant spirit prodded her on. Even now, she heard his voice every day. The way he spoke, his turns of phrase. Moments when he encouraged her to keep digging and times when he spoke caution into her soul. Like that moment on the street with Horace and Jasper. It had been her dad's voice warning her, as it had been the day she'd knocked on their front door.

Tess didn't realize she'd said all of this out loud until Mark's voice drifted to her from the dark. "If that's who your dad was, how do you get out of bed every morning? How do you love someone that much and keep going when they're gone?"

The words hung in the air between them, and Tess was suddenly sure Mark was as glad the lights were off as she was. By the sound of Mark's voice, he was feeling as devastated as she was and neither wanted the other to see.

"What else am I going to do?" Tess swiped at eyes she hadn't known were wet. "I can't let him down. He would want these guys caught, so I'm going to catch them. Well, *we* are going to catch them," she amended, throwing him a bone. Offering the hand of friendship, as it were. It felt right, somehow.

Tess could admit it. It felt nice to not be alone in the dark anymore.

"But Tess, that isn't..." Mark drifted off, and Tess waited for him to argue. To try to talk her out of what she knew she had to do. She prepared herself, ready to defend and fight against Mark's doubts. But whatever he was going to say drifted away, disappearing in the dark along with Tess's objections to his presence. Instead, he nudged her with his elbow.

"Thanks for letting me help."

And they continued to sit in the dark, silently watching an empty house across the street. But somehow, Tess felt lighter than she had in days.

Because she didn't feel quite so alone anymore.

Chapter 28

"What have you found?"

Miss McGuire was a throw-down thing, dressed to the nines yet sitting in front of him with an equal measure of hope and despair in her eyes.

Blast his secretary for going home early once again.

Not one to mince words, he cleared the whiskey-induced gruffness from his voice and gave it to her straight.

"Something. Maybe."

Well, straight could be a subjective term. This bit was tricky because he needed to know what she knew. He needed to see her reaction.

He watched as steel filled her eyes and her spine. "What is it? What have you found?"

"A shareholders' meeting to discuss your father's erratic behavior."

"My father's...a shareholders' meeting?" Words seemed to temporarily abandon the young miss as confusion played across her features. "I don't believe I follow."

He eyed her, watching for the truth. "Henry McGuire cost the shareholders several thousand dollars when he closed the bank with no notice. Two days, it was. I don't suppose you know anything about that?"

No matter how he watched, he saw nothing to give her away.

"He closed the bank? On a business day?"

"Two business days." He tapped his fingers on his desk twice to make his point

"Alright..." She was suspicious, which wasn't surprising based on his knowledge of the girl. One of the first women to receive a Harvard education, she was intelligent in her own right. But raised under her father's business tutelage and all the advantages that were offered were sure to have developed her intellect to a keen edge.

Her wide-eyed and delicate appearance was simply an illusion to ensure she was underestimated to her advantage.

"It crosses my mind that his decision also cost you *thousands of dollars."*

He let it hang in the air between them, thick as the cigar smoke he used to indulge in before his secretary put a stop to it.

He watched as the young lady absorbed his words. He watched as the awareness of what he was implying crept in. And he watched as she straightened her spine even further and pierced him with cold blue eyes.

"I won't insult either of us by pretending to misunderstand your meaning," she said with fire. "But what use is a few thousand dollars to me? My father saw to it that my home is my own and our coffers are full while others have lost everything. An action you deem erratic *was a calculated choice, as were all his decisions."*

She settled back into the hard-backed wooden chair, sincere conviction plain in her face.

"I see," he said, leaning back in his chair and stroking his chin thoughtfully. "Then you were aware of the phone call he received that day, the one that caused him to close his own bank's doors and disappear for two days."

His opponent narrowed her eyes. "Of course, I wasn't aware. I'm not privy to every call my father took during his business. But had it been important, he would have told me."

She pulled a small, leather-bound journal from her pocketbook. "What day did the closure happen? Pardon," she said, glaring at him harshly, "I meant days?"

She flipped to the days in question and held the small book out to him. "You see? Nothing but his usual activity." She pointed to a set of initials with times marked beside each one. "He had his monthly meeting with the historical society, a lunch with the Commonwealth for the Poor board of trustees, and a variety of other social causes he was part of." She laid the book in front of him. "Nothing out of the ordinary whatsoever."

He pointed. "What is this?"

Miss McGuire glanced to where his finger had landed. "MCH. Matthew Connor Horowitz. He's the leading physician for the Detroit Foundation for Medical Care. He and my father were working on an initiative that would offer no-cost healthcare for our homeless citizens." Miss McGuire smiled. "This is my favorite of the initiatives, truth be told. Dr. Horowitz is deeply invested in our community. In fact," she leafed back through the book, "he and my father met quite regularly. I intend to make sure that initiative comes to fruition."

He got the idea that Dr. Horowitz played a particular part in that interest but didn't say so. Womanly drama was not in his wheelhouse.

But if Dr. Horowitz was meeting regularly with McGuire, if they were working closely on a new project, he might be able to shed some light on McGuire's behavior that day.

It seemed clear to him that the daughter knew nothing of her father's behavior on that particular day. He glanced at the small, leather-bound calendar in front of him. But there was a good chance someone else did.

• • • •

TESS SHOT OUT OF BED the second she heard the growl of the old engine churning up the street.

They were early.

She darted to the window, hunkering down and swiping her wild hair out of her eyes so she could watch.

It wasn't even daybreak yet. They were a good three hours early, which meant something had changed.

Tess's eyes were still blurry from sleep as she snatched up the binoculars waiting on the window sill and watched as the doors of the van opened and Horace and Jasper climbed out. Instead of slamming the doors shut, like any normal person climbing out of a car, they gently eased them closed, making as little sound as possible, and Tess perked up.

They were deviating from their timeline, and they were going out of their way to be sneaky. Something big was happening.

They met at the back of the van and instead of pulling out a box, like they'd done every morning before, the one Tess suspected was filled each morning with cash or diamonds or illegal cigars, they worked together to tug a large duffle bag to the edge of the van. Horace leaned over and tucked something inside so he could zip it closed, and then Jasper grabbed it in both beefy hands, slinging it over his shoulder like a fireman rescuing someone from a burning building. He looked like the very opposite of a hero though as he started stumping his way towards the house.

Horace quietly closed the door and followed his brother up the sidewalk - and then they deviated again. Tess watched as they took a glance around before slipping away from the front of the house, furtively winding their way into the backyard, through the gated privacy fence, and away from Tess's prying eyes.

Tess's eyes continued prying, hoping against hope for something else to happen, until movement caught her eye above. Something fluttering in the upstairs window. Tess sat up straighter, straining to see beyond the dark of the morning and the curtains that hid the room from view. Janie Doe had been standing in the window, Tess was almost certain, although she was gone now. Had she been watching the men too? Did she know what her caretakers were doing?

Did Tess know what they were doing? They hadn't left the night before with the duffle, she was sure of that. Had it already been in the van? Or had they acquired it during whatever nefarious activities they had conducted during the night?

Tess watched the house obsessively until her alarm went off three hours later. Her eyes burned and blinking felt like an exercise in sanding the inside of her eyelids with forty grit sandpaper. The thought of her bed called to her like a beacon, and she briefly debated pleading illness so she could regain the hours she'd lost.

It was tempting right up until her mother knocked on her door.

"Tessa, baby, are you up?"

When Tess didn't answer right away, still eyeing her bed, Kate poked her head around the corner and practically paled on sight.

"Tess, what's wrong, baby? Don't you feel well?"

Kate brushed Tess's hair to the side as her hand rested on Tess's forehead. "You don't feel hot, but maybe we need to visit Dr. Brower?"

Tess tried not to be offended. She knew she wasn't ready for a beauty pageant, but did she look that bad?

Ever since her father had gone, Tess's mother had become overly watchful of Tess's health. It had been the only thing that brought any spark of light to Kate's eyes for the first few months after the funeral.

Before the funeral, Tess rarely went to the doctor. She'd get her physical once a year but coughs, colds, and bruises were treated at home with honey, aloe, and hot soup. Now, she and Dr. Brower were practically golf buddies, and though the knowledge that Kate seemed to be getting a little better was cheering, the flash of obsessive worry in her eyes now caused the alarms to sound in Tess's mind.

The idea of faking sick to go back to bed vanished in an instant and she brushed her mother's hand away from her face, giving it a quick squeeze of reassurance.

"I'm fine," she soothed, plastering a smile on her face. "I just didn't sleep very well, that's all."

Instead of lightening, Kate's eyes furrowed in greater worry. "Why not? Don't you feel well? Did something happen that's upsetting you?"

Tess considered. Had something happened to upset her? Why, yes. Yes, it had. The murderers across the street had come home before the crack of dawn, breaking a week of solid behavior to drag a body into their backyard.

Because that's what it had been, Tess was suddenly sure. She knew a fireman's carry when she saw one. She knew what it looked like when a man tossed another person across his shoulder - the adjustments in posture, the struggle to keep the other person balanced, and the strain and toll it took on one's own body.

And that bag. The only people who had duffle bags that big were professional athletes and professional criminals.

Tess thought for a moment. Yep, that was it. Athletes and criminals. Did bags even come that big ordinarily? If it was some kind of special order, Tess might be able to trace it. If she could-

"Tess?" Her mother's voice cut through the whirlwind of thoughts spinning through her head, and Tess snapped out of it. The killers could wait just a little longer to fall from their thrones of lies. Her mother was hyperventilating in front of her.

"Mom." Tess took her mother's hands again, and she looked right up into her eyes. "Mom, I'm fine. I promise I'm not sick. I didn't sleep because I was finishing my life science project." Tess smiled at her mother with confidence. "Ben isn't going to leave me alone until I finish, so I polished off the paper early this morning."

Tess hoped her mother didn't demand she produce the finished product. The lie had come easily, but it only worked if her mom bought it. "I need to get going if I'm going to sneak over to his house and take one last picture of the butterflies before they hatch."

Would it be the last pictures before the chrysalis broke and the butterflies emerged? Tess had no idea. But it sounded reasonable, and she could see her mother calming as she spoke.

I taught you to use your powers for good, not for evil, Tessie.

Tess knew she was a good liar, and she wasn't above using it to further her agenda. She hated lying to her mother, but this was for the greater good. Her mother needed reassurance.

"Are you sure, baby?" Kate asked, looking up from where she'd sunk to the edge of Tess's bed, as though the idea of Tess being sick was enough to take her legs out from under her.

Tess could feel her mother's hands shaking in her own. "I'm sure, mamma." She gave the hands another squeeze. "I promise, nothing is wrong."

We don't lie to family.

Ian McGee rarely sounded stern with Tess, but the disappointment was obvious this time. Tess just squared her shoulders. Why her mother's grief focused itself on Tess's health, she didn't know. But if she could spare her mother even a moment of worry and fear, she would lie like a snake in the grass and not feel a second of guilt over it.

Not one second.

"I'm going to take a shower," Tess said, pulling her mother to her feet. "Do we have anything I can take for lunch today? Our cafeteria is partnering with a company that unethically sources their milk products from child labor in Peru, so I'm boycotting."

Her mother latched onto the idea of Tess not eating like Tess knew she would.

"I'll make you something fantastic to take to school, baby." Tess watched Kate head for the door, clearly considering what she could produce on an hour's notice. "We still have some of that smoked turkey from Key's Farm that we picked up at the market last weekend. I'll make up a couple of sandwiches for the boys, too."

She stopped, hand on the doorknob, and shot Tess a wobbly smile. "I'd better make extra, now that we know how Mark eats."

Tess could only smile back. Her mother was getting better, she really was. Kate and Tess were talking more like they used to. Kate was making an effort to ask about her day and rising to meet Tess's spirit as best she could. But then, like she'd opened the pages of a storybook, the rabbit hole would open up and sweep Kate McGee back to Wonderland.

Tess never knew when it would happen, and she never knew what would set it off. The sudden grief that swamped Tess's heart was powerful, and she struggled to push it back.

She wanted her dad back. She did. But that wasn't going to happen. The best she could do for her father was to avenge his death.

What she could have back was her mother. And Tess was determined to have her, no matter what.

Tess hadn't realized her phone was in her hand until she heard the voice on the other end of the line.

"Tess McGee, you better have a good reason for disrupting my beauty sleep."

"Hey, Miss Angel. I think my mamma's going to need some company today."

Chapter 29

Tess was waiting on Ben's porch when he stepped out and while she wished he at least had the decency to look surprised, she was too excited to share what she'd seen to be offended.

He took one look at her and summed up the situation. "Tell me you at least got a few hours of sleep last night."

Tess waved him off. "I'll sleep when I'm dead. You'll never believe..." Tess drifted off as Mrs. Lewis appeared in the doorway behind Ben.

Mrs. Lewis, and one Mark Dunham.

"You make sure you eat that cinnamon roll before practice now," Mrs. Lewis was saying, patting Mark fondly on the shoulder. "You need the energy. Oh, hey there, Tess."

Mrs. Lewis smiled brightly at Tess, who smiled right back while eyeing Mark suspiciously. "I was actually on my way to meet Angel Sullivan at your house. We're going to see a movie in Savannah, and we thought we'd drag your mother with us."

Tess had to swallow down the lump that suddenly appeared in her throat, which Mrs. Lewis must have seen because she wrapped Tess in a big hug. "Angel called and said your mamma might need a little happiness today," she whispered. "Don't you worry. We'll take good care of her."

Mrs. Lewis leaned back and swiped a thumb over a suspicious bit of moisture that had appeared on Tess's cheek while both boys busied themselves looking the other way.

"Keep your chin up, kid," she said, before turning her smile back on the boys.

"Benjamin, have a good day at school. Stand up for the little guy and all that. Mark, you feel free to come by anytime, alright?"

"Yes, ma'am," both boys said at once, and the three watched as she bounced off the porch and headed in the direction of Tess's house.

"She's not used to sitting still," Ben remarked dryly. "Chasing bail jumpers hasn't been as rewarding as she'd hoped."

Tess was secretly hoping Ben's mother might be interested in taking on an intern in a few years because she thought chasing bail jumpers sounded awesome, but she pulled herself back to the task at hand as they stepped off the porch.

"You'll never believe what happened across the street this morning," she started. Though weird, Mark conveniently being at Ben's house worked in her favor. Although...

"Do you have any of those cinnamon rolls left?" Tess asked, eyeing the Tupperware Mark was tucking into his backpack, but Ben just shrugged.

"What do you think?" he asked, shooting a side eye at Mark, and Tess huffed. Did playing football cause such extreme hunger? In the last twenty-four hours, they'd watched Mark inhale everything around him. Did he not have food at his own house?

"Anyway," Mark drawled, stepping out with his long stride and causing Tess and Ben to scurry to keep up, "I believe Inspector Lestrade here was about to introduce a new wrinkle in the plot. Inspector?"

He bowed gallantly and Tess wrinkled her nose. "How do you know who Inspector Lestrade is? You know what, never mind." She was pretty sure Mark said things like that just to mess with her, and she refused to be drawn in during her big reveal. He grinned, which she ignored.

She was getting very good at ignoring Mark Dunham.

"There's been a break in the case."

Ben and Mark exchanged looks, and Tess allowed them a moment of suspense before plowing forward. "Horace and Jasper came home three hours early last night."

She watched them expectantly, eager to share her enthusiasm, but they must not have understood the implications because they just waited for her to continue.

"They deviated from their schedule?" she prompted, "Which is a big deal and exactly what we've been waiting for?"

"And then what happened?" Mark asked, pulling an apple out of his pocket and taking a big bite.

"What do you mean, 'and then what happened?'" Tess spluttered. "That should be enough! Don't you get it? This is huge!"

Mark just grinned that big, stupid grin at her, but Ben sighed. "And then what happened, Tess?"

These boys had no imagination. Where was the passion? The intensity? The thirst for knowledge?

"And then they dragged a body out of the van and into the backyard to bury it."

And finally, there it was. The reaction Tess was hoping for.

Both boys stopped and stared. Ben closed his eyes and looked skyward, as though he were praying to the Lord for strength, and Mark tossed the apple over his shoulder. He turned and gripped her by both shoulders, making sure she was looking right at him.

"Tell me," he said, "please, please tell me that you did not see those men burying a body. Please tell me you did not follow them into their backyard in the dead middle of the night."

"Did you see a body?" Ben asked, slightly less hysterical than Mark.

"Well, no," Tess admitted, and she could swear both guys released identical sighs of relief. "And of course, I didn't follow them into their backyard. I'm not insane." Although, that might not be a bad idea. If she could identify the burial site -

- but Mark was giving her a doubtful look so she pretended she wasn't considering it, and he hesitantly let go of her shoulders and took a step back.

"Tess, what did you see?" With the moment of drama in their rearview mirror, Ben picked up the pace and Tess had to scurry to catch up.

"The van came back at 3 a.m.," she reported. "Horace and Jasper were alone, like usual. But they were acting real cagey." Tess thought back to the furtive movements, the quietly closed doors, the glances as they moved toward the backyard. "They had a large duffle bag that Jasper had to carry over his shoulder." Her eyes were heavy with implication as she gazed meaningfully at her partners. "A bag just the right size to store a body in."

"That's the body you saw? Come on, Tess." Mark glanced around like he was suddenly sorry he'd tossed his apple away. "That's a pretty tall leap."

"You didn't see them." How could Tess explain what she'd seen? How she knew what she knew. "The bag was huge! And the way Jasper had to carry it over his shoulder? The way he had to steady himself and balance just so? It was a body."

Tess was certain. "They didn't bring the box back that they usually have, and they went into the backyard instead of into the house. Why would they do that?"

"Because whatever was in the bag belongs in the backyard?" Ben answered logically. "Because it was dirty and they didn't want it in the house. Because they're working on landscaping and the backyard is the easiest access. Because-"

"Okay, okay," Tess interrupted. "I guess if you have no investigative prowess, that's how it might have looked. But I know what I saw."

The men hadn't wanted to be seen. That alone was enough reason for Tess to want to see whatever they were doing. The men were out all night, which meant they probably slept through the day. The odds were good they were sleeping now. Maybe if...

"Hey, why are we walking this way?"

Tess had been so wrapped up in telling the guys what she'd seen that she hadn't noticed they'd taken a different way to school. They'd never even passed the Brooklyn house.

The west route was more efficient, sure. But that meant they were already coming up on the school.

Honestly, the entire reason she walked her normal route was because it took longer. Who wanted to get to school sooner than they needed to? Except Ben, of course.

The guys exchanged another deep look reeking of bromance, and Tess had the sneaking suspicion they'd planned to take a different route all along.

"And why were you at Ben's house, anyway?"

Tess pinned Mark with a stare, and he had the decency to look like he'd rather be anywhere else at the moment.

He shoved his hands into his pocket as he lopped forward. "Just thought I'd walk with you guys today. You got a problem with that, McGee?"

Tess didn't look at Ben, but a ghost of their conversation from the night before floated through her mind. No, Mark wasn't like Derrick or Gage or the rest of the popular kids at school. She'd asked him before why he was friends with them. Maybe he was trying not to be.

"No, no problem," she replied mildly. She thought that would appease Mark but it had the opposite effect.

"What, no argument? No snarky comments or clever innuendo?" Mark slapped his hands over his chest. "Am I alive? Is my heart still beating? Am I on death's door? That can be the only excuse for a docile Tess McGee!"

Well, if he wanted to fight, she could-

"Take the win, man," Ben cut in. "Before she changes her mind."

Mark gave her a little grin, one that Tess would almost call fond. "You're right. I'll take what I can get."

Tess was feeling oddly unsettled by this turn of events. Mark and Ben, suddenly the best of friends. Interrupting her quippy comebacks, leaving her feeling incomplete and off-kilter. And they were thirty minutes early for school, which Tess considered the greatest sin of all.

"You know what?" She smiled sweetly and was gratified to see Mark visibly pale. "I'm going to take advantage of all this extra time to pay the office a little visit. I have some business, you see, and now is a perfect time to take care of it."

Ben simply shook his head, like he didn't want to know, and Tess had to acknowledge that was probably true. So she turned her attention to Mark. "Since you two are suddenly bosom buddies, I'll give you some time alone to make friendship bracelets and braid each other's hair."

Tess turned and headed towards the administrative part of the school. "Tell Derrick I said hi." Tess smiled over her shoulder so she could make sure Mark caught her full meaning. "Tell him I'll see him soon."

Mark sighed deeply and Ben patted him on the shoulder. "You did warn him."

Tess was going to take that as their blessing for what was to come.

Chapter 30

Tess had been idly considering how to exact her revenge on Derrick Merrigan for a few weeks, but nothing seemed quite right. Despite her best bluff, she didn't want to cause him permanent damage. She just wanted to bring him down a peg. What he'd said about her dad...the way he treated other people who weren't in his cool dude group...no one should be allowed to get away with that.

Justice called. How could Tess not answer?

So with no real goal in mind other than research and free time on her hands, she popped into the library. The sum total of her knowledge about Derrick was that he was approximately twelve feet tall, played every sport the school offered, and had a complete lack of insight into the federal justice system. Of those three points, sports seemed like the best place to start. The library would have back copies of the school newspaper, as well as all local articles that covered Lafitte sports. Maybe she could discover a weakness using the deep insight of high school journalism.

"Hello, old friend," Tess whispered, breathing deeply as she stepped through the door, the feeling of coming home singing through her veins. Mrs. McCallister, the ancient librarian, didn't appreciate her helpful suggestions, but Tess felt proud that she'd successfully petitioned the school to add a classic microfiche system for student usage, even if it had taken two years of dedicated petitioning to accomplish. If she were the only student who used it, that was a loss for her classmates.

Tess gave the small microfiche machine in the corner a regretful look as she settled in at one of the open research stations instead. Unfortunately, this search wasn't confined to the dusty film strips of the past. She would need space to lay out as many back issues of the more modern student paper as the library had available. They were digitized, Tess knew, but she much preferred the feel of newsprint beneath her fingers.

Research was an important component of investigation, and she needed to set the right parameters. Tess would start with the most recent editions, but how far back should she go? Perhaps she should confine her first round of research to the current season. Would that be enough data? Maybe, maybe not. She would keep going until she found what she was looking for. Any information was-

"Hi, Tess."

Tess tensed, not quite as alone as she thought. Who were all these people who came to school early, and what was wrong with them?

By the time she straightened and turned, she'd pasted a smile fit for the queen on her face.

"Hi, Maddie."

Tess wasn't in the mood to be sociable, and Maddie's polite smile dimmed slightly as she waited for Tess to say something else. Maybe to ask why she was at school so early, or to see if Maddie wanted to share a table. Neither of which Tess intended to do.

Maddie must have been feeling determined, however, because she slogged forward despite Tess's unwelcoming demeanor. "What are you doing at school so early?"

"Research." Tess glanced at the circulation desk where Mrs. McCallister had yet to appear. She always seemed to vanish the moment Tess appeared in the doorway. Physical copies of the paper had to be pulled by staff, but Tess knew from experience that Mrs. McCallister would come back. Eventually. One didn't make it in the hallowed halls of high school librarian-ism by dodging persistent students forever.

"Just waiting for Mrs. McCallister."

Maddie brightened. "I can help. I work first period as a library assistant."

Of course she did.

Tess swallowed her pride and followed along obediently as Maddie let herself behind the massive circulation desk and logged into the workstation. "What do you need?"

Tess hesitated. Maddie knew good and well that Tess didn't care about sports, and she knew Tess didn't write for the paper. She'd want to know what Tess was doing. But it seemed as though Mrs. McCallister was happy to allow her student to take care of early-morning business because Tess couldn't even catch a glimpse of her in the open copy room behind Maddie.

And so, Tess had to choose a path: give up her quest of destroying Derrick Merrigan, at least for today, or allow Maddie to assist.

"Oh, come on, Tess." Maddie rolled her eyes. "I'm just trying to help. I'm not going to ask what you're doing."

"Fine," Tess finally agreed. She didn't want to waste any more time, and she had nothing else to do anyway. "I need all the back issues of the school newspaper from the current academic year." She'd decided to go year instead of season because the paper always covered the up-and-coming football players as a build-up to the season.

"There," Maddie said, smiling brightly. "That wasn't so hard, was it?"

She busied herself collecting the issues and Tess waited as impatiently as she could. She tapped her fingers on the polished surface of the desk and sighed frequently, and Maddie went slower still. All of which had Tess smiling to herself, even if just slightly. How easy it was to fall into old patterns with even older friends. It was comforting, in a way. Familiar. Something she missed more than she thought she did.

And though Maddie was no longer a friend, she followed Tess back to her table and settled in across from her.

"I thought you were working?" Tess asked pointedly, nodding her head back towards the circulation desk.

"Not until first period starts." Maddie pulled a magazine out of her bag and started flipping through the glossy pages without looking up. "I just thought I'd sit here quietly and read."

Tess stared at her for a moment, but Maddie never flinched.

"I thought you weren't going to ask what I'm doing?"

"I'm not."

"So, you're just going to sit there. And read? A magazine?"

"Yes, Tess," Maddie said patiently, flipping another page. "I'm going to sit here quietly and read a magazine. No, it's not Agatha Christie or Sherlock Holmes, but I like it. It's my version of a mystery novel."

"You're mixing your metaphors," Tess argued. "Agatha Christie is an author, Sherlock Holmes is a character."

"I know."

Maddie still didn't look up, but Tess could see the smug smile and realized she'd been lured in by a foe she'd underestimated. The Moriarty to her Sherlock. The unexpected poisoner to her Poirot.

That was fine. Two could play that game. Tess straightened the papers and pulled out the first edition, published in January. There were nineteen issues altogether, two published each month. The final edition of October would be out next week, and Tess went straight to the sports section on page three.

"You know," Maddie drawled nonchalantly, flipping another needlessly glossy page. "If you're looking for dirt on Derrick Merrigan, and I'm not saying you are, but if you are, I might be able to help."

So much for not caring what Tess was doing.

"And why would you think I would care anything about Derrick Merrigan?" Someone had been talking, and Tess was afraid she knew who.

"Ben and I are friends," Maddie said airily. "He's helping me in Art and I'm helping him with Spanish."

"You don't need help in Art. You won the junior watercolor competition four years straight."

"Ben doesn't know that, now does he?" Maddie finally looked up and grinned. "And he doesn't exactly need help in Spanish either, but here we are."

Maddie's smile faded, and the more tentative Maddie emerged. The one Tess hadn't seen since Maddie's dad had abandoned her family. "And maybe I mentioned that I need to apologize to you for some things that happened, but that's not how our friendship works, and so maybe he gave me a tip on how I could help."

Tess wanted to be mad at Ben, she really did. And she wanted to be mad at Maddie. But it was really hard to scrape up her usual indignation when Maddie was sitting in front of her, wanting to help, and Ben already knew her well enough to know she'd want that, even if she couldn't say it.

Tess had been lonely, even if she didn't want to admit it. And suddenly, it seemed like Maddie might have missed her too, and Tess wasn't sure how to feel about that.

"I guess," Tess said slowly, "if you want to help and you have information on the target, you could be considered a confidential informant."

"Confidential informants get paid, I believe." Maddie had gone back to perusing her magazine, but her posture was more relaxed than it had been before.

"Only after they prove their worth." Tess would consent to try, but she wasn't ready to jump right back in.

"Thank goodness." Maddie dropped her magazine and grabbed Tess by the hand, hauling her to her feet. "That much, I can do right now. You didn't even look in a mirror this morning, did you?"

"Hey!" Tess protested, dragged behind ridiculously long legs she had no chance against. "It can't be that bad. And my stuff! Mrs. McCallister won't like it if I leave a mess!"

"Mrs. McCallister doesn't like you either way, and I'm her first-period student. I'll clean it up. And yes, it is that bad."

"I was in a hurry this morning." Tess had been both too excited and too exhausted by the morning's events to worry about taming her mess of hair. "But what do you think you're going to do about it?"

"Oh, Tess McGee," Maddie said, exasperated. "As though I don't know what to do with that hair by now."

With her free hand, Maddie pulled a thick, woven headband in teal and gold from her backpack. "I still carry emergency supplies."

Well. If that wasn't your oldest friend, Tess didn't know what was.

Chapter 31

"**I** 've got a bone to pick with you."

Tess dropped her bag onto the table and Ben looked up from his book in surprise.

"You sound mad. Are you mad?"

"Mad, no." Tess considered. "Hurt? Betrayed? Skewered through the back like Julius Caesar on his worst day ever? Maybe."

"Julius Caesar, huh?" Ben turned back to his book. "You talked to Maddie, I'm guessing?"

"In case I was too subtle about the situation, Maddie and I are no longer friends."

"First," Ben said mildly, folding the edge of the page he was reading to mark his place, horrifying Tess to her very soul, "you are never subtle about anything. And second," he flipped the book closed and Tess thought she detected a hint of annoyance, "maybe *you* are mad at Maddie, but I'm not. And she wants to make up."

"Make up? Make up!" Tess dropped onto the bench across from him. "Did she tell you what happened?" Ben wouldn't be so quick to jump on Maddie's bandwagon if he knew that Maddie had dropped Tess like a bad habit when her dad had left. That she hadn't reached out, at all, after Tess's dad had gone. Ben had lost someone, too. He knew what that was like.

"Her dad decided he didn't want to be her dad anymore. How did you expect her to react?" Ben's voice was hard, accusatory, like it was somehow Tess's fault and that tone raised her hackles even more.

"I expected her to need her best friend, not pull the same trick her dad did and replace the friend who loved her with new friends. What?" Tess snarked. "Tess 2.0 not working out for her? New friends not all they were cracked up to be? Color me surprised."

"She told me, you know? About your dad."

Tess stiffened. "What about my dad?"

Ben hesitated, and she could tell he was considering his words carefully. "She told me-" He broke off before starting again, and Tess could see the mental debate he was having with himself. "She told me how he was. The kind of dad he was, the kind of dad hers wasn't. How your dad spent every moment of his free time with you. How you and your mom were the most important things in his life. More important than his job. More important than his country. More important than anything."

"'More important than his country'? Are we still talking about me and Maddie or did you slip your issues in when I wasn't looking?"

Ben blew out his breath. "Not everyone has what you have, Tess. And it can be hard to be around the constant reminder of what you've lost."

"I don't have it anymore though, do it." Tess refused to allow the tears clogging her throat to reach her eyes. "Your dad came home. He gave up his job and his country and came home. Mine didn't. Maddie's didn't. And you would think that would bring us closer together."

Tess ignored the knife twisting in her chest. "Did she tell you she didn't check on me? Not even once. She didn't come to the funeral. She didn't text, she didn't so much as glance my way in the halls. Nothing. My dad *died*, and she couldn't be bothered to care."

It came out a little louder than Tess intended, and she could hear the words echo around the cafeteria as conversation stuttered like a candle in a stiff breeze.

"Tess." Ben dropped his voice and leaned towards her as the kids at the nearest table pretended not to listen. "I'm not saying what she did was right. I'm just saying, well, maybe she can help." His eyes slid away in discomfort before focusing back on her, imploring her to hear what he wasn't saying. "I think you should tell her what you think happened to your dad, and about the men across the street. I think she would know what to say."

"No." Tess said it quietly, but she might as well have slammed her hands on the table by the way Ben jerked back. "I will not. You want to stop? Fine, then stop. Hang out with Maddie and join the baseball team and take nature pictures and go home to your mom and dad and talk to them about how much you miss your grandma."

Tess rose to her feet and clutched the strap of her bag. She was intensely aware of the eyes of the cafeteria on her. Of Ben's eyes on her, so full of pity. Of Mark, sitting quietly with Derrick Merrigan and Gage Shaw while they laughed at her outburst.

And she just didn't care. She didn't care about any of it.

"Tess, wait." Ben finally dropped his eyes and Tess watched silently as he dug his sketchbook out of his backpack. He flipped through it until he found what he was looking for, then tore out a page and offered it to her.

"I finished," he said quietly.

Tess numbly took the portrait he offered and looked at it silently. It was Janie. It was the little girl Tess had seen watching her from the street, from the front porch, and again from an upstairs window. Ben, having never seen her, had managed to capture her elven features and the fragile feeling Tess had whenever she saw her.

Ben hadn't even seen the girl, and he barely believed Tess had, but he'd drawn her anyway.

Tess couldn't speak, and everything she was feeling threatened to crash over her in waves of grief, guilt, and pain that she couldn't control. Ben was sitting quietly, just looking at her. Mark had risen to his feet, hesitating but losing the battle on whether he should join their public debacle. Mr. Abrams had made an appearance at the door of the cafeteria and was staring intently their way.

And Tess just didn't care.

She folded the page and slid it into the back pocket of her jeans. Then she slung her backpack over her shoulders and walked steadily towards the door as the eyes of every person in the room followed her.

When she got to the door, Mr. Abrams attempted to intervene.

"Tess, why don't we-"

"I need a moment." She was perfectly calm and controlled, and Mr. Abrams nodded his head.

"I'll wait for you in my office."

That was just fine. He could wait in his office, and Ben could read his book, and Mark could become the jerk everyone already thought he was. Maddie could move on with new friends and a new life.

And Tess just didn't care.

Chapter 32

D r. Horowitz was a smiling young man who gave off a strong impression of youth and vigor. He carried the idealism of the young, of a man not yet beaten by the harsh realities of life.

He would learn.

Dr. Horowitz shook his hand and ushered him into the office.

"Miss McGuire said you'd be paying me a visit, and that I was to give you my full cooperation. Tell me, how can I assist?"

The smile was open and assuring, confident, but he detected just a hint of discomfort. It seemed he made most people uncomfortable, truth be told. The average Joes in the world found it hard to be truly comfortable when coming face-to-face with the gritty underbelly of life.

"What can you tell me about your last meeting with Mr. McGuire?" No use beating around the bush when he could cut straight through it. "What did you talk about? What were your impressions of the man?"

"Oh," the doctor replied, thinking back, "nothing special, I can tell you. We were finalizing an initiative that would fund basic medical care for our homeless citizens, which is a passion for both of us." His smile dimmed slightly. "Or rather, it was a passion for both of us." He brightened again quickly. "What a relief it's been to discover Miss McGuire shares her father's interests and is committed to making the man's final dream a reality."

"I'm sure it is," he said dryly. "A relief, that is. How much capital would you be out if she hadn't?"

The doctor's smile flattened into disappointment. "Really, Mr.-what did you say your name was again?"

"I didn't." And now his natural inclination for inspiring discomfort became useful as his gruff answer echoed around the very silent room. Few people could sit in silence and wait it out. Dr. Horowitz was no exception.

"Ah. Well, then." He tinkered with an expensive fountain pen on his desk, clearly anxious at the lack of social conventions being practiced. "Yes, as you say, I would have been out some initial capital. But my investment was less financial than you might expect. Henry was bankrolling the project. I was simply supplying the manpower."

That made sense, he supposed. The financier would carry most of the financial risk while the doctor could provide the expertise necessary for the day-to-day functions.

"Did McGuire say anything to you of a personal nature during that meeting?" he asked, unsurprised to see a small tick in the corner of the man's eye.

So, there had been something.

"We talked about his daughter, of course," Dr. Horowitz said, and just the mention of the woman was enough to soften his anxiety. "She's lovely, of course. A Harvard graduate, if you can believe that. One of the first women to enter the college. Did you know her entrance exam scores were higher than mine?"

The man fairly beamed with pride for his beguiling new partner, and he quickly redirected the conversation before the man began to wax poetic about the many virtues of the lovely Miss McGuire.

"What else did you talk about? Other than Miss McGuire?"

"Oh, yes, of course." The young doctor shook himself from his reverie. "We briefly discussed the state of the world's economy, of course." He shook his head sadly. "You can't go far these days without the topic coming up. It was my understanding, though, that the McGuire's were unscathed." He looked concerned. "Do you believe that might be the reason he, well, that he died? It certainly wouldn't be unheard of."

And there it was again. A slight glint. A tightening of the smaller muscles around the eye.

Dr. Horowitz was lying to him.

"So, you believe McGuire killed himself then?" he asked. "Despite what Miss McGuire believes?"

The man's shoulders twitched uncomfortably. "Well, children do want to think the best of their fathers, true? If the police have concluded it was suicide, who are we to argue?"

Who, indeed?

"So there was nothing else that day? Nothing out of the ordinary? Nothing that was bothering the man, no troubles he mentioned, even in passing, that might tell a different story."

"I'm sorry to say, sir, that I can be of no help in the matter. Miss McGuire has my condolences, of course, and she shall have anything else from me she desires. I have related these facts to the authorities, but I can not give you any information that might point you in a different direction."

...these facts...can not give...

...such intentional wording from a man who should have nothing to hide.

It was raining when he left Dr. Horowitz's office. He tilted his hat further over his eyes and pulled the collar of his battered coat closer against the chill Detroit wind as he wandered slowly down the deserted streets.

The doctor was lying to him but about what, he couldn't say. He knew something, that was clear. And it was something he didn't want Miss McGuire to know.

But whether the doctor was protecting himself, his partner, or his young lady, he couldn't yet say.

• • • •

TESS SHOULD HAVE BEEN surprised when she heard feet on the gravel and felt someone settling onto the ground beside her, but she wasn't.

"Skipping class is against the rules. Don't you have a game tonight?" She spoke without turning, eyes locked on her target down the street.

"Please," Mark scoffed, and Tess knew it was true. Mark Dunham could be busted smoking in the bathroom and it wouldn't affect his game status. Football in small towns was king, and they both knew it.

"So," he drawled, settling against the tree at his back, leaning just slightly into Tess's side. "What are we looking at?"

The tree Tess had her back pressed against was one of the oldest in the area, a Southern Live Oak the neighborhood had nicknamed Lou. Its thick, gnarled branches formed a nest around the ancient trunk before shooting towards the sky, and it was the perfect place to observe without being observed herself.

From her vantage point, Tess could see the van parked in front of the Brooklyn house. She hadn't been sure about its activity during the days since she had never been able to observe during school hours. The windows had been completely blacked out and duct tape lined every inch and seam where the glass met metal. Reinforced like that, the windows would be very difficult to bust out.

"Lots of people use duct tape to fix car windows," Mark said mildly. "Especially in this town." He shrugged. "Not everyone has the money to fix what still works. Or they just don't care."

He thought he could read her mind and if Tess cared, it would be infuriating.

Luckily, she didn't.

"You're bored."

He looked at her askance. "What?"

"You're bored." Tess's voice was clinical as she kept watch over the house. "The school is yours, and there's no sport you haven't conquered. You're looking for a challenge, and I never back down from one. So here you sit, waiting for me to entertain you. Possibly you even report back to your cronies and have a good laugh at my expense."

If Tess cared, she would admit she didn't find it likely. Despite his reputation, Mark wasn't a bad guy and Tess couldn't bring herself to believe he would mock her for sport.

But she still didn't care.

Mark didn't say a word, so Tess continued with her cold, clinical diagnosis uninterrupted. "It doesn't matter. Have your fun. Play your games. I don't need your help, or Ben's help, or even Maddie's. I will sit here until I have proof that they killed my dad, or I will sit here until I die. Whichever comes first."

Mark Dunham was rarely speechless and if this were a different day, Tess would be proud of her accomplishment.

But she just didn't care.

Everything she cared about was sitting down the street, and they would eventually make a mistake. She would be here when they did.

"You know," Mark finally said, and Tess couldn't decide if he sounded sad or dismissive. "if you weren't so determined to push away everyone who could see through your bulletproof facade and do everything on your own, maybe you would see what's right in front of you."

He pushed himself to his feet. "I know you're looking for a life raft in the middle of all this grief," he said, "but Tess, they didn't kill your dad. I think you know that, and it's okay if you're not ready to accept it. But don't do what Maddie did, okay? Don't push everyone who cares out of your life."

Tess finally looked up at him, only to find he wasn't looking at her at all. He was looking behind them, towards his own home.

"Loving and losing isn't so bad. It beats never being loved at all."

Mark's eyes settled on her again, and they looked haunted. "Do what you need to do to deal with it. I'll still be here when you're done. Just make sure you're actually doing it."

Tess didn't care, but she couldn't help but ask anyway. "Doing what?"

"Dealing with it."

Feet crunched gravel as Mark left Tess to her thoughts.

Well, just the one thought. And it was less a thought than a single-minded determination to pursue justice at all costs.

It's a fine line between determination and obsession, Tessie.

Maddie's dad had left. Ben's dad had come home. Mark's dad was just plain mean. And Tess's dad should still be here.

He *would* still be here, if not for Horace and Jasper.

Watching them wasn't doing any good, and she knew it. She could develop a timeline for their days and nights, but they weren't going to offer up the evidence she needed in broad daylight. They could be suspicious and paranoid as the day was long, but acting shady wasn't the same as breaking the law. And she needed to catch them breaking the law to convince Sully to act.

Watching just wasn't going to cut it.

Now, Tessie, don't go jumping before you're ready to walk.

She would regret it, she knew, doing nothing. She'd regret sitting at the kitchen table every night, pretending everything was fine, watching her mother watch the empty chair across the table, taming her tongue to make sure she didn't say something to make her mother disappear again.

She'd regret watching Horace and Jasper's freedom, watching them continue whatever crime spree they were on while she made notes from her window and more families were destroyed.

There was evidence in that van that would tie them to the crime, Tess was certain of it. Those blacked-out windows were hiding something. But it was a very visible target, sitting on the street in front of the house where every Tom, Dick, and Mrs. Sandoval would see someone breaking in. She couldn't peek inside and she couldn't break the windows because of the duct tape reinforcement.

The van was a very hard target. What Tess needed was something a little softer. Something like, for example, a backyard with a privacy fence and criminals who were gone in the evenings for hours at a time.

Tess couldn't see the fence from this angle, but she'd walked the neighborhood enough to know it was at least six feet tall, surrounding the backyard. One side of the fence was visible from her house, but not all of it. Breaching the fence might be doable if there was a weakness. A blind spot, a loose board, uneven ground. She was small. If she could shimmy under-

The door of the house opened and Horace and Jasper emerged. Was it time already? Tess found it hard to believe hours had passed since that horrible scene in the cafeteria, but in her numbed state she supposed anything was possible.

She watched as they made their way to the van, silent and brooding. Horace carrying an empty box like always, birdlike and skittish, anxiously checking the area around them. Jasper, resolute, ill-tempered, and sneering, stomped to the van and climbed in.

Tess rose to her feet and somehow, the slight movement must have caught Horace's hawkish gaze, because his face jerked towards her and she froze.

Easy, Tessie. Be very easy.

Tess didn't know if they stood there for seconds or minutes or hours - she, barely breathing, and Horace,

burning eyes locked on her position - before a muffled shout reached her and Horace finally blinked. He squinted once more at the branches of the tree that concealed her before a hand snaked open the door of the van and he slithered in. Jasper, clearly unhappy with the delay, was shouting obscenities at his brother, but Horace still looked troubled. Or maybe that wasn't quite right. No, he didn't look troubled. He looked thoughtful.

The van door closed but the last look Tess caught was of his eyes, lingering on the tree, a thoughtful expression on his face.

That would have concerned her more if she hadn't caught a wisp of movement on the porch.

There she was.

Little Janie Doe. She was crouched in the back corner of the porch, almost hidden by boxes and the kind of debris that accumulated when murderers moved into a nice neighborhood. And she was looking right at Tess.

The girl's expression never changed, and Tess's fingers instinctively sought the comfort of the fur tucked into the front pocket of her bag. The bunny had been with her for weeks now, and it was a familiar friend. She didn't know how Janie could see her when the men couldn't, but Tess could almost swear the little girl was trying to tell her something.

The times Tess had seen her before, the girl looked sad. Lost, somehow. But now, there was a pained look on her face. A look of frustration, fear, and worry. Somehow, Tess knew the girl would disappear if she tried to approach, but Tess took a step forward anyway.

Away from the safety of the tree.

If she could just get a little closer. If she could just ask what was wrong, ask her to tell Tess what the men were doing...

The sound of the engine firing up brought Tess back to herself, and she stumbled. The van was still sitting in the street, and now Tess had exposed herself. If Horace was still looking, he would know. And the girl-

-was gone. Spooked by Tess or by the sound of the van, but gone nonetheless. Tess bit her lip in frustration. Where had she gone? Why wouldn't she come out?

The van pulled away, and Tess felt a sharp spike of anxiety. They had seen her. Somehow, she knew they had. They knew she was watching. Why else would Horace so waspishly check their surroundings? Why would Jasper leer when he looked across the street?

At Tess's house. At her mother. Like he was mocking her. Mocking them.

Mocking her father.

And Tess was finished waiting.

She was already running before the van turned the corner.

Chapter 33

"**I** know who killed Dad."

The words came exploding from Tess with an intensity she hadn't known existed. It was like trying to take a drink from a fire hose and once she started, she couldn't stop.

"I know who killed Dad, and I'm sorry I didn't tell you but I was trying to protect you. You were so sad, and we still eat lasagna and go to the market on weekends but you don't go to work and I didn't want you to be even sadder so I didn't tell you.

But it's going to be okay now because I know who killed Dad, and you won't have to be sad anymore."

Tess paused, gulping in air, and braced herself to look at her mother, who hadn't said a word since Tess had sent the screen door crashing against the kitchen wall. It would be hard, Tess supposed, to say a word when she hadn't stopped talking since she came in. But it didn't look like her mother had even tried. She stood exactly as she had when Tess burst into the room, a look on her face that Tess couldn't interpret.

"Mom?" Had Tess broken her mother again? Had she made everything worse? She reached tentatively for her mother's hand. "Mom?" she tried again, not sure what else to do. Time was of the essence though. Now that she'd been made, they needed to go to the police. Tess would be their next target. Or worse, they would go after Kate to get to her.

"Mom, we have to tell Sully," Tess said, giving her mom's hand a small tug. "He's Dad's partner. He'll help us."

In all of Tess's life, Kate McGee had never been so still and Tess hadn't realized how unnatural it would be to see. Terrifying.

Finally breaking that terrifying stillness, Tess's mother closed her eyes for a moment and took a deep breath. When she finally opened her eyes, Tess was relieved to see the detective's wife was still there, after all.

Kate McGee's eyes were fierce despite the shine of tears, which she held staunchly at bay. At that moment, Tess was so proud. Her mother was still here, and she knew how to handle the hard stuff. It would all be okay. She didn't need Ben, and she didn't need Mark, and she sure didn't need Maddie. Her mother was on her side. She believed her, and she would take care of everything. Tess wasn't alone anymore.

"Sweetheart." Her mom's voice sounded strangled, and she paused to clear her throat before trying again. "Sweetheart, what do you mean when you say you know *who* killed Dad?"

It wasn't exactly what Tess had expected, and it seemed like a weird question, but she could give her mom the benefit of the doubt. Tess had sprung the news on her very quickly, after all. So she tried not to show the annoyance she felt at having to explain. There was no time. They needed to get to Sully.

"The Brooklyn house. The men across the street. They have a van." Tess said as patiently as she could. "A cargo van. The men who live there have been watching us. I think Dad was investigating them and they killed him, and they know I know. Or," Tess thought it through, "they suspect I know.

They know I've been watching. Which is why we need to get to Sully *right now.*"

"Dad was investigating..." Tess's mother trailed off, looking very lost. It was an expression Tess had only ever seen on her mother's face in the first weeks after her dad died.

Murdered, Tess reminded herself fiercely. He hadn't died, he'd been murdered. Horace and Jasper had murdered her father, and today she was going to deliver justice.

It was such a powerful, heady feeling.

"Come here, sweetheart," her mother finally said, tugging Tess away from the kitchen door and into the living room. "Let's talk this through."

Tess had to forcibly stop herself from protesting. Her mother needed her right now. This was a huge shock, and now they were in danger too. Tess needed to be patient. If the pattern held, Horace and Jasper would be gone until the early hours of the morning. They still had a little time.

"Tessa." Her mother patted the couch cushion next to her, and Tess dropped hesitantly to a seat, folding her legs under her so she could face her mother straight on. "Baby, do you believe your father was murdered?"

Tess didn't understand the question. Shock was a terrible thing, she supposed. It made even very smart people do and say things that didn't make any sense.

"I know it's hard, Mom." Tess squeezed her mother's hand gently. "But Dad would want us to be strong. We need to do what's right, even when it's hard."

Tess knew that was what her dad would want. He'd said it her entire life.

Tess's mom didn't argue. Instead, she smiled. It was watery and frail, and it didn't match the determination in her eyes. But she still smiled.

"He would, wouldn't he?"

Those words seemed to steel something in her mother and when she placed a hand on each side of Tess's face and met her gaze head-on, it felt like the mother Tess used to know.

"Tessa, baby, Dad wasn't murdered. He was sick. He was very sick. Do you remember that?"

Tess frowned. She could feel her cheeks burning under her mother's touch, which seemed like a weird thing to notice, but she couldn't help it. The moment was fraught, the world around her vibrating on the edge of a pin. She thought she might throw up.

"He was sick because they hurt him." Tess squirmed beneath her mom's hands. The heat was radiating through her face and spreading down her neck to her arms. Was she on fire? "He came home from work because he didn't feel good. He went to bed to rest, and he didn't wake up. They killed him."

But Kate McGee only shook her head, those sad, sad eyes filled with steely determination. "No, baby. Dad was very sick for a long time. He had a very bad disease. He didn't go to work that day, he went to the hospital. Do you remember that?"

Tess didn't move. She didn't even know if she breathed. She remembered...was he sick?...he didn't wake up...

"The doctor sent him home because there wasn't anything else they could do for him. Sully was here. He helped carry Dad to our bedroom, and he did go to sleep. He didn't wake up, but not because someone killed him. Sometimes, sweetheart, brave people like Daddy just...well, they just...die."

Her mother's voice broke on that last word and Tess stared, trying to understand what she was saying, but it didn't make any sense. Her dad wasn't sick. He wasn't tired or weak. He was big and strong, and it would take a lot more than some sickness to beat him.

Her mom was confused. Losing Dad made her sad, and she couldn't remember right. That was okay. Tess wanted to scream and argue and wrap her mother in the biggest hug she could manage, all at the same time, but she also needed time to think.

Tess slowly pulled away from her mother's hands and sad, steely eyes and rose. Her face was wet, and she wiped it with her sleeve as she backed towards the stairs.

"I'm going to go to my room for a little while," she said, trying to smile at her mother, who looked devastated from her seat on the couch. "Just for a little while," Tess repeated. "I'm going to work on my book, okay?"

But Tess didn't give her mother time to respond. Instead, she spun and darted up the stairs to the safety of her bedroom. She forced herself to close the door gently, instead of slamming it like she wanted, so her mom wouldn't have any reason to follow her. And once she was alone, Tess just...stood there.

It wasn't her mom's fault, she reminded herself. College sweethearts, they'd met in law school and never looked back. Mom had never been thrilled that Dad changed paths, but

Tess couldn't imagine him doing anything different. If anyone was born to be a hero, it was her dad. And Mom had always worried. That was why she couldn't admit that he had been killed. It was easier to think he'd just gotten sick, that it was a random roll of the dice and not the dangers of his job.

Tess took slow, deep breaths, pressing her hands to her chest to still a racing heart, and wandering aimlessly around her room, folding a shirt here, stacking a pair of shoes there. Her hands were trembling as she picked up the picture frame, still face-down on her desk, and sat it upright. But the tremors stilled as the image came into view, dust from the edges of the frame clinging to her fingertips.

Tess and Ian smiled up from the frame, just the two of them, his smile as bright as she remembered. He was in a recliner and Tess was stuffed into the chair beside him. The chair should have been too small for them; it wasn't that big of a chair, after all. But there they sat, perched together in an off-green, plastic recliner, a tube running into her father's frail arm, another disappearing beneath the collar of his white t-shirt.

He looked so small, but that wasn't right. Her father was a big man, bigger than life. He'd never been this emaciated man in the picture. Had he?

Tess flipped the frame back over. It didn't make sense. Her dad was big and strong. He had an Irish disposition and a lust for life. He wasn't a frail, sick, old man in a hospital bed.

It didn't make sense.

But what did make sense was the mystery across the street. Horace and Jasper had killed her dad. She knew it. She *knew* it. And she didn't blame her mom for not believing her. She didn't have any evidence.

That was the problem. Tess knew good and well that every successful case was built around solid evidence. Once she had that, her mom would take her seriously. She wouldn't look at Tess with those sad, sad eyes anymore.

Tess snatched up her binoculars and looked across the street. The van was still gone, the house quiet and still, and Tess glanced at her alarm clock. As it should be for early evening. If the pattern held, they wouldn't be back until the next morning. That meant she had plenty of time to get in and find what she was looking for. The smoking gun. Or at least a little girl who could tell her where the smoking gun was hidden.

And yet, Tess hesitated. She wasn't a cop. She didn't have a warrant. She didn't even have probable cause-

Her phone vibrated in her hand and she glanced down. Sully. Mom must have called him after their little...discussion.

She knew what Sully would tell her, which was the same thing she already knew. She was just a kid. Breaking and entering was illegal.

Whatever.

Sully's wasn't the only voice she heard. She heard her dad, telling her how important police work was. How brave people had to defend the helpless. To stick up for the little guy. How to put her head down when the going got tough, and how to keep pushing on.

Tessie, we have to do what's right. Even when it's hard.

Her mom didn't get it. Sully wouldn't get it. Not yet. But they would. As soon as Tess showed them how much like her dad she really was.

Chapter 34

"Hello, old friend," Tess whispered, sliding her bedroom window up as quietly as she could. She'd stuck her head into the hallway before she'd made her move, and she could hear her mother's voice, pitched low to keep Tess from hearing anything, which meant she was worried.

Good. That meant she'd called Sully or Miss Angel. If all went according to plan, Sully would be here once his shift ended to talk things out. Having Sully on hand would be important once Tess had the proof she needed. Things would move fast, and they could get dangerous.

So Tess could check back-up off the list.

She slung her bag across her shoulders and felt the weight settle comfortably, the binoculars banging against her leg in the same old place, the pepper spray knocking lightly against her back. She was ready.

Her father had taught Tess to climb in and out of her window using this tree so many times that each hand and foothold felt familiar and safe as she edged out of the window. True, he'd taught her for safety reasons. Should the house catch on fire or a wild bear enter their home, Tess would be ready. She wondered briefly if he had ever considered what someone like Tess might one day use that tree for, but then she was on the ground and putting phase two into motion.

And phase two was...what exactly? Tess hugged the house and considered her options. She could cross the street and approach the Brooklyn house directly, but that wouldn't work. For one, her mother would see her as she cut through the yard to the sidewalk. For another, one didn't just stroll right up to a house under surveillance. Or did one?

Tess thought that one through. If the keyword was *stroll,* then maybe that was exactly what she should do. This was a quiet, tree-lined neighborhood with a school at one end and a park at the other. People were constantly walking up and down the sidewalks of their neighborhood: mail carriers, speed walkers, families catching the sunshine. What was one more, innocuous person?

The gate to Mrs. Sandoval's backyard was to her right, so Tess crept backward until she felt confident that her mom wouldn't see her if she happened to glance outside, then popped the lock on the gate and ducked through. Mrs. Sandoval's backyard was park-like, with ancient weeping willows, trellises of hanging flowers, and an expansive coy pond winding through a small walking path.

Mrs. Sandoval hired a landscaping team to keep her backyard pristine, and one of her favorite activities was to stroll the grounds, telling Tess tall tales of her life and admiring the butterflies and hummingbirds. That meant Tess knew the terrain pretty well. She also knew Mrs. Sandoval wouldn't mind Tess using her property in her schemes. She had a taste for adventure and intrigue too, and Tess couldn't wait to tell her about breaking this case wide open.

There was a gate at the back of Mrs. Sandoval's yard, a place where maintenance could enter without coming through the smaller front gate, and Tess slipped quietly through. The gate deposited her on the opposite side of the block, and she slipped her phone out of her pocket and held it up like she was taking pictures.

If anyone asked, she could say she was working on an art project for school. Or maybe the never-ending life science project she really did need to finish. Tess pressed record and started walking.

The sidewalk was cracked and pitted in some areas as she made her way around the block. Hers was an older neighborhood, though painstakingly maintained by the retirees and young families that made up the community. Tess had always felt safe here but as she wandered closer to the fenced-in backyard of her target, she felt a decided chill slide down her back. It was just...darker here.

The grass that lined the area between the fence and the sidewalk wasn't exactly unkempt, but there was an air of neglect in the uneven growth. No flowers dotted the meager landscaping and weeds poked out here and there. The fence itself was in good condition, for the most part.

It could stand a good cleaning and a couple of the slats in the wood were bowed, but there were no obvious holes where, say, an enterprising young sleuth could squeeze through unseen.

That was unfortunate, and Tess took a moment to drop down and tie her shoe so she could get a better look. The back of the fence stretched for another fifty feet before turning and while she'd still have cover on the side of the house, she'd rather approach from the back and take no chances. There were currently no walkers on this section of the street, and the sidewalk here faced an empty lot.

Tess glanced around, making sure there weren't any nosy neighbors who might report her odd behavior to her mother and switched to her other shoe. This was why you always wore sneakers to a stakeout. They provided a cover story and were easy to run in should the need arise.

There. Tess spotted a low spot in the yard near one of the bowed planks. Several rocks had been strategically placed to close any holes, but Tess could see a small pocket of light beneath. She stayed low and crept over to the fence, tugging on the rock cover one by one until she cleared the hole.

It wasn't half-bad. There was no way her bag would fit, too - Tess was petite, but it would still be a tight squeeze for her. Tess peered under the hole, but she couldn't see enough of the yard to verify if anyone was back there or not. She hadn't heard anything as she'd cleared the rock so, taking a deep breath, she swung her bag over the fence and tensed as it hit the ground on the other side, waiting for something to happen.

To Tess, the sound of the bag hitting the ground was deafening but in reality, any noise it made was swallowed by traffic a few blocks over and birds singing in the nearby trees. The sound was only prominent to Tess, whose adrenaline was coursing in time with her rapidly beating heart.

Okay, then. Now or never. Tess popped her neck and swung her arms a few times. She could do this. She could. Grabbing the bottom of the fence, Tess stopped thinking and squirmed her way under.

Chapter 35

The grass was slick, which helped as Tess slid on her back beneath the fence. Or tried to. Her jacket snagged on the rough ends of the boards as she tried to wiggle her way under. Great. Tess paused for a moment before shimmying out of the jacket and leaving it behind. If she were very lucky, she'd be able to retrieve it as she escaped back the way she'd come.

She crouched for a moment inside the fence, glancing around to make sure she was alone before she picked herself up and slapped at the grass, mud, and wet that accumulated during her entry. Ah, the glamorous life of an investigator.

As she rubbed her hands down the legs of her jeans, she took stock of her situation. She was alone in a backyard she had decidedly *not* entered illegally. She had broken no locks and there were no signs posted warning against intrusion. By the letter of the law, she was good.

It was darker than she'd expected back here, especially with no trees in the backyard. The house rose three stories and blocked the sun, casting a pall over everything around her. Tess grabbed her bag and swung it back around her shoulders as she crept along the edge of the fence, keeping to the shadows as much as she could.

This was an older home on the edges of an aging neighborhood - historic, her mother called it - so the septic tank parked in the middle of the yard was no huge surprise. The tank looked ancient, with rusting legs and a hood that hadn't been checked in years.

There was a pile of dirt across from the tank, tucked up against the far corner of the fence, the recent excavation acting as further proof of the disrepair. An obvious place to bury unwanted bodies.

Tess's shoe landed on something soft, and she froze. It didn't move, which was encouraging, but that wasn't grass or mud. She looked down slowly and exhaled in relief. It was just an old toy. A doll, though it looked like it had seen better days. Her red hair was parted down the middle and ended in braids over her shoulders. One arm was hanging by a thread and the soft blue of her apron was dingy and stained with mud, rust, and who knew what else.

Tess tucked it into her back pocket, another treasure she could return to Janie. Weather had already laid its hand on the doll, but it could be washed. Most things could. At least Tess had gotten to it before any animals. If a dog got its paws on the little doll, it would-

Tess stopped, a very obvious but terrifying thought occurring. A dog. Did the killers have a dog?

She would have smacked the heel of her hand against her forehead if she wasn't trying to be stealthy. A dog! Rookie mistake. Tess had never even considered there might be a dog back here but if there was, she was in so much trouble.

Tess hesitated as she thought. She had never seen either man with a pet of any kind, which had to be a good sign. If there were a dog, surely Tess would have seen evidence. The men would need to let it out at some point, right?

It was too late to do anything about the possibility now, so Tess squared her shoulders and hoped for the best. Ninety percent of an investigation was preparation. The other ten percent was luck. Maybe hers would hold.

As Tess approached the back of the house, she considered her options. There was a sliding glass door, but Tess didn't like the look of it. There was a crack running diagonally from top to bottom, and she was pretty sure one good breeze could shatter it.

The entire thing was covered by something dark on the other side. A curtain or a piece of cardboard, maybe? It didn't look sturdy, but it did make it impossible to see if anyone was in that part of the house.

No, thank you.

The cellar door, on the other hand, looked doable. Tess took a breath and left the relative safety of the fence line, creeping gingerly towards the old wooden door set into a small hill in the ground beside the cracked and pitted cement patio. It was ancient, just like the septic tank, but that worked for her.

Tess examined the padlock, noting the loose screws and rotting boards holding it in place. What she really needed was...Tess looked around the yard. There. She ducked her head so anyone in the house who happened to be looking wouldn't see and scampered across the yard to the pile of freshly turned dirt beside the tank.

The edges of the rock were sharp and jagged, and she wrapped the end of her sleeve around her hand before she tugged it out of the dirt. This would do nicely.

The wood beneath the lock splintered easily after two quick blows from the rock, and Tess tossed it down in satisfaction, dusting her hands on her jeans. Television made this look so hard, but she didn't see what the big deal was.

Okay, yes - she had now technically *broken*. And she was getting ready to *enter*. But it was in the name of justice. The greater good. Surely her dad would understand. Sometimes, you do what you have to do to get to the truth.

The creaking of the cellar door was just the world's agreement with her assessment of the situation. The soft thud it made as she eased it shut behind her was just the icing on the cake. The cherry on top.

The toll of the bell. The closing of the casket.

She was in.

Chapter 36

Darkness wrapped around Tess in a suffocating choke hold as the door of the cellar settled shut behind her, and she had the uncomfortable vision of being sealed into a coffin. It was a decidedly disorienting feeling and if Tess's hands trembled slightly as she fumbled for the flashlight app on her phone, who could blame her?

The weak light from her phone dispelled enough of the doom and gloom that Tess could pretend she wasn't buried six feet underground, though she realized that wasn't far from the truth.

The entrance of the cellar was at least that far above her head now, and the walls were much closer than she would have thought. Didn't they use cellars to store preserves and potatoes in ye olden days? This was decidedly too narrow for storage. It looked more like...

"A tunnel," Tess whispered, just to hear a sound other than her breathing. The walls of the tunnel were close together, not even five feet apart, and completely swallowed sounds from the outside. Tess stretched her arms out and could just scrape dirt on both sides with her fingertips.

It was obviously a passageway, but to where? How long had it been here and what might it have seen over the years? Could it be a forgotten stop on the Underground Railroad? Had it curried bootleggers and their wares to the safety of the sea? What treasures did its hidden corners conceal?

All potentially valid questions, and not overly dramatic at all, but the thoughts were only a distraction from the inevitable. The next move was obvious, but taking the first step down that tunnel was harder than she thought.

That long, dark tunnel made of dirt. Which was really only a hole in the ground. What was keeping it from collapsing? Why hadn't it been on any of the floor plans Mark had conned out of the courthouse staff? Had it just been hanging out here, all these years, waiting for an intrepid young soul to bury alive?

Oh, that was a good one. She needed to remember that phrase for later. Because there would be a later. Of course there would. She wasn't in over her head in the least.

"Intrepid young soul," she murmured into the dark, the silence swallowing it whole, "intrepid young soul." She'd find a way to work that into her novel. It had impact. Heft. Weight.

But this wasn't a story, and she wasn't an author. Not right now. Right now, she was -

"An intrepid young soul."

Bold. Daring. Yes, much better. That one sounded more convincing. Tess took one step forward. And then another. There, that wasn't so bad. These walls had probably stood for hundreds of years. Thousands, maybe. The odds of them collapsing now, when she was simply walking through them, minding her own business, was probably slim to none.

The thought was less helpful than she would have liked.

Deeper into the tunnel Tess walked, holding her phone before her like a lantern. It was damp in the tunnel. Humid. But there was a chill to the air that belied the moisture, and Tess shakily wiped her free hand across her face. It came away clammy, so she reached out and touched the walls of the tunnels instead. Her fingers traced lightly across the dirt, snagging on a jagged rock here and there. It was oddly helpful, her fingers in the dirt of this endless, immortal tomb. It kept her grounded, somehow.

But it only seemed endless, as these things did. Tess counted off another minute in her head before the dirt beneath her feet began to slope gently uphill, and a small crack of light appeared in the distance in front of her.

She had to remind herself not to run; she still couldn't see well enough to see anything in front of her feet. But there was actual light at the end of the tunnel, and Tess felt like she wouldn't draw a full breath until she had kicked that light open and let it spill into the oppressive blackness around her.

It was a door, as it turned out. An old, wooden door, roughly the same age as the cellar door she had come through. It was a single door set into a rough frame embedded in the dirt walls, and light spilled weakly beneath the crack at the bottom.

Now that the light was within reach, Tess had the good sense to consider the situation in front of her. Wherever this door led was likely to be what Tess was looking for. Bad guys kept nefarious secrets in cellars and basements.

It was Bad Guy 101. And this basement had a backdoor entrance and exit that was hidden from view of the main house, which didn't exactly scream nice and normal. So she couldn't just open it. Could she?

No. Tess took a deep breath to calm herself and knelt quietly in the dark, pressing her face to the dirt and peering as far into the crack as she could. The weak light was almost blinding in the darkness around her and it took a moment to blink the tears away. But once she did, Tess could see...

Very little. Unfortunate, but not world-ending. Tess shifted her head and closed her eyes, pressing her ear against the crack instead. Nothing. No shoes scuffing the rough concrete, no sounds of breathing or life whatsoever. No rafters rattled, no floorboards creaked. Floorboards always creaked when bad guys were around.

Tess popped back to her feet and dusted her hands against her jeans. Which were also covered in dirt, so it did very little good. The fact was, she couldn't tell if anyone was on the other side of the door or not. She couldn't see or hear anyone, but that didn't mean they weren't there.

What does your gut tell you, Tessie?

Her dad was right, of course. Something was wrong in this house. She knew it. She'd come this far, how could she not follow through?

Tessa Lynn McGee, what are you doing in a stranger's house? You know better than this!

Oh, that was a new one. Tess paused, just for a moment. Not that her mother's voice in her head was necessarily wrong.

She had broken a lock and willfully entered the residence of men she believed to be murderers. Even if she didn't see through their evil schemes, a young girl entering an unknown home was just plain stupid.

Tess knew that, she really did, and she looked back to the door, hesitating. Her mom had also said the men who lived here hadn't killed her dad, but she was wrong about that.

Tess's gut knew it. So if her mom was wrong then, what's to say she wasn't wrong now?

No, she had to finish it. She wouldn't be able to rest until she did.

The door creaked open slowly under Tess's hand and she watched as if from afar. The world felt hazy, with a slow and dreamy quality that Tess wasn't used to, and her breath caught.

Had the moment finally come? Had justice finally arrived to claim its deserving victims and release her from the torment of this past year? Had the door really opened as loudly as it sounded, or was that just Tess's heart pounding in her ears?

She froze, waiting for some kind of reaction but...nothing. That was good, right? Taking a deep breath, Tess stepped into the room.

And realized she wasn't alone.

Not at all.

They hadn't made a single sound that Tess could hear from the other side of the door, not a cough or sniffle, not a creak of bed springs or a rattle of chains, and Tess's disjointed mind wondered how that could be. How could so many people be so quiet? It wasn't natural.

There were girls everywhere. Cages and cages of them. Cages against the walls, with tiny bodies crammed inside. Small cots with girls handcuffed to the frames. Buckets of grimy water were placed haphazardly around the room, the smell of filth, waste, and decay caking the walls.

And Tess just stood there, wondering how they could be so quiet.

The girls didn't move or react to Tess's presence. They simply stared back at her with empty, emotionless eyes. Silent, without so much as a rustle of the worn rags covering their thin bodies. Eighteen girls crammed into the small space below the stairs, and not a single sound among them.

Her phone slipped loosely from her fingers as the fog cleared and Tess started to understand what she was seeing. And how much worse it was than she had thought. Was this it? Was this why her dad had been killed? Had he stumbled onto the human traffickers across the street and been killed for it?

After what must have only been a moment but felt like time immemorial, Tess forced herself past the shock and stepped forward. It was a slow, tentative step, but she did it. Most of the girls looked younger than she was, maybe ten or eleven. Only two looked close to her age, and she stepped up to the cage holding the one closest to the door.

The girl was slumped against the bars holding her inside, legs pulled in tight to keep from crowding the younger girls in the cage with her. Her head was resting against the metal and the only part of her that moved were her eyes, which tracked Tess's movements like a caged cat, wary and haunted.

"My name is Tess," Tess whispered. Well, that was stupid. Clearly, this girl didn't care what Tess's name was. "I...I'm going to get you out of here, okay?"

Still nothing. She was pretty sure the girl heard her, but she didn't react to Tess's words at all. Only her eyes gave Tess any hope at all.

"How long have you been here? What are these men doing to you?" Tess tried again. She gestured around her but didn't break eye contact with the girl. She didn't want to lose what little connection she had.

Again, the girl didn't react. Except, there. Right there. One of her eyebrows lifted slightly, as though to say, *You know what's happening here.* And Tess did. It was one of the few things her dad rarely talked with her about, but she understood what she was seeing.

There was only one thing it could be. Only one reason why there were almost twenty little girls locked in cages in the basement of a rental house that had no record of recent renters.

Tess needed help. Right now. In exactly five seconds, everything she thought she knew had changed. These were bad men, very bad men. She had known that. She had watched them, gathering suspicions and evidence, and accused them of murdering her father. But her mother had been right. These men hadn't killed her father.

In a flash, she saw the last two years of her father's life play out before her eyes like one of the old black-and-white films they loved. The big hero who came home from work to swing Tess around the living room, to play catch with her in the backyard. To teach her the fine art of investigation. She saw the appointments and hospital visits, the treatments, and the weight loss. The wheelchair, the respirator. The cemetery.

No, these men hadn't killed her father. They were just trafficking children instead.

Tess reached out and wrapped her fingers around the other girl's, where she was limply clutching the bars. She didn't pull away, but the fingers Tess clutched were chilled and lifeless.

"You're getting out of here," Tess promised. "I live across the street. My dad's a police detective." Tess swallowed. "He...he *was* a police detective. And his partner is on the way. I'll get help."

The other girl didn't react, but Tess liked to think her eyes sharpened, ever so slightly. There was fight in those eyes, and it lit the fire inside of Tess. She squeezed the girl's hand, and then both of them froze.

Floorboards do creak when bad guys are moving around, Tess realized, dust from the shabby wood above her head settling on the tip of her nose. She and the girl shared one more glance before the girl abruptly shoved Tess's hand away from her.

Go, she mouthed, and Tess didn't hesitate. She spun on her heel and crashed back through the door, still hanging open on its rusted hinges. The door squealed as Tess slammed against it and she could hear a lock being opened above her, but she didn't look back.

They were early.

It was the only thought Tess had. They never came home this early. What had changed?

Horace had seen her. Tess knew he had, but she hadn't thought it would change the timeline.

To be fair, she hadn't really thought about it at all.

Another rookie mistake.

The darkness of the tunnel didn't scare her any longer. No, the frightening thing was standing in the light, stark beneath a single, bare bulb. Girls in cages, girls chained to beds.

Murderers who weren't murderers, but who did other bad things. The sound of heavy footsteps stomping down the stairs behind her was lost as Tess burned rubber. She shot down that tunnel like her life depended on it which, as it turned out, it did.

It was a straight shot, so she didn't worry about trailing her hand along the wall to keep her going in the right direction. She pumped her arms and ran like she'd never run before, but it still felt like an eternity before she burst back into the open cellar.

Her heart pounded in her chest, but Tess didn't bother stopping. Now was not the time to wax poetic about the light at the end of the tunnel. That's how silly girls got killed in horror stories. But she did take one last look behind her as she flung the heavy cellar door open.

Which was why she ended up running head-first into the arms of the child trafficker waiting on the other side of the door.

Silly girls never learn.

Chapter 37

D r. Holland was remarkably sober for the time of night as he slid a copy of the investigator's interview with one Dr. Michael Connor Horowitz across the polished wood.

"I've got an autopsy to attend to yet this night," he said by way of explanation. "The young pup they hired to force me out is remarkably unreliable in his work ethic."

"Anything interesting I should know before I read it?"

"Oh, yes." The old medical examiner smiled as he stood. "I think you'll find it most enlightening. I certainly did."

His expectations went up.

If the interview was enough to win Dr. Holland's interest, it meant there was something here.

"Were you able to corroborate it?"

Dr. Holland snorted as he settled his hat on his head and folded his knee-length coat across his arm. "With the state of that body? Of course not. Had the good doctor not divulged his patient's secret, it would have gone with him to the grave."

He was already reading by the time the doctor made his exit.

And the truth of the case finally became clear.

• • • •

YEP, THIS ONE WAS PRETTY bad.

The bell curve by which she judged all of her hasty actions had just been shattered by the sheer stupidity of a child walking into the hidden lair of child traffickers.

Not murderers, though, she tried to tell herself. At least not that she could see. That was something. But *something* wasn't going to get her out of the jam she'd dropped herself into this time.

Tess shot a glance at the two men huddled at the base of the stairs and gave a sharp pull against the plastic zip-tie they'd used to secure her to one of the water pipes running from the first floor. It was hot and Tess was careful not to let her wrist bounce back against it as the cuff held firm.

She'd learned that lesson the hard way, the back of her wrist blistered from her first attempt at testing the strength of her bonds. The pipe itself moved, just a bit, but Tess couldn't see any way to use that. If she found herself with enough time to pull as hard and as loudly as she wanted and she managed to dislodge the pipe, the very real possibility of drenching herself in boiling water was a little off-putting.

That, and putting the other girls around her in danger. But she suspected the men would notice and be on her before she could do any real damage.

So now what? Tess's imagination was busy spinning a story she didn't want to think about so instead, she focused on what she could hear and see.

Gather as much intel as you can, Tessie. That's the first step.
Right. Intel.

Tess was cuffed in a corner of the basement, which meant she had a pretty good view of the entire room without needing to move her head much. The less she moved, the less attention she drew, so that was a good thing.

There were no other girls restrained near her - also a good thing. The nearest rack of pre-teens was ten feet away, secured to a post driven between the dirt floor of the basement and the rough wooden planks overhead.

From what Tess could see, the post was driven too far into the ground to hope to maneuver it out. There were five girls, wrists zip-tied to the post, who looked to be anywhere between the ages of nine and sixteen.

The wall to Tess's left had a long, flimsy metal cot secured by metal bolts, and three more girls were huddled there. These girls looked even younger, if possible.

The youngest couldn't have been six. Tess bit her lip, trying to repress the disgust rising in her throat. She was an emotional chucker-upper, which was so much worse than an emotional crier. But now was not the time. She could puke later. Right now, she had work to do.

The wall where the three girls were huddled would be the north wall, facing the backyard Tess had come in through. Not exactly useful information, but no intel was bad intel.

And hey, right there beside the beds was a stack of office boxes, the exact boxes she'd seen Horace carrying back and forth each evening. Some were empty, but others were full. Of frilly dresses, hair ribbons, and costume jewelry.

Glossy, sparkly eye shadow and blush. Cheap frosting for the precious cargo being shipped out like black-market organs.

But what was worse were the dolls and stuffed animals lining the walls opposite the girls. Each well-loved, an obvious reminder of home being used to torture instead of comfort.

The dirtbags.

Tess shook her head, trying to stay focused. Rage could be useful, but it could also blind. And she didn't need any more handicaps than she already had.

A set of bunk beds along the south wall contained girls on two levels. The girls on the top were lying as flat as possible, probably in an effort to disappear. The girls on the bottom bunks, though - something was wrong with them.

They were also lying down but instead of being stretched as flat as possible or huddled into balls for protection, they almost looked to be lounging. Arms hanging off the bed or tossed over their heads, mouths open, eyes half-mast. None moving.

Tess's dad had taught her the signs often enough, despite her mother's protests that she was too young. These girls had been heavily drugged. In different circumstances, Tess might have assumed they were the troublemakers. Determined to get away, to cause as much trouble for their captors as possible, these girls were under lock and key because they were a threat.

But Tess could also see the new dresses, some still creased from the hanger, the washed faces and combed hair. These girls weren't a threat. They were simply...next.

A soft scuffing sound to Tess's right got her attention and she glanced at the older girl, the one she'd come face-to-face with when she'd first broken into the basement.

They made eye contact, and the look in the other girl's eyes confirmed Tess's fears. These girls were likely either up for auction or on the next shipment. Tess squeezed her eyes shut briefly. She so hoped whoever was buying from this filthy marketplace didn't prefer to pick up their merchandise in person.

Focus, Tess, she scolded herself harshly. Time, it was a wasting, and Tess knew she didn't have all day. Oh, that she had tried to recruit Ben or Mark to come with her on this foolhardy adventure. Or that she had left her mother a note explaining where she'd gone. The thought of her mother shook Tess harder than her actual predicament. What would her mother do if Tess simply...disappeared?

No one had believed Tess when she'd accused the neighbors of being killers. Sure, she had been wrong about that, but she had been spot-on about the nefarious intentions. After her dad, well, her mom was trying but she still didn't smile like she used to. She was still a few pounds too thin. She didn't go to PTA meetings and school mom gatherings like she did...before.

Tess knew her mom hadn't quite recovered, but she didn't know why she was only now realizing that healing was a process. Her mother wasn't listless. She was healing. But what would happen to her progress if she suffered another loss so soon?

If only Tess hadn't been determined, as Mark had so helpfully pointed out, to do it all on her own. It was one of the things her dad loved most about her, Tess's single-minded determination once she settled on something. And she had doubled down on the scummy new neighbors being the cause of the McGee family woes. Her menfolk had turned on her, and Tess had been determined to prove them all wrong.

Turns out, Horace and Jasper hadn't been the cause of their family's woes. Not yet, anyway. But if she didn't figure something out fast, her mother would have another reason to cry. So it was time to get creative.

Basement with two exits: one up the stairs and into the light of day, the other through a hidden cellar in the backyard. Four cement walls, a dirt floor of unknown origin. Hot water pipes that looked like they should snap like a twig but didn't.

Eighteen unknown girls in various states of consciousness and disrepair. And Tess cuffed to a rusted pipe. Not great, admittedly. But there had to be something there. There had to be some-

Jasper shoved Horace a few feet back against the stairs, and they both turned her way, staring at her for a beat too long. Well, now that she had their attention...Tess took a deep breath and energized full thrusters. Throttle up and pzazz engaged...in three...two...one...

"Hey, Tweedledee and Tweedledum!" Tess sank back against the corner joists like she didn't have a care in the world. "What's the plan here?"

The trembling of her cuff against the metal pipe wasn't exactly what she was going for, but maybe they wouldn't notice. "Brain trust that you are, I'm guessing you haven't thought this through."

Jasper bristled. "I'd watch that mouth if I were you, sweetheart," he sneered. "You're not exactly in a position to mock."

Tess yanked on her cuff, rattling the metal of the pipe even louder. "Oh, I don't know," she mused. "If ever there were people to mock, you seem like the ones."

Horace shook his head behind his partner. He almost looked...sad, somehow. Like he wasn't one of the reasons she was in this mess and wished they didn't have to do what they were going to do. Tess had no sympathy. He didn't deserve to feel regret.

Jasper took another step closer, kicking her phone towards her as he did. "That what you were after, little girl?" he asked, a grin on his face. "Think that phone is going to save you?"

The phone had skittered to a stop just outside of Tess's reach, and she didn't pay it any attention. Jasper was right, he just didn't know it - that phone *was* going to save her. It was going to save them all. Just not in any immediate way.

Instead, Tess nodded in the general direction of the room. "This looks like quite a slumber party," she said. "But I think we're all ready to go home."

Horace stepped forward this time, his long face and sad eyes setting her teeth on edge. "You'll all be going home soon enough," he said quietly. "Just not the home you'd prefer."

Tess licked her lips nervously. She needed them to be more specific, but she also didn't want them any closer to her than they already were. "Let me guess. You have new homes all lined up for us. Like puppies on Christmas day."

"For them, yes." Jasper had a look on his face that turned Tess's stomach. "Eventually. But you, little girl, you've been a problem for long enough."

If you can be anything, Tessie, be a problem.

It was something her dad used to say to her all the time. Be bold, cause a fuss. Don't go quietly. It was something of a gift, and hearing those words again gave her strength she didn't know she had. She could feel him with her. He was right beside her. He would-

"See, we know who you are," Horace interrupted quietly. "You're not just some neighborhood girl, in the wrong place at the wrong time. You're a cub."

Tess knew the term, and she narrowed her eyes.

"Yeah, we know who you are," Jasper took over. "You're daddy was a cop, isn't that right? But he's not here anymore, is he?"

Tess bit her lip to keep from snapping back. Smart. She needed to be smart. And smart girls didn't let child traffickers goad them into saying something that would make the situation worse.

"He died, didn't he?" Jasper leered over her, the smell of mold and tobacco pushing her gag reflex to the limit. "An old man in a wheelchair who couldn't even breathe by himself in the end. He couldn't protect you then, and he sure can't protect you now."

An old man in a wheelchair? That wasn't...but Tess had forgotten a lot of things over the last year that she was seeing in digital high-definition now.

Tess, sitting beside her father in a white, sterile room. A slick, plastic recliner, tubes snaking into his arms.

Tess's dad, his laugh a pale shadow of its former self, pointing a shaking finger at the bears frolicking in their habitat at the zoo, Tess riding shotgun in his wheelchair.

Tess, curled up beside her father watching their favorite movie, the sound of the ventilator where his voice should have been.

A big, white stone that read Loving Father, Loving Husband, Loving Servant *beneath the sound of a twelve-gun salute.*

"Knock it off." The sound of Horace's voice jolted Tess back to the present, and she gasped for breath as she tried to remember where she was. This was important. She was in danger. She had to make her dad proud. But, she had just seen...just remembered...he had been so sick...

Now wasn't the time. Now was the time to be brave. Focused.

She had to focus.

"She's just a kid," he went on. "You don't have to make this worse than it is."

"I know I don't have to," Jasper answered. "But I *want* to." He tilted his head to look at Tess, mocking her from five feet away. "I've been waiting, hoping, for a chance just like this. A chance to put you in your place."

Go get 'em, Tessie, her dad's voice prodded her on.

"Like you're putting these girls in their places?" she shot back. Part of her marveled at the lack of fear in her voice. She sounded strong. Brave. Just like her dad. "But I'm guessing you didn't just grab them off the street, did you?"

Tess realized she was right as she said it. In a small, close-knit town like theirs, alarms would have been raised if this many girls had gone missing. A war cry would have gone up if even one disappeared. These girls weren't local. They'd been brought in from somewhere else.

"What, just because you took them from somewhere else and shipped them here, you think no one will notice?"

"But no one did notice, did they?" Jasper grinned, nudging a barrel from against the wall with his foot and settling on it. He pulled something from his belt and started running it along his leg, lovingly stroking it back and forth. Back and forth.

A knife.

Horace sighed and shook his head, as though he knew better than to argue as Jasper waxed poetic "We took these little girls from their backyards, their schools. Their streets. No one said a word. We've been bringing girls to this basement, and other basements just like it, for months now. Do you know how easy it is to sell such small, invisible humans? All you need is the right storage space and a decent internet connection, and you can make a mint."

Back and forth.

One of the younger girls to Tess's right began to cry softly, and another tried to hush her. The girls were good at shrinking into the background, which Tess could only assume was a survival instinct. But there was a limit to what a person could take, and Tess was guessing every girl in this room had hit that line and then some.

"So, what?" she pushed on, ignoring the sounds and smell of terror around her. Ignoring the quiet shush of the knife gliding smoothly across the fabric of Jasper's pants. Back and forth. Back and forth.

Tess felt like she was the one terrorizing the captives now, making them listen to the plans these terrible men had for them. But she was on a roll, and she couldn't seem to stop.

"What now? Do you have a buyer from Egypt or Tanzania or Delaware looking for a four-foot blonde with wide eyes and a smile that lights up the room? Where exactly do you think you're going with this?" Tess gestured at the room around her, and Jasper scoffed.

"I have buyers lined up from anywhere you'd like," he sniffed. Horace had moved to the back of the room, seemingly resigned to let his partner spill all of their juicy secrets. After all, who exactly was she going to tell? "We aim to please."

Tess felt her stomach roil with disgust, and a girl across the room sniffed loudly. These poor girls, plucked from their homes. They probably had parents and siblings and friends who loved them, who missed them. Dads at home, worrying about their little girls.

Her dad would be worried right now. Tess had been trying to ignore the truth for as long as she could, but there was no denying it.

She was in trouble. Really big trouble. These weren't bad guys from one of her cheesy noir films. These were smugglers, traffickers. They would kill her before they let her ruin their business. Tess wouldn't swear to it, but death might be better than what these evil men had planned.

What good did it do to get them to talk when she couldn't do anything with it? What she needed was for them to leave. Her lock picks were zipped up in her backpack, leaning against the wall at Horace's feet, but maybe she could come up with something. She'd at least be able to talk to the other girls.

A floorboard creaked overhead, and Tess flinched. "You should be used to old houses, sugar," Jasper mocked. "Yours is no modern beauty."

Tess took offense. Her house was not old. It was...aged. And classic. It had character. A willow tree in the front yard and a trellis of roses across the door. The paint was peeling here and there, but that could be fixed. At least her house didn't have a basement with a dirt floor and a rusty septic system in the backyard. Why, she should -

The older girl across from Tess didn't move but her eyes slanted up like something had caught her attention and she was trying to look without actually looking.

If the girl didn't want to get caught, then Tess trusted it was for a good reason.

"What do you think will happen to you?" Tess asked, suddenly conversational. "You know, when you go to prison for trafficking little girls. I hear hardened lifers don't like that kind of thing."

Jasper scowled, and Tess felt a momentary flicker of satisfaction. She could annoy the rings off a raccoon. It was about time this half-baked villain wanna-be got with the program.

"You little brat," he spat, pushing himself to his feet. Quicker than Tess thought possible, he'd stepped right up to her and grabbed her chin in one meaty hand. "If you didn't have all these pretty curls, I'd put a round through your skull and bury you in the backyard." He pulled her face up and took a deep breath, inhaling the scent of her hair. "But redheads are in fashion this month."

In another world, this was the exact moment her dad would have burst in. He would have noticed she was missing, and he would have followed her trail. He would throw open the doors, rush the bad guys, and make some jaunty quip about how Tess had done all the hard work for him.

'Bout finished with these guys, Tessie? I could use a snack.

But instead of hearing a deep, perpetually amused baritone, she heard a polite southern voice, full of culture and class, floating down to them.

"Sir, I'd appreciate it if you'd remove your hands from my child."

Tess thought the sound of the shotgun being cocked only magnified the genteel sweetness in her mother's voice. "Before I do it for you."

Chapter 38

"**C**ome here, baby."

Angel's arms were warm and comforting, and Kate wanted nothing more than to sink into them and cry. But she gently disentangled herself from Angel's embrace because she knew if she started, she wouldn't be able to stop.

Kate had spent the last year wrapped in grief and guilt. As much as she wanted to stay shielded in the full armor of her loss, she had to do what Tess said. What Ian always said. She had to do what was hard.

"Where is she?" Sully asked, closing the door his wife had so brazenly flung open behind him softly. Sully was used to his wife's boldness by now, and he complemented it with his quiet thoughtfulness.

Husbands and wives *should* complement each other. They *should* pick up where the other left off. Something else Kate didn't have the reserves to think about today.

"Up in her room." Angel squeezed her arm before heading to the kitchen, and Kate had known her long enough to know some sort of baked good would be forthcoming. If Kate had anything in her kitchen to bake with. She honestly couldn't remember.

Sully nodded and Kate dropped limply onto the couch, but she couldn't relax enough to drop her head to the cushion behind her. Instead, she leaned forward, elbows on knees, rested her head on her balled-up fists, and closed her eyes. The couch shifted beneath her and then Sully's warm hand was squeezing the back of her neck. It was a brief touch, but it helped still her mind.

"Just start from the beginning," he recommended logically. Practically. So very Sully. So very unlike her husband.

The beginning. What was the beginning? Was it the day they brought Tess home from the hospital, Ian wearing the most ridiculous pink shirt with their baby's giant head screen-printed across the front? Or was it the day Ian showed up for Tess's kindergarten show-and-tell in full uniform, bullet-proof vest on proud display? He'd given the kids rides in his cruiser and it had been impossible to tell who was prouder, Ian or Tess. The grins on their faces staring at her from the frame across the room mocked her.

Was the beginning the first time Ian took Tess on a ride-along? Or maybe the hours they spent reading Agatha Christie novels and pouring over murder mystery games? Tess was writing a gumshoe noir, for Heaven's sake, and it was all Ian's fault.

The truth was, Tess idolized her father and her father adored her right back. Kate hadn't wanted to get between that, never worried that Ian wouldn't be there to foster that connection and keep Tess tethered to the ground. Though she should never have expected Ian to ground anyone. Kate had been her husband's tether and now, she would have to be that for their daughter as well. Which meant it was well past time to get her act together.

Kate had been cruising, auto-pilot fully engaged, and she knew it. Oh, she told herself she'd tried. She still made lasagna every Tuesday. They went to the local farmers' market on Saturdays and sat in the same pew on Sundays. Kate tried to smile, tried to keep the routine for Tess's sake, even if she couldn't bring herself to go to work or eat more than a bite or two at a time.

Kate knew Tess hadn't dealt with her father's death. She'd talked to Tess's therapist and the school counselor and both agreed it was best not to challenge Tess's narrative of the last months of Ian's life. Even though she'd pulled away from friends, she was practicing healthy coping mechanisms like writing and she was only skipping school periodically now. Keeping Tess in the same routine was supposed to make her feel safe and loved.

Well, the last hour of Kate's life had shot that theory right out of the water. How safe could Tess feel if she thought her father had been murdered? Murdered, of all things. And why hadn't Kate known that? How badly had Kate scared her that Tess wouldn't confide in her mother sooner? That Tess felt the need to protect her mother and not the other way around?

Well, no more of that nonsense. Kate took a deep breath and lifted her head. She hadn't married Ian because he was the strong one, after all.

"Tess believes the renters across the street murdered Ian." Kate kept her eyes locked on one of the many pictures across the room, of Ian sitting on his motorcycle, Tess gripping his back from behind. Both grinning like fools.

"The old Brooklyn house?" he asked without preamble, and Kate nodded into the silence. She felt the couch shift again as Sully got up and stepped to the window, looking across the street. "She's asked about it often enough."

The house in question was less than a block down the street, easily viewable from Tess's window but partially blocked from where they sat now. Still, he peered down the street, not seeming surprised in the least that Tess suspected murder instead of the chronic wasting disease they had all born witness to.

"She's been asking about the investigation into Ian's death," he finally said, having given the house a thorough once-over. "But why would she focus on these particular neighbors? Because they're new?"

Kate already knew the maintenance van that usually sat on the street outside the house was gone. Kate was still a cop's wife, even now, which meant she knew the signs and kept her eyes open. She had a daughter to protect, after all. But the neighbors hadn't killed her husband. Even the job hadn't killed her husband. Genetics had.

"You knew?" It made an odd sort of sense that Tess would trust her dad's partner with her theories before her mother, especially if she thought she was protecting Kate. Sully hadn't told her though, and that told Kate even more clearly that she needed to pull herself together.

"She's writing a novel, you know," Kate mumbled around her hands. "I thought it was a good thing. The counselor said it would help Tess deal with the loss, and that I shouldn't interrupt. Now I wonder what has been going on inside her head for the last year."

The couch dipped again, and Kate spun in the seat, folding her legs under her and meeting Sully head-on. Exactly like Tess had faced her only an hour ago. "How can she not remember the last year?"

Kate knew she would never be able to forget it. The symptoms had started innocently enough: muscle cramps and stiffness, twitching fingers, a bit of clumsiness now and again. Neither had worried too much at first. A nasal twinge and slurred speech had finally convinced him to check it out. Nothing but a virus, he'd assured her. But he'd go have it looked at, just in case. For Kate.

Two weeks later, even Ian's sunny disposition couldn't shield Kate from the truth. Amyotrophic lateral sclerosis. It was fatal, and it was fast. The disease was eating through his nervous system at an alarming rate, and the wheelchair hadn't been far behind.

If I have to go, at least I'll go like Lou Gehrig. One of the greats.

Kate's husband had always wanted to be *one of the greats.* One of the great athletes of their time. One of the greatest detectives, and the greatest father. The greatest husband. Ian could always find a bright spot, but Kate hadn't found it funny at all.

"Kids have a way of pushing the hard stuff away," Sully said simply. "We don't have that luxury."

Sully and Angel had been with them through it all. Sully and Ian had met at the academy and had been lifelong partners and friends. When Tess had gotten her first bike, Sully was there to take the training wheels off while Ian ran alongside.

When Tess had wanted a Sherlock Holmes cake for her fifth birthday, Angel hadn't blinked an eye. When Ian could no longer move from his bed to his chair and back, Sully was there to carry his partner wherever he needed to go. They had been right there with her. They had seen how rapidly, how completely, the disease had taken her husband.

"Six months," Kate whispered.

"I know."

Six months was all they'd had between the first symptom and the funeral. The doctors told her what a blessing it was. How patients with ALS could linger, immobile and vegetative but still aware, for years.

At the moment though, she just couldn't see the total destruction of her strong, energetic, enthusiastic husband as anything but a tragedy.

"She read to Ian. She went to treatment with him. She held on to his shoulders as he raced his wheelchair down the sidewalk. She sprawled on the bed with him so they could watch their movies over the sound of the respirator. She saw it all!"

Kate had never been sure that was the right decision. What would that do to Tess, to watch her father deteriorate before her eyes?

But how could she deprive her daughter of her beloved father when she wouldn't have him much longer? How could she deprive Ian of his daughter? In the end, she didn't need to struggle with the choice for long.

"Six months," she said again. This time though, she shook her head and pushed herself back on the couch. She could hear something clattering in the kitchen, so she guessed Angel had found something to work with. Or she'd come prepared.

She'd probably come prepared. Kate knew Angel, but Angel knew Kate, too.

"If she thinks the neighbors killed Ian, it's not just some fancy," Sully said, and the observation caught Kate off-guard.

"How can you say that?" Her confusion must have been clear because Sully held up his hands.

"I don't mean she's right," he assured her. "I just mean she's observant. She may be hiding from the memories, but she had to see something that set off alarms."

"What doesn't that girl see?" Kate muttered, lost in thought. Sully was right, and she knew it. Tess was imaginative, sure. But she was also whip-smart, and her father had made sure she knew how to pay attention to every detail. So what had Tess seen that had driven her to this assumption?

"Van just pulled up," Sully commented, and Kate looked over in confusion.

"They leave every day at 4:30 and are home between 3:00 and 6:30 the next morning. They've never come back this soon."

Sully's quiet laugh rumbled through the room, and a tiny piece of Kate's heart ached at the sound. Evening dinners with the Sullivans, weekend bonfires and late nights spent on the patio under the stars, Ian's tall tales, and Sully's deep laughter. It was hard to hear one without the other, and it was one more painful reminder that her husband, her brilliant, vivacious, life-loving husband, was gone, and she was alone.

"Tess isn't the only one who knows how to watch her surroundings," he commented.

"Please." Kate couldn't help smiling, despite the pain tearing through her chest. "I knew how to do that long before Ian came on the scene." She thought for a moment. "I rarely see the neighbors themselves. They're quiet and keep to themselves. They keep the place tidy, but they don't take pride in it."

"Mold growing on the siding, lawn ragged, nothing but weeds in the flowerbeds," Sully remarked. "A typical renter who doesn't plan to stay long."

"Or someone who doesn't want to be noticed one way or the other." Kate nodded, thinking. "The van's windows are too dark to see through, and they're taped up tight. The license is up-to-date. They keep odd hours, but nothing that couldn't be explained by overnight or contract work."

Kate stood, making her way to where Sully watched again from the window. Both men had just gotten out of the van and were unloading boxes from the cargo area. The boxes were small enough to carry, with a handhold on each side. Office boxes, with removable lids. These lids, however, seemed to be jammed onto boxes too full to let them settle completely.

"Clothes," Sully said, nodding to one of the men leaning down to replace a lid that had blown off in the breeze. "Boxes and boxes of clothes."

"In office boxes." It was weird, maybe. But that didn't explain Tess's obsession with them.

"Tess has a better view from her room." Kate realized as she said it that Tess would have been camped out on her window sill, binoculars in hand, watching every move these men made. If she thought they'd killed her father, she would have watched everything.

Kate headed for the stairs. She was calmer now that she'd had time to think it through. Now that Sully had pointed out the obvious. So why didn't she just ask her daughter? She could do that. She would have done that, a year ago. When they were a whole family and grief hadn't carved a hole in her heart where her husband used to live.

"Tess?" Kate knocked softly and when she heard no reply, pushed her way in. "Tess, can we talk about-"

Tess's window, the one pointed at the Brooklyn house, was open. Everything was exactly like Tess had left it this afternoon, except for her bag, which wasn't in its usual perch on the windowsill: notebook shoved under an old jacket on her desk, a picture of Tess and Ian lying face-down beside it.

Kate gently turned it over, thinking. Tess and Ian, perched together in the ugly plastic recliner at the treatment center, Ian hooked up to an infusion with an arm thrown around his daughter.

The picture had been upside-down, which meant Tess had turned it over. She couldn't stand to see her dad like that, and it broke Kate's heart a little bit more. Of course, Tess was hiding from the memories. How could she not?

Resolving to replace the picture with one of a healthy, strong Ian, Kate turned back around. Sully had stopped in the doorway and was looking towards the window. It was obvious that, while Tess's things might be in this room, she was not. But she hadn't come back down the stairs and Kate hadn't heard the door open, so how-

The gauzy curtains fluttered at the open window, mocking her. She took a step in that direction, but Sully's hand wrapped around her elbow.

"Katie."

She knew what that voice meant. It was the same voice her sergeant detective husband used when something was very wrong.

"Look."

Kate looked. Out the window. Across the street. To the fence wrapping around the neighboring yard. A tall fence meant to keep out onlookers.

A tall fence that might seem unbreachable to most, if not for the jacket tangled in the rough boards at the bottom, snagged half-beneath it.

Chapter 39

Kate simply stood, looking at the sleeve of canvas buried halfway beneath the dark fence, for just a moment. She knew what it meant. She understood what had happened. An upset Tess had come to her room where, left alone with her thoughts, a rampaging imagination and overpowering sense of justice had overruled her sanity.

Then, Kate's skinny troublemaker had shimmied down the tree outside her window as she had so many times before, book bag slung across her shoulders, and went to find her evidence.

After all, Tess would know their routine as well as Kate did. She would know they never came home before the night was over. She wouldn't expect them early.

We have to do what's right, even when it's hard.

Ian and Tess's voices echoed at the base of her skull, settling around a frozen heart that had just sparked a flame.

Sully had already vaulted down the stairs, and Kate could hear his rapid-fire conversation with Angel. Frantic. When was Sully ever frantic? But Kate knew why.

Sully was trapped by his badge. Tess had trespassed on the property illegally. Sully, as a law enforcement officer, could not do the same. He had witnessed no crime being committed, and he had no reason to suspect illegal activity. The best he could do was knock on the door and ask if either man had seen a red-headed terror breaking into their house.

Kate could also knock but unlike Sully, she had no badge to stop her. She could retrieve her child. And she would. She knew these people hadn't killed her husband. But she also knew, with the instincts only a cop, a mother, or both could possess, that the children's clothing and toys she'd seen in those boxes meant something bad. Something very bad. And she wasn't going to stand here and think it through or talk it out with Sully and Angel. She was going to get her daughter.

Kate turned, calmer than she'd ever been, and pushed open the door to her bedroom. She had buried Ian's service revolver with him, unable to stand the sight of it, but the shotgun Kate had been firing on the range when a young Ian McGee first wandered her way was still in the gun safe in the closet.

She popped the lock and pulled it out. It had been a while, but it still felt good in her hands. Double-action short barrel, Kate slid two shells into the casing, slamming them home through muscle memory more than conscious thought. Then she turned and walked down the stairs.

Angel, her face horrified, caught a glimpse of Kate as she walked to the front door, and Sully caught her by the elbow before she could open it.

"Katie!" he hissed. "You can't just walk over and blow the door off the hinges. We have to do this right!"

"You have to do it right," Kate replied, that same supernatural sense of calm flooding her veins. She and Sully locked eyes, both refusing to be the first to flinch. It reminded her, oddly, of the night Ian had died.

She'd known what was happening and had held his hand as he slipped away. She'd known with certainty that he was leaving her. And she felt the same now. Only instead of the creeping certainty of death, Kate knew what she was feeling now meant the opposite. That chilling certainty still flooded her bones but this time, she didn't have to sit aside and watch something precious slip from her hand. This time, she could do something about it.

Her child was in danger. And she was going to get her back.

Kate had never felt more awake in her life.

"Make your calls." Angel forced herself between them, putting her finger in Sully's chest. "Call the chief, the judge, whoever you need to call to get your warrant. But *watch her*," she said meaningfully. "Watch as a woman breaks into a home with a loaded weapon. *That* is your exigent circumstance, and you can follow her."

Kate was already gone. She'd walked out the front door the second Angel had separated them, and she could hear Sully cursing the day he'd introduced them. They were bad influences on each other.

Kate already knew the outcome of their stand-off, because Angel was right. Sully would do things the legal way so Kate could do things the right way. And maybe, between the three of them, they could get Tess out of that house.

Sully had seen what Kate had seen. She was sure he wouldn't tell Angel, because he wouldn't want to worry her even more, but those boxes had been filled with clothes and toys. They'd only caught a glimpse, but it was all they needed.

Little girls' clothing, stuffed animals, and baby dolls. The boxes didn't seem like inventory, they seemed like a convenient way to move necessary items that the public shouldn't see. They both knew what those things added up to, but they didn't have time to dwell on it.

If Tess was in that house, and Kate was very certain she was, they needed to get her out now.

Using whatever means necessary.

Chapter 40

Tess just stared, not entirely certain what she was looking at. It looked like her mother. It was dressed like her mother, and it sounded like her mother. But it was holding a double-barrel shotgun like it knew what to do with it, and that was most definitely not like her mother.

Horace and Jasper didn't much know what to make of the scene in front of them either, judging by the dumbfounded looks on their faces.

"How...did you get in?" Horace finally asked. He looked around like he expected to see someone else, or at least a ready explanation for what was happening.

"Door was open," Tess's mom replied in that sweet, southern drawl of hers. "And I won't ask again."

The gun never wavered from where it was trained on the flunky not gripping Tess's face as her mother calmly cocked the other hammer.

Tess and Jasper locked eyes for a moment, each seemingly as confused as the other, before Jasper's bad-guy instincts took over.

"You're in no position to make demands," he sneered, shaking Tess's face like a rag doll in his hand. "If you don't-"

Shot exploded from both barrels and Horace went down howling. Without hesitation, her mother chambered two more rounds and had Jasper in her sights before he had time to react.

"Like I said," her mother's voice was smooth as glass, as though she hadn't just left a man in bloody chunks on the floor, "I won't ask again."

Who was this woman, Tess wondered? Where was her distant, withdrawn, grieving mother, and who was this force of a woman who had replaced her? Calm, cool, collected. Unflappable.

Tess wanted to be just like her.

"You wouldn't dare," Jasper said, but even Tess could tell he wasn't sure. "You wouldn't shoot your own daughter."

"I would not," her mother agreed, and Tess felt just the tiniest bit of relief. She hadn't been sure either. "But I am an excellent shot and an indirect hit won't kill her."

Oh. Well, that didn't make Tess feel better at all. So she did what anyone in her situation would do. She took advantage of Jasper's momentary distraction and kicked him as hard as she could in the shin.

"Ahhh!" she yelled, grabbing her foot in both hands as soon as his fingers dropped away from her face. That was so much more painful than the movies made it look. And then Tess hit the floor.

Tess hit the floor and rolled, not because of any heroic, indwelling instinct for survival, but because she'd heard her mother's voice. At the moment, Tess hadn't had time to decipher what her mother said. But she *felt* it, and she knew what that tone meant.

She dropped and rolled, head slamming against the solid metal of the hot water pipe, just in time to avoid the buckshot that came exploding towards Jasper's midsection.

Tess felt a hand grab hers and she flinched, but then her mother was right beside her. "Get up, baby," she whispered. "We need to go."

Tess struggled to obey, but her head felt muddled. She needed to get up, but wasn't she already up? Why was her mom holding her hand? She wasn't a baby, after all. But it felt nice, so maybe she'd let her, just this once. And she was so tired, so maybe she would just stay right here and...

A loud bang sounded over her head followed by angry shouts, and Tess's mom stopped talking. Instead, Tess felt herself scooped up into arms she hadn't known could still hold her, and, tucked against her mother's chest, they hit the stairs hard.

Vaguely, Tess wondered how her mom had been able to pick her up, let alone carry her up the stairs. Tess was almost as big as she was.

"That's what mamas do, baby."

Had Tess spoken out loud? She hadn't meant to, but maybe-

"Tessa, I need you to look at me right now."

Tess felt her mom's hands on her face and realized she was on something soft. A couch, maybe? She opened her eyes, not sure when she'd closed them, to see her mother's face beside her own, peering at her with...not worry, but determination.

"Are you with me, baby?"

Tess nodded, but she was still confused. Her mother's hands on Tess's cheeks were cool, and they felt good. One hand moved to Tess's forehead and rested there for a moment. When they finally moved away, Tess shivered at the loss.

Someone moved behind her, and Sully's calm, deep voice sounded more frenzied than she'd ever heard. "Is she okay? Is she hurt?"

"Her head hit the pipe when she dropped," her mother replied, still as calm as the small creek that ran through Mrs. Sandoval's backyard as she firmly probed the aching place on the back of Tess's head. "Her wrist is burned and I did some damage getting the zip-tie off. She's going to need stitches, but I think it's just shock."

"Just shock," Sully murmured, and Tess could picture him pinching his eyes shut with one hand and shaking his head. "You McGee's are going to be the death of me. Every single one of you."

"Well that's alright, isn't it baby?" Her mother pressed her hand against Tess's forehead again. Later, Tess would understand that Kate was applying pressure to a bleeding head wound but whenever she looked back at this moment, she would just remember her mother's cool hands, the calm in her deep, brown eyes, and how she'd rode to Tess's rescue when she'd needed it the most.

Just like a real hero.

Chapter 41

Tess didn't complain much when her mom suggested they both sleep in Kate's bed that night. Sully had insisted on driving them to the hospital, and Miss Angel had made such a scene that the poor emergency nurse found them a room right away. Ten stitches in her hairline, some burn cream, and a metal splint and she was home.

Miss Angel had finally gone home after much weeping and gnashing of teeth and Sully was back across the street, helping run the scene. And Tess really, really didn't want to crawl into her own bed, where she'd see the red and blue of the parked police cars reflecting across her walls or hear the steady buzz of activity across the street.

Somehow, despite Tess's rigid refusal to complain or appear to be anything less than fine, her mother had understood. And against all odds, Tess slept soundly tucked against her warm side.

But daylight comes whether a girl is ready or not so when the bed dipped and Tess felt her mother settle beside her again, she rolled over and stifled a yawn.

"Sully's on his way over, sweetheart," her mom said. "He needs to get your statement now if you're up to it."

"Does he really need to do that, though?" Tess argued. "He has my phone. It caught the whole thing, right?"

"That was a stroke of luck," Kate agreed. "They have an audio recording of the whole ordeal. Not that I want to encourage this kind of behavior." Kate narrowed her eyes on her daughter until Tess nodded meekly. "But yes, you still have to give a personal account."

Tess knew how these things worked. She knew she couldn't argue her way out of it. Did Tess want to talk about last night? Definitely not. But she was Ian McGee's daughter, and she would not impede an investigation simply because she wanted to run away and hide. So she nodded instead.

"Can I brush my teeth first?"

"Oh, baby," her mom brushed the hair gently away from Tess's stitches and grimaced. "I don't think you have an option." Then she giggled and pulled Tess up by the hand. "Let's go, little one. The day is calling."

A quick ten minutes and Tess was thundering down the stairs, expecting to see Sully and hoping he came bearing a giant milkshake with her name on it, but the house was empty except for her mother. Well, her mother and someone she had not expected to see.

Kate McGee was looking at Tess like she'd just caught a raccoon in her kitchen - an awfully cute raccoon that was also crazy and unpredictable and that you knew better than to touch.

"Mark came to check on you. Isn't that *nice*?" The way her mother said "nice", as though it were a four-syllable word, sounded dire.

"Yes, ma'am," Tess said, trying for all the world to look like she meant it. "That sure is...nice." Tess ran a self-conscious hand through her hair, suddenly wishing she'd taken a few minutes to do more than brush her teeth and change her clothes. Sully wouldn't notice how she looked, after all. But Mark might.

And when did she start caring what Mark thought, anyway?

"Mark," her mother said, putting her hand on his shoulder and looking straight up to meet his eyes. "Would you care for some lemonade, sugar?"

"Oh, yes, ma'am," he agreed respectfully, and Kate smiled as she left them alone for a few minutes. It didn't take Mark long to break the silence.

"My mother taught me two things in this world," he said randomly, hands in pockets as he strolled casually around the living room like he was on a social call. "One, you call every lady *ma'am*, whether she wants you to or not. And two," he held up two fingers before pointing them right at Tess, "never say no to Miss Kate's homemade lemonade."

He wasn't wrong. Her mother did make the best lemonade. In fact, they'd served it at the wake of one Ian McGee, and not one time since. Why was her mother making lemonade at a time like this? Shouldn't she be shaken? Shouldn't she be weak with fear and might-have-beens? But she wasn't, Tess realized. She hadn't shown that timid, grieving woman once since last night. Instead, she was acting more like...well, like a cop's wife.

Mark's eyes drifted up to her hairline, and Tess fought the urge to cover the ugly bruising and swelling with her hand. Her good hand, not the burnt, broken one tucked shamefully behind her back. Kate and Miss Angel had pinned her hair away from her face last night so it wouldn't stick in the ointment the surgeon had smeared over the fresh stitches to keep them soft.

So the tangle of curls that would have usually covered the mess from prying eyes was, for once, out of the way and the consequences of her rash actions were on display for all to see.

But Mark simply raised an eyebrow. "Nice shiner, McGee. How's the other guy?"

This time, Tess did reach up and poke at the swelling that was taking her eye. The doctor had warned her the bruising would probably spread, but she hadn't taken the time to glance in the mirror before she'd left her bedroom.

"A bloody pile of meat, last I saw." Though she'd had no part in how it had ended, it still gave her pleasure to think of her mother, shotgun in hand, calmly blowing a hole in the men threatening her daughter. "I take it you heard?"

Mark was wandering around the living room, checking out the pictures on the mantle as though he hadn't already seen them. "The whole neighborhood heard. A SWAT team storms the streets and you just know Tess McGee is up to no good."

Tess couldn't help but smile at that. It did seem like the right conclusion to draw. When Tess didn't say anything, Mark shoved both hands back into his pockets and sauntered back towards her. "You look like you just took a hit from the number two high school tackle in Louisiana. And you still look great, by the way."

Tess's mouth dropped open of its own accord. "What? I never- I don't care what I look-"

"You did and you do. You've got a terrible game face, kid. I can always tell what you're thinking."

Well, what could she say to that? Thanks, I guess? At least I'm alive?

Tess dropped into the armchair by the window, the big, worn-out, gnarled thing she'd loved since she was old enough to sit in it, and curled her knees into her chest.

"I am alive, you know." Her fingers were picking at the fraying patches at her knees. "There were a lot of other girls in that room. And I don't know how many came before them."

"Yeah." Mark sat down too, but he didn't say anything else, and Tess found it quite nice. She closed her eyes and leaned her head against the back of the chair, angling so the watery sun could shine on her face for a few minutes.

One of the worst pieces of information to come to light in the last twenty-four hours was the excavation site in the backyard. Tess had noted the old septic tank and the overturned earth nearby as she'd made her way through the backyard.

She hadn't considered that there were only two reasons to dig in backyards: to dig something up or to bury something else. In this case, the freshness of the earth had set off alarms for the investigators, and a team of forensic specialists had been dispatched to recover the bodies.

Tess's mind was eventually drawn back to the room by the rustling of pages. She opened her eyes and looked at Mark. "What's that?"

"What's what?" he asked, and Tess pointed.

"That book. What are you looking at?"

"You're asking me?" Mark held it up. "It was on your coffee table."

Tess peered in his direction at the book he was holding. It was slim, not even a book at all. More like a plastic folder with spiral binding around the edges. Laminated. Tess launched herself at Mark and he jerked back, but Tess landed heavily on the couch next to him and he was trapped. She had the folder in her hands before he could pull it back.

"Ahhh! You have two black eyes, a broken wrist, and a head wound. Would you be careful, for once!" he exclaimed, gripping his chest like he was about to have a heart attack."

"Aren't you a quarterback?" Tess said idly, opening the book. "Don't people throw themselves bodily at you every week? It's pictures of girls." That much was obvious, but Tess felt it needed to be said. "It's just...girls." Then something caught her eye. "Wait. I know her!"

It was the girl from the Brooklyn house. The little girl that lived there with Horace and Jasper. Janie Doe, in the flesh.

In all the chaos of the last day, Tess had completely forgotten about her. "Mom. Mom. MOM!"

There was a clattering in the kitchen, what sounded like glass breaking, and Kate McGee shot through the entryway like an arrow.

"What is it? What's wrong?"

"What is this?" Tess held up the folder, and her mother's eyes went from terrified to murderous in a second flat.

"Tessa Lynn McGee." Tess felt Mark flinch beside her at the dreaded use of her middle name, which was never a good sign in a southern mother's mouth. "Less than twenty-four hours ago, you were kidnapped by traffickers and killers. The next time you bellow like your life is on the line, it better well be."

"Yes, ma'am." Tess tried to look contrite, apologetic, and innocent, but her mother knew better, and Tess heard her sigh.

"Well, what is it?"

Tess looked back up, grinning. "What is this?" She held up the folder again, and Tess's mom wrinkled her nose.

"Gracious, I shouldn't have left that out. You kids weren't supposed to see that."

"What?" Tess asked. "But why-"

"Oh, baby. These are some of the victims that have been identified. You weren't supposed to see it, but Sully brought it by." Her mother seemed distraught that Tess had found it. "I wanted to know how many they've found so far."

Now it was Tess's turn to wrinkle her nose. She looked back down at the folder, open to one of the last pages. That didn't make any sense.

"No, I mean, who is *this*." She pointed at the girl on the page. A girl with long, mousy brown hair and pale skin. She had a smattering of freckles across her nose and eyes that could be blue, green, or gray, depending on her mood and what she wore. She didn't look quite as washed out as when Tess had seen her before, but the pictures didn't lie. This was her.

"Who is *this*?" Tess asked. "Did they find her in the basement?" Tess was certain she would have noticed this girl she'd been trying so hard to identify but then again, a lot had been going on. If the girl had been quiet or trying to stay invisible, Tess may have missed her.

Again, her mom hesitated. Tess had seen her mom prepare to give bad news too often to ignore the signs, but what bad news could there be? She'd found her.

"That's Mary Beth Dobbins. She was six when she was kidnapped from Anacostia four years ago."

Four years ago? Tess couldn't believe that. The child she'd seen, the Mary Beth Dobbins Tess had spotted around the house for the last few weeks, was the same age as the girl in this picture. She hadn't aged a day.

"The police believe she may have been one of the first children kidnapped. I'm sorry, baby, but she didn't make it."

Didn't make it? What-

"She was one of the first bodies exhumed from the dig site."

Chapter 42

I'm sorry, baby, but she didn't make it.

The words rattled around inside Tess's head, but they didn't make sense. She didn't make it? Her body had been exhumed from the backyard?

After all this time, the girl she'd been so concerned about, the girl she'd tried to befriend, the girl named Mary Beth Dobbins, had been identified... after being dead four years?

It just didn't make any sense. Tess had seen her repeatedly in the weeks since the men had moved in. There was no way that timeline added up.

Tess supposed that after four years of being buried, some of that time spent beneath a septic system, it might be hard to properly identify someone, especially so quickly. The body they'd found and identified as Mary Beth Dobbins had to belong to someone else.

One of the other girls in this book, or perhaps not. There would be no way to know if the duo had killed before. Someone had found a missing girl that resembled the body and jumped to an incorrect conclusion. That was the only thing that made sense.

Tess was aware of her mother, staring intently at her, probably trying to judge if Tess was finally going to splinter or if her head wound was worse than suspected. And she could feel Mark's eyes boring into her, waiting for her to argue the fact.

It was clear he knew who this girl was and was waiting for Tess to make a scene or, at the very least, make her case. That wasn't necessary, though. Tess didn't feel like making a scene. Instead, she just wanted a little air.

"Do you mind if I go back to my room?" Tess asked her mother. "Mark brought my homework, and I should get started."

"Sure, baby," her mom said, still looking worried though she tried to lighten the mood. "Make sure you don't go shimmying out any windows this time."

Tess forced a smile for her mother's sake as she grabbed Mark by the collar of his t-shirt and tugged. "Come on," she said. "You can help."

By the time they made it to Tess's room and she'd shut the door as gently as she could to help alleviate her mother's worry, Mark's phone was in his hand.

"Who are you texting?" Tess demanded. Where had she put her backpack? That's what she needed right now.

"Ben, obviously," Mark said, slipping his phone back into a pocket. "He'll be here in a minute."

"He will?"

There. Sully had returned it to the house while Tess had been at the hospital and she'd kicked it beneath her bed, not ready to look at it yet. Poor bag. It had been terribly mistreated in the last twenty-four hours.

First by Jasper, who'd tossed it thoughtlessly against one of the dank basement walls as he gloated over a restrained Tess, and then by its owner, who'd dragged it into the lair of child traffickers and later took her anger out on it.

Tess could just make out the strap, half-buried beneath a pile of laundry she should toss in the hamper.

"Sorry, bag," Tess whispered while she was still shoulder-deep beneath the bed where Mark couldn't hear her. "You didn't deserve it."

She dropped the bag on her bed and started digging. She knew it was in here somewhere.

"What are we? Animals?" Mark asked, pushing a pile of shoes and sweatshirts to the middle of the bed so he could sit. "I am a teenage boy and I keep house better than this. What are you looking for and also, I'm pretty sure I can guess why you can't find it."

A book tumbled to the floor when Mark shoved her pillow back, and he crushed a bag of half-eaten chips when he propped his back up against the headboard. Embarrassing, but Tess was too preoccupied to feel shame for her slovenly ways at the moment.

The door to her room pushed open, and Ben poked his head in. "I was already on my way. My mom wanted me to bring you these." Ben held out a pan of something that smelled like more chocolate than she should probably have in a moment of fevered frenzy. "What are you looking for?"

Ben's question was meant for Tess, but his eyes strayed to Mark and Tess could almost imagine the silent conversation between them: *Nervous breakdown? Yeah, started a few minutes ago. Think she'll cry? No, but she might hit us. Dude. Bro. Guy hug.*

Tess wasn't sure how guys talked when she wasn't around, but it was probably something like that.

"The bunny," she muttered. Where had she put it? Under her math book? Nope. "It's hard evidence. They can't ignore that."

Tess had scooped the little girl's bunny up the day she'd first seen her, intending to keep it safe and return it when they finally met. She'd shoved the small stuffed animal into her backpack and had even taken it out on occasion to look at it. Where had it gone?

"The bunny?' Ben parroted, looking again at Mark. "The stuffed animal you picked up that belongs to the girl across the street?"

"This girl?" Mark asked, holding up the picture Tess had found in the folder of victims, and Ben lit up.

"Hey, that's not bad!" He took the picture from Mark, squinting to make out every detail. Tess dumped her backpack on her bed, shaking it to make sure every nook and cranny was empty. "I was pretty close!"

Tess had pulled his sketch out of the pocket she'd shoved it in when she'd changed last night and tossed it onto her desk. Ben snatched it up now and laid it beside the picture in the folder. Tess had described the girl to Ben a few weeks ago after he'd had trouble spotting her on his turn for stakeouts. She'd always thought he'd gotten pretty close but seeing the two pictures together now, he'd been dead on.

"Dude, that's not bad at all," Mark said. "You did that just off Tess's description?"

"It's not here."

Ben and Mark looked up, jarred from their mutual awe of Ben's brilliance. "What?" Ben asked again. "The stuffed animal?"

It didn't make any sense. Tess knew where she'd kept it. She might take it out and look at it sometimes, but she always put it back in the same pocket. She'd looked at it just minutes before climbing out of her window and putting feet to her whole, miserable crusade.

But it wasn't there.

"When was the last time I saw her?" Tess demanded, looking up at both boys, who were utterly useless. Neither of them had ever seen the little girl, after all. "Was it..." She couldn't remember. "Was it yesterday? Or maybe a few days ago? I don't-I'm not sure..."

It was hard to look away from the proof lying right in front of her. A girl no one else had seen. A stuffed animal missing in action. And two pictures of the same girl, dead for four years, staring up at her as though she'd tried to tell Tess all along.

Chapter 43

"**W**ell?"

For the first time in their short acquaintance, Miss McGuire had appeared before him in a less-than-perfect state. She had clearly rushed out of the house at his summons, and the evidence of her day shoes and lack of expensive jewelry did not go unnoticed.

Nor did her lack of hat, which was unheard of for a lady of her esteem. The wind and rain had played havoc with what he could now see were unruly red curls framing eyes swollen with hope and grief.

She hastily brushed both tears and curls from her eyes with an impatient hand. "I knew you would do it. You did, didn't you? You've found my father's killer."

"I did, indeed." Though not the killer she was expecting. He nodded at his secretary, for once right where he needed her. "Mrs. Bilson, will you fetch Miss McGuire some tea and show our young friend in when he arrives."

"That's not necessary," Miss McGuire argued impatiently. The signs of sleepless nights and long days were apparent in her frustration. "I don't need refreshment, I need to be relieved of my burden. I need to know who killed my father!"

Mrs. Bilson clucked in sympathy. "The poor dear," she whispered to herself. He could see her lips moving, even if he couldn't hear her. She pointed a sharp glance his way. Making sure he understood that this one was to be treated with kid gloves.

As though he couldn't be delicate when he needed to be.

"Please, Miss McGuire," he gestured once more towards the chair in front of him. "Have a seat, and I'll give you the facts of the case."

After a brief pause where the young lady took his measure with suspicion clear in her eyes, she sank stiffly into the chair at her back. He followed suit, keeping his own wary eye on her. There was still one piece to this puzzle he wasn't yet clear on. Her reactions in the next few minutes would close that last door, one way or the other.

"Now, then." He leaned forward, folding his hands on the desk between them. "I was skeptical when I first started, I don't mind saying. But I've looked into every avenue that presented itself and I must admit, I found some potential motives and suspects."

Miss McGuire's breath caught as he watched closely but she said nothing. She simply scooted forward in her chair, as though being closer would help her hear the truth more quickly.

"Your father kept the bulk of your fortune spread between not only his banks but those of his competitors. Because of this, his losses were not so great as others on that terrible Friday."

She nodded, clearly privy to her father's business habits. As he knew she had been.

"But then, he closed the bank." She knew this too, but still he watched. "For two days, the bank sat empty. Your father's steward, a Mr. Ford," he said, checking his notes, "estimates the bank lost close to ten thousand dollars. Not a small sum in today's landscape of loss."

Miss McGuire frowned. "Yes, you've mentioned this before. But what has that to do with his murder?"

"It's curious, is it not?" he asked conversationally. "Was your father prone to rash decisions? Did he often close his doors without explanation? His employees suffered because of his actions. Were they simply collateral damage? Did your father not care about those in his care?"

"He, in fact, cared very deeply for his employees." Miss McGuire sighed. "He'd never done anything like that before, and I would be hard-pressed to think of a reason why he would."

A second wind clearly caught her then, because she rallied to defense. "But if he did, then I'm sure he had a good reason!"

She still showed fight. That was a good sign.

"I mention it only because it's a motive for murder, which is what I'm in the business of seeking," he said mildly. "The very day he closed the bank, he received a telephone call. One he had been anxiously awaiting, if Mr. Ford is to be believed. Desperately, one might even say."

Again, he watched. And again she showed no signs of understanding, so he carried on.

"If the reaction to this telephone call was to close the bank with no explanation, I wonder why you aren't more curious. I certainly was."

Here, he leaned back in his chair and openly watched, waiting for a response.

"If this is a motive for murder, I'm curious that it isn't the other stakeholders in this meeting now instead of me." Her tone was one of condescension, her look dispassionate. "Unless, of course, you truly believe I may have had a hand in my own father's death."

The young Dr. Horowitz had been right, of course. Miss McGuire was an intelligent woman, Harvard-educated or not. Most people would feel threatened by the insinuation that they may have orchestrated their father's death. Miss McGuire was utterly confident in her poise and control, swollen eyes and unkempt hair aside.

"I beg your pardon, Miss McGuire," he said judiciously. "I wasn't speaking about the bank closure. I was wondering why you weren't more curious about the telephone call that led up to it."

She flinched.

It was slight, and it was brief, but it was there. And that last puzzle piece slid into place.

"I suppose you wouldn't be curious, of course," he went on, "if you already knew what it was about." Mrs. Bilson quietly peered around the corner of the door, and he nodded.

"Your father didn't tell you," he said, knowing it to be the truth. "So how did you find out."

"How did I find out what?"

Finally, finally, *that perfect posture wilted into the cracked leather at her back. "How did I find out about the tumor? Or how did I find out what he was planning?"*

"You knew?"

Miss McGuire hadn't noticed when the doctor moved quietly into the room at Mrs. Bilson's urging but she turned now at his voice. "Henry was so certain you didn't."

She smiled, though it was a sad, defeated affair. "Brain tumors show signs," she sighed. "As a doctor, I expect you know what I mean."

He nodded. *"Single-sided weakness, faltering gait, slurred speech and disorientation."*

"To name a few." She sighed again, turning back to the desk. Dr. Horowitz advanced, placing a hand on her shoulder.

"It was nothing overt. A stumble here when he got up from the table. A dropped ink pen there as he moved about the house. He would ask for a certain file and look confused when I retrieved it." She opened her pocketbook and took out a small slip of paper, about the size of a memo sheet. *"And then I found this."*

She offered it and he leaned forward to take it, noting the fine tremors in her delicate hands. She was holding her grief well, but everyone had a breaking point. He hoped Mrs. Bilson wasn't too far away.

"I found this the night...well...the night the police came to inform me. I'd had a bit of a headache and found I wasn't able to rest that night. I knew my father was out so I was tidying the office." She nodded towards the note, crumpled and worn with tears and time. *"I found that shuffled amongst some of his papers."*

He read it quietly before sliding it across the desk to Dr. Horowitz. The doctor only gave it a quick glance before nodding his head once to confirm.

Gliablastoma. Inoperable. Terminal.

"Certainly I was shocked, but everything came into crystal-clear focus after that. The words he couldn't quite get out. The way his eye seemed to droop, even when he wasn't tired. The dropped pens and stumbling steps. And then I noticed everything else."

Miss McGuire slid a small square of cloth from her pocketbook and dabbed genteelly at her eyes as though ashamed of the need, and the doctor squeezed her shoulder in consolation.

"What else did you notice?" Dr. Horowitz asked softly, as though he were afraid to disturb her grief.

"I noticed what was missing." She turned her gaze back across the desk, imploring him to understand. "The emerald cuff links my mother had given him on their wedding day. He only wore them on their anniversary. They were gone." Her eyes drifted, looking into the past. "A foreign business acquaintance happened upon a bottle of Old Forester whiskey. It was bottled the same year that Prohibition took effect and quite expensive." She smiled distantly. "He kept it in the safe, of course. He vowed not to drink it until Prohibition was ended."

He nodded. "The bottle of whiskey found on the rooftop, along with a crystal-cut glass. Neither used."

"Prohibition hasn't ended yet, you see."

He nodded. He did see. But he wasn't sure he could have withstood the temptation, himself.

"You looked in the safe? You discovered the bottle was gone?"

She nodded grimly. "Along with a letter. He would never leave me without some attempt at comfort, you see. My mother's wedding ring was tucked away, as well." She touched the delicate chain around her neck and tugged the ring from beneath her collar. "He always insisted it would be mine someday. When I needed it." She tucked the ring back beneath the fabric. "Or once he was gone."

"I don't understand, Betsy," Dr. Horowitz admitted, kneeling down beside her so he could meet her eyes. "If you knew all this time, why would you go to the police to find respite? Why insist on hiring a private detective to uncover a truth you knew never existed?"

"Isn't it obvious?" As said private detective, it seemed perfectly clear to him now. "When someone is taken from you without warning, there should be someone to blame. You can't hate a disease and if you can't hate the disease, how can you admit the truth, even to yourself? How can you strip yourself of your hate and anger, only to replace it with sorrow and loss?"

"Just so." It was said quietly but with strength. Miss McGuire would be okay, he knew. She had taken a chance, she had hoped for somewhere to direct her anger, and now that she knew without doubt what had happened, she could allow herself to grieve.

"And what does one attempt to do with sorrow and loss?" he asked, and a glimmer of hope came into the young doctor's eyes as well. He leaned forward, clearly eager for the young lady's answer.

"Well, that is the question, isn't it?" She took a deep breath and when she opened her eyes at last, the steel had returned. She stood, taking a moment to brush incorrigible wrinkles from a dress that could not be saved. "Come, Dr. Horowitz. We have much to do."

"We do?" The doctor scrambled to his feet and scurried to open the door for a woman who knew her own mind.

"Indeed. We've wasted too much time already. We must see to the medical needs of our vulnerable community members. Goodness knows, there are more every day."

Dr. Horowitz fairly glowed. "Oh, Miss McGuire. Your father would be so pleased."

"Indeed he would," she agreed. "But so will I."

She stopped just inside the door and turned back. "Thank you, sir. I apologize if I've wasted your time, but I needed to know. I needed someone to confront me with the truth, no matter how painful." Her smile was watery, but it was beautiful indeed. "My steward will ensure your payment."

A better man than he would have gallantly waved aside the payment. Helping a loving daughter find closure should be more than enough.

But then again, he had bills to pay and a secretary to feed. And good cigarettes were getting mighty expensive.

So instead, he nodded and watched through the window as the pair crossed the street to Dr. Horowitz's car. Yes, Betsy McGuire would survive to fight another day.

And if he were any kind of gumshoe at all, he'd lay odds that she'd need her mother's wedding ring sooner than later.

· · · ·

THE MEMORIAL WAS HELD a week later, and Tess wasn't quite sure how they'd put it together so quickly. Between the national news vans, the flocking murder mystery groupies, and the flood of families looking for their missing daughters, their small town had become a tourist trap for the macabre overnight.

Sully had done his best to keep her name out of the press's hands, but she was in the official report. There wasn't much he could do except assign a couple of patrols to keep the crowds off their lawn.

Tess's mother handled the whole thing with aplomb, and Tess knew the shift wasn't simply a momentary adjustment to circumstances. The threat to Tess had shaken her out of the cave she'd been trapped in since Tess's father had died and even though it was hard, she knew her mother wouldn't fall back in again.

Her father had died.

Tess was still trying to accept it, but facts were facts. She drifted from the window back to her desk and picked up the framed picture that now sat upright, one of the last memories she had of her dad before the disease claimed him.

They were smiling, despite the fact he was hooked up to an infusion that couldn't prolong the inevitable. He was wan and pale, and Tess could see the arm of the motorized wheelchair he'd been forced to adopt in the background, but he was still himself. Not even sickness could diminish the impish gleam in Ian McGee's eyes.

She sat the picture back down gently and took a minute to remember. The doctors said the disease could take years to claim her father's life but in reality, it had happened in six months. A blessing, they said. To linger, locked in a body that no longer responded, unable to breathe but still fully able to think, would have been a fate far worse than death, and Tess knew it was true. For her fun-loving, energetic father, she could think of no worse way to die. So the speed with which it claimed him was a mercy.

For him.

For Tess and her mother, there had been no time. No time to understand what was happening. No time to accept it, to rail against the inevitable, or to grieve what was coming. The counselors all said Tess's reaction was normal. That she was using her writing to cope with what she couldn't understand. But they hadn't understood the full extent of her denial. Neither had her mother.

Neither had Tess.

The day Tess had blurted her suspicions to Mark, he'd understood. Looking back, his reaction made perfect sense. He hadn't argued with her, he hadn't mocked her, he'd simply been silent as he'd taken it in. As he realized she truly believed her dad had been murdered instead of taken by a disease that couldn't be fought.

It had been Mark who had shared the truth with Ben, and Ben who had tried to recruit Maddie, thinking she could help. And despite the fact she'd been dead wrong, they'd decided to help her anyway. Tess knew herself well enough to know that, had Mark confronted her with the truth sooner, it would have pushed her into action that much more quickly. Going along with her delusions had softened the blow, protecting her for just that much longer.

Tess ran her fingers along the soft bracelet she'd wrapped around her left wrist. The thread was twisted with gold and jade filigree, with turquoise stones woven into the strands. The bracelet she'd been tempted to buy at the farmer's market the day she'd spied on Horace and Jasper. The bracelet Maddie bought for her, even as Tess rejected her attempts to renew their friendship.

Tess wasn't quite sure where that friendship was going just yet. It was different than the friendship they'd had before. It was scarred, marked by the sadness and loss they'd both endured. But scars tended to be pretty tough and once healed, were harder to injure than they'd been before.

They would be okay, Tess knew. It would never be what it was before, but it would be okay. Eventually.

Such was life.

A soft knock sounded on Tess's door and her mother popped her head in. "Are you ready, baby?"

The town was holding a memorial for all the girls discovered in the backyard, and most of the families of the victims were joining them. Understandably, the girls who had survived had declined to join, simply wanting to go home and forget it had ever happened.

Tess had only seen the older girl from the basement once after they were rescued. From her front steps, Tess had watched as the girl was escorted to an ambulance, wrapped in a blanket. The girl was wary, even in rescue, and she'd noticed Tess across the street. They'd watched each other, just for a moment, before the girl ducked into the open doors of the ambulance, but Tess would swear she'd nodded her head, ever so slightly, in acknowledgment.

"I suppose." If Tess had her way, she would skip the whole thing. She didn't want to be the center of attention. She didn't want to remember. Truth was always harder than fiction, but she knew she couldn't keep hiding between the pages of a story. Not if she wanted to make her dad proud.

We have to do what's right, even when it's hard.

It was the story of her life.

"Mark and Ben are waiting," Kate said. "They offered to walk with us."

Well, far be it from Tess to keep them waiting. They'd stuck with her this far, after all.

So Tess straightened her shoulders and touched the framed picture one more time for luck, her fingers idly brushing the hand-drawn portrait she'd tucked behind it. The picture Ben had drawn one fall afternoon at the insistence of a crazed redhead he'd only just met.

Mary Beth Dobbins. Aged six. Missing along with her favorite stuffed animal, an old, worn bunny rabbit still clutched in her arms when she'd been unearthed.

Tess knew what she knew. And she knew it was best not to dwell too deeply on what had happened. But she would keep the memory of Mary Beth Dobbins tucked alongside the memory of her father, and she would learn from both.

She let her eyes linger on the finished draft of her novel, sitting front and center on the desk. She still had work to do. A lot of work, in fact. It was rougher than she'd like, but she wasn't afraid of a little work.

No need to be afraid of the memories, her dad whispered in her mind. *They just mean I'm right here with you, that's all.*

And he was.

Tess smiled up at the mother who'd come back to her, the mother who'd filled two men with buckshot on her account, and held out her hand.

"I guess we'd better get to it, then."

Also by Tara N. Hathcock

Shattered Highways

B ook 1 in the explosive Shattered Highways *series*

Quincy O'Connell blows through identities as quickly as she creates them. She has to, to stay alive.

They've been following her for years. Watching her. Trying to get close. She doesn't know why and she doesn't know who, but she knows she has to stay one step ahead. So she becomes nobody. A loner with no roots, no paper trail, no friends. And no home.

It's lonely living one life to the next but she's safe as long as she's invisible. After all, she's survived this way for as long as she can remember. But what if her memory isn't what she thinks it is? What if nothing is what she thinks it is? And what if her memory is exactly what they're looking for?

What you don't know can't hurt you. So if you don't know you're broken, are you?

Burning Bridges

NOT EVERYONE CAN BE SAVED

BURNING BRIDGES

TARA N. HATHCOCK

SHATTERED HIGHWAYS BOOK 2

BOOK 2 IN THE Shattered Highways *series*

Quincy has made her choice. Now she has to live with it.

It's all starting to make sense. After a harrowing escape, Quincy finally knows why she's been on the run for as long as she can remember - and why that memory ends so abruptly. She also knows about the others like her, the ones who haven't been so lucky.

Now there's really only one way forward, but her actions come at a cost. Planting her feet and using the gifts she never wanted will end the hunt once and for all, but it will leave her vulnerable: to the company who wants to use her, to the allies who want to help her, and to the monster inside her head who wants to end her.

On a collision course with disaster, Quincy must make one more choice. Because not everyone can be saved.

The End of the Road

THE EPIC CONCLUSION to the Shattered Highways *series.*

Logan is convinced Quincy is still alive. She has to be. What Logan doesn't know is whether she's the same person she was before. His best friend. His partner in crime. His...something more. Or is Quincy someone else now? A new person, with a new life and a new identity and no memory of who she left behind?

Logan may not know which version of Quincy walked away from the destruction of the Rhinehardt Collaborative, but he's beginning to suspect she may not have been the only one to escape that night. Someone else was there, someone who should have stayed in that basement, and now no one he loves is safe.

Enemies are closing in and Logan is losing ground. How do you fight a war on two fronts when you're fighting blind? Maybe he isn't the soldier he thought he was. Maybe he doesn't save the girl. Maybe he's not the hero.

But maybe Quincy is.

TARA N. HATHCOCK

About the Author

A native of the Midwestern United States, Tara N. Hathcock spent 16 years in the healthcare field as a radiologic technologist, where the first inklings of *Shattered Highways* was born. Having since made the jump to academics, Tara now works as full-time staff for an area community college and teaches anatomy on the side while she continues to write stories that blend her own love of reading and writing with mystery and adventure.

Shattered Highways is her first novel.

Read more at https://books.taranhathcock.com/.

About the Publisher

Writing doesn't have to be graphic to be good.

Quiet+Kin Publishing is a family of booklovers dedicated to producing quality content for every reader.